SNOWED IN AT THE WEDDING CHALET

LEONIE MACK

Boldwood

First published in 2025 as *A Winter Wedding Adventure*. This edition published in Great Britain in 2026 by Boldwood Books Ltd.

Copyright © Leonie Mack, 2025

Cover Design by Alexandra Allden

Cover Images: Shutterstock

Every effort has been made to obtain the necessary permissions with reference to copyright material, both illustrative and quoted. We apologise for any omissions in this respect and will be pleased to make the appropriate acknowledgements in any future edition.

A CIP catalogue record for this book is available from the British Library.

Paperback ISBN 978-1-83603-396-7

Large Print ISBN 978-1-83603-395-0

Hardback ISBN 978-1-83603-394-3

Trade Paperback ISBN 978-1-80635-263-0

Ebook ISBN 978-1-83603-397-4

Kindle ISBN 978-1-83603-398-1

Audio CD ISBN 978-1-83603-389-9

MP3 CD ISBN 978-1-83603-390-5

Digital audio download ISBN 978-1-83603-392-9

This book is printed on certified sustainable paper. Boldwood Books is dedicated to putting sustainability at the heart of our business. For more information please visit https://www.boldwood books.com/about-us/sustainability/

Boldwood Books Ltd, 23 Bowerdean Street, London, SW6 3TN

www.boldwoodbooks.com

For all the tough, capable women in real life who inspire me to be my best.

1

The crowds obviously hadn't got the memo that it was no longer the season to be jolly. Although it was two days after Christmas, a milling throng filled the square, smiling faces illuminated by the warm fairy lights criss-crossing above. The sound of animated voices was punctuated by a brass band playing cosy Christmas tunes with a jaunty oompah beat that matched the mountains of pretzels and gingerbread hearts available at the wooden stands.

An inch of snow glittered on the roofs of the market stalls and more was coming down – fat flakes that were also a few days late for Christmas, but perfect timing for the ski season, which would soon get going in earnest.

Usually, if Kira found herself in Salzburg, it was on a ski trip for her employer, Great Heart Adventures. If only that were the case today. She might have been able to enjoy the cosy kitsch if she had fresh powder and a steep slope awaiting her. But no, she wasn't leading a group out to one of the ski resorts today. She was collecting an Italian opera singer to take him to a wedding.

A *wedding*. Just the word made her break out in an unseasonal sweat. Willard, her boss, had got the company into a grand mess and now they'd sunk to this: taking clients to out-of-the-way places to *get married*. She'd thought about quitting earlier in the year when the merger with I Do Destinations had been announced, but then someone would have asked her why she couldn't handle a wedding or two and she didn't want to answer.

There were a few things in her past none of her colleagues – her friends – knew about.

All of which was why she now hurried impatiently across the twinkling square, probably the most miserable wedding planner who had ever held the title, the grumpiest person at the market, reluctantly ready to play taxi driver to the opera singer for the posh wedding in the snow.

Also torturous was the smell: caramelised orange

peel, burnt sugar, cinnamon and fresh bread, bratwurst, melted cheese and even hints of garlic. Because Kira was *starving*.

Flight delays had necessitated skipping lunch and although Christmas dinner had sat in her belly until Boxing Day, her usual appetite had returned that morning, only to be thwarted by her mum's latest diet-fad breakfast ideas and her nauseating hints that it was past time for Kira to consider a relationship again. *No thanks, Mum.*

Gritting her teeth against the tantalising aromas that made her stomach twist and groan, she scanned the square for the meeting point.

Why the guy had changed plans at the last minute to meet her at the Christmas market, she had no idea. She only had a mobile number and a name for him: Mattia Bentivoglio. It sounded more like the name of a footballer. She would have expected something like Luciano or Donatello.

Apparently, he was a close family friend of the bride and an important part of the ceremony – his voice, Kira assumed. The only other information she had was that he was 'high maintenance', whatever that meant. It was probably a euphemism for 'rude and terrible company'.

She was trying not to dwell on the baseline anxiety turning to ice in her shoulders. A three-hour drive on pleasant Austrian highways should have been a much cushier job than her usual: leading groups up rock faces or down glaciers on skis. But out in the extremes of nature, clients didn't expect service or deference or politeness – or any conversation at all, if Kira was lucky.

Weddings were their own special brand of hell. There was too much she had to hide.

She'd managed her first affair with Great Heart Adventure *Weddings* three months ago only because it had been amusing to watch her best friend try to win back his lost love, although it was less amusing now he was properly shacked up. Kira didn't have many other friends to replace him. People probably called *her* 'rude and terrible company' too, without even using a fancy euphemism.

The prospect of spending three hours in a vehicle with an opera singer, trying not to say the wrong thing, was making her leg twitch. Opera sounded like someone torturing a swan to her untrained ear, to say nothing of the fact that the storylines were all tragic and defeatist and the woman was guaranteed to die. God, she hoped she didn't blurt out any of this stuff during an awkward silence.

She didn't even know what this guy looked like or

how she'd recognise him. She was picturing a dark-haired man in an evening tailcoat and one of those waistband things that were called something like Benedict Cumberbatch. Maybe he'd have a round belly to go with his powerful diaphragm. Or maybe he'd be a silver fox, oozing Italian machismo. Except if he was a childhood friend of the bride, a chirpy, tiny woman somewhere around thirty called Alessandra Martinelli, he couldn't be that old. She was originally from Naples and apparently so was this tenor – or bass. She wasn't actually sure which.

Lifting her backpack higher on her shoulders, she made her way swiftly past the enormous Christmas tree to the white, stone arcade. Behind it, the copper-domed spires of the cathedral rose against the evening sky.

Arriving under the arches, she glanced at her watch – entirely unnecessary, as the church bells gonged loudly a moment later. Five o'clock. No time to grab a sausage or one of those rolls with a slab of mixed meat in it. Maybe she could swipe a pretzel on the way to collect the minivan from the rental place. There was no way she could manage the three-hour drive on an empty stomach, so hopefully, the opera singer would be hungry too – although she didn't know what opera singers ate.

She waited ten minutes, hopping from foot to foot, leaving complex prints from her boots in the dusting of snow. At least the temperature was hovering around zero – comparatively mild and positively comfortable compared to some of the expeditions Kira had been part of. She'd dressed as usual according to the 'onion principle', a series of layers she could take off as necessary, and her gloves were designed to protect her fingers from much harsher conditions.

She scowled as she thought of her new colleague Ginny's instructions to dress as a wedding planner and not an expedition leader. Ten years as an outdoor guide and she'd been reduced to babysitting opera singers and worrying about presentable outfits. She'd reluctantly packed her best blouse, which was currently growing increasingly crushed in her rucksack, but she wouldn't pull it on until it was absolutely necessary.

She would feel so out of place next to the pretty, made-up wedding planners with their fancy aesthetics – and genuine excitement at the prospect of a wedding. Kira was worried she wouldn't even manage any fake excitement.

Five minutes later, her stomach was a gnawing void and there was still no sign of an Italian stallion wearing a cummerbund – *cummerbund!* That was the word she'd been thinking of earlier. No one else in the jolly crowd looked like a high-maintenance opera singer and she was hopping from foot to foot with sheer impatience. She should have grabbed some food. Luckily, the car rental place was open late and they had plenty of time once the dude showed up. In the time she'd been waiting, she could have eaten three—

'Kira Watling?'

She whirled around, but before she had time to register more than a head of thick, dark hair and a fine wool coat, the man mumbled an excuse, shoved an enormous, wheeled suitcase at her and rushed off again.

'Can you look after that for me? I just have to—' He gestured expansively with quick fingers, walking away backwards, running into someone and then stumbling over his own feet as he tried to turn around. 'Mi scusi!' he said emphatically, clutching the shoulders of the poor passer-by.

He wasn't wearing a cummerbund that she could see, didn't have a belly and definitely no silver hair, but this had to be the opera singer. He didn't even look as though he could grow a beard, this baby-faced man with thick, black curls and dramatic features – made more dramatic by what appeared to be a hint of eyeliner under his lashes. A dangly earring winked in one ear. If he'd said he was twenty, she would have believed it.

Collecting himself, he straightened with a deep breath through his nose and strode theatrically to the bar tables set up around a stall selling pungent hot drinks. Kira watched, mystified, as he leaned on one of the wooden barrel tables, staring up at the sky with a wistful expression.

The air around him seemed to sparkle, but it appeared Kira was the only person who noticed, because the hum of the voices of the crowd continued as normal, as though nothing out of the ordinary was about to happen. For a moment, Kira wondered if he had a bomb strapped under his coat – or a superman suit. It was clear from the tension in his body that he was about to perform some kind of stunt.

Perform... The word should have tipped her off, but she still jumped when a man three metres away from her lifted his chin suddenly and sang '*Amo!*' in a dramatic voice. Heads turned. A musical refrain sounded from behind one of the stalls.

The first man shook his fist and sang, '*D'un colpevol amor! Elisabetta!*' Even though Kira spoke no Italian – much less operatic Italian – she understood the word 'love'. Conversations stilled as the incredulous crowd watched, some raising their phones to record. Goosebumps raced up Kira's arm.

His coat a flurry of cloth around him, the younger man – Mattia, presumably – came closer. '*Tua madre!*' he sang, his voice rounded and full and so powerful, Kira heard it through her skin.

She'd never attended live opera – never had the faintest desire to. But she was frozen to the spot, her jaw around her collarbone, as the raw sound shuddered through her.

The first man was singing again, apparently arguing with Mattia, gasps from the crowd providing an audible counterpoint. It could have been a bar brawl between drunk friends, except they were singing instead of speaking, punctuating the music with theatrical gestures that belonged on a stage.

They sang a few lines in piercing harmony, then Mattia continued solo, as though brainstorming the solution to his friend's heartache. He looked older, his brow creased, his hands on his hips and the long coat framing his tall figure.

And his voice... It was deeper, rich and dramatic and as smooth as an Italian hot chocolate. Kira's eyes were huge as the drama unfolded.

A large bell clanged once, twice, three times and Mattia and the other man jumped in surprise.

Taking his comrade by the shoulders, Mattia sang something encouraging, a soft, melodic line ending on a hopeful note that made Kira's skin prickle. She couldn't understand a word of the modulated vowels, but her heart was pounding, not with the familiar adrenaline rush of physical challenges that she loved. This was *internal* and she wasn't sure how to process it.

After a gripping pause, they began a lively duet, starting quietly and building to a vibrant harmony full of colour, courage and rebellion. With life and passion and emphatic gestures, they held the crowd in thrall. Kira's hair stood on end as the notes washed over her – tones of dark and light, triumph and despair.

With a declaration of '*Libertà!*', they embraced each other and turned to rush through the arches, nearly bowling Kira over as three instrumentalists appeared – a trumpet, a trombone and a flute – to finish the piece to a burst of applause and cheering from the delighted crowd.

Sagging where she stood, Kira took a breath for what felt like the first time in several minutes – or her entire lifetime. She swiped at a cold spot on her cheek and was stunned to find moisture. It was incomprehensible, that bead of salty liquid on her waterproof glove. She couldn't have... *cried*. Kira hadn't even cried when she'd finally beaten the classic climbing route on the north face of the Eiger on her fifth attempt.

She sniffed and rubbed her nose, belatedly joining the applause. All of a sudden, Kira noticed two men with cameras filming the stunt. The instrumentalists unwound their scarves to make the words 'Salzburger Festspiele' with a date the following year, and then took a bow.

Fresh applause alerted Kira to the return of the two men. They raised their hands and bowed and Kira wondered if she should inch away so she wasn't standing awkwardly in the background of their publicity photos with her dyed hair, in her bright jacket and her beat-up backpack – and possibly tear-stained cheeks.

Her chest was still tight and she was appalled by her response to the performance – embarrassed and confused. She must have been more strung out about this posh wedding than she'd thought. She squeezed her eyes shut for a moment, wishing she had a free evening to watch a brainless thriller and settle herself down. But she had to ferry this guy to the *wedding*. There would be no peace until she'd got through it.

An older man appeared and shook their hands vigorously. 'Wonderful, wonderful! The public adored it. What a wonderful taste of the performance to come next year.'

Further claps on the back, hugs and cheek-kisses appeared to be obligatory and Kira was glad they had until six-thirty to collect the car, or she might have been biting her already stumpy and cracked nails. At long last, there were final goodbyes and her charge waved as the others moved off. When he turned, the dynamism of the performance seemed to leach out of him and he transformed back into the hunched young man who'd asked her to look after his suitcase.

Rubbing his forehead with a bare hand, he peered at her from under those astonishing lashes. 'Sorry about that,' he muttered.

She blinked at him. Was he apologising for turning her into an emotional wreck without asking? 'You're... sorry?'

'I didn't know I would have to do that tonight and I'm sorry it took so long. Shall we go? Get the car and go to Alessandra?' Phew, he was apologising for the practical inconvenience, not the way he'd imposed on feelings she preferred to pretend she didn't have.

He cleared his throat and gave a shiver, closing his hands into fists and blowing on them. Kira had the strange impression that he might disappear back into the realm where he came from – or grow wings and fly back. He didn't seem quite corporeal as he swayed. There were hollows under his eyes, as though he'd been breathing the wrong air for too long and needed to return to his natural habitat.

'Yeah, we should go. Let me find a cab,' she said, shaking off her distraction. She had a job to do and wondering whether he was too beautiful to be entirely human wasn't part of it. She started across the square, tugging off her glove with her teeth and fetching her phone. 'How did you know who I was, by the way?' Since she hadn't pictured Mattia looking anything like this.

'Blue hair,' he answered. 'Alessandra told me you have blue hair. I thought she was joking, but... you actually have blue hair.'

She refused to run a self-conscious hand through her bleached and dyed bob. 'You've never seen anyone with blue hair before?'

'No, actually.'

Before he could voice an opinion she had no interest in hearing, she picked up the pace, hurrying under the strings of glowing lights and ignoring the renewed grumbles from her stomach. Mattia fell behind, his polished leather shoes providing no grip in the gluggy snow, and she had to stop and wait.

'Wow, this place is... This is...'

Kira turned to find him staring, wide-eyed, at the pine garlands, replete with cones, and the warm lighting on the facades of the historic buildings as though seeing them for the first time – as though he'd just woken up.

Stifling a forlorn sigh at the further delay to dinner, she crossed her arms and waited for him to catch up – or finish his sentence. He caught sight of her and flashed her a smile – bright and staggeringly magnetic. Kira drew back in dismay.

'I'm coming!' he assured her, throwing out an arm for balance as he slid closer. 'This is the most snow I've ever seen!'

Kira's steps faltered again.

'It's beautiful.' There was something about his voice that cut through the white noise to the sea of emotion in a person and Kira definitely did not like it.

She should remind him that their destination – one of the farthest corners of Tyrol, at the end of the isolated Tux Valley, at the foot of a glacier – would have a lot more snow than this, but the light in his eyes stopped her from dragging him back to earth.

'It is,' was all she said in reply.

2

Mattia realised he hadn't eaten lunch at about the same moment he noticed the car rental company appeared to be closed.

At least the wedding planner's exclamation of, 'What the—?' covered the creak and groan of his stomach, where he sat in the back of the cab. She peered through the windscreen, her look just as dark as the windows of the shopfront.

He was selfishly relieved that Alessandra had sent this woman with blue hair to look after him. If she was the kind of person who sat in the front of the cab with the driver, she must be capable of anything and after the day – *days* – he'd had, he wasn't sure he was able to solve any problems right now and he didn't want to disappoint Alessandra just before her wedding.

'It's supposed to be open until six-thirty!'

'Shall I get out and—'

She was already shoving open the car door and trotting up to read the sign stuck behind the glass. 'Stay there. It's closed. Due to heavy snowfall, apparently.'

Glancing doubtfully at the sky, she grumbled under her breath as she returned to the cab. 'Be still, my growling stomach.'

Mattia had to resist a smile. 'Can we try somewhere else?'

'With a minivan available at short notice two days after Christmas?' she snapped without looking at him. Turning to the driver, she said, 'Could you take us to the train station, please?' and pulled out her phone. After a few short taps, the device was at her ear.

'We're going to take the train?' he asked.

She eyed him and that seemed to be the only answer he was going to get.

A quick phone conversation followed, emotions from frustration to dismay to a hint of amusement flitting across her features. She had an interesting face: a strong jaw and a high forehead, slightly crooked teeth – and straight, firm lips that hinted at complexity. A puckered scar the shape of the crescent moon adorned her cheekbone. He suspected *he* was wearing more make-up than she was, if his concealer and subtle eyeliner had survived the rigorous day of auditions.

Just thinking about the auditions made his empty stomach heave.

'Are you sure you're okay on your own until tomorrow? She's not a bridezilla?' Kira was saying into her phone.

Mattia sat up straight. 'Alessandra is not a bridezilla,' he said indignantly. 'And what do you mean, "tomorrow"?'

Kira ignored him. 'We'll get going as early as we can, but the rental company doesn't open until ten.'

He held his hand palm down and gestured urgently.

She finally paid him some attention. 'What?'

'Can I have the phone? Is Alessandra there?'

'Can't you call Alessandra yourself?'

'Ah.' She was right. Rummaging in his coat pockets, it took him a minute to find the device and then they were pulling up outside the historic rail terminal and he had to scramble to keep up with her – no hope of working out what was going on, in his state.

After paying the driver, she was out and hauling her backpack on while he was still finding his footing on the slippery pavement and nearly lobbing his phone into the fountain in the process. Despite the foot and vehicle traffic, a layer of snow had built up and it was still coming down.

The train station had a lush spruce bringing post-Christmas spirit into the square. If this place had to be cold and damp, at least it did so beautifully. He thought of Alessandra's dreams of a winter wedding with a shot of tenderness for his old friend. Then he remembered: Kira Watling had said *tomorrow*!

Alessandra would be running herself ragged – and worrying about *him* on top of everything else. But if he stopped to call her now, he might lose his guide, who was setting off at quite a clip.

'Can we slow down?' His foot slipped, punctuating his sentence. His elegant Santoni dress shoes obviously didn't like the snow. Kira wore yellow nylon boots with soles that appeared to bite into the pavement and he was struck by the thought that she wasn't what he'd expected from a wedding planner.

She was far too grumpy.

'The tourist information office closes soon and I don't want to spend all evening looking for a hotel online. Those apps drive me crazy.'

Definitely too grumpy.

He slipped and slid after her, dragging his suitcase. 'Are you... not having a good day?'

To his surprise, she laughed, a deep, throaty sound with rough edges and a brittle centre. He was so distracted by the texture of the sound that it took a moment for her words to register. 'You could say that. Weddings are up there with laundry and tax returns in my book – complete hell.'

'You don't like doing laundry?'

She glanced back at him as though he had a screw loose. 'No one likes laundry.'

With a self-conscious hand at his starched, white collar, he dashed after her through the sliding doors.

'Why do you do this if you hate it so much?' he couldn't help asking, struggling to catch his breath.

'I'm not really a wedding planner,' was her only response.

'Huh. Are you kidnapping me, then? Is that what's going on?'

Her withering sigh was another inexplicably pleasant, textured noise on his skin. 'You seem very cheerful at the prospect of a kidnapping.'

'As long as I get some food and rest, I'll take a kidnapping right now.' He was drained, strung out and wobbly with the remnants of audition adrenaline in his system and all his mixed feelings about the imminent wedding. Grumpy he could accept right now, as long as she looked after him.

She blinked at him, but her steps slowed. Her eyes were almost the colour of her hair and just as striking. 'You are one of the strangest people I've ever met.' Her declaration was without the bite of some of the statements he'd heard from her, so it didn't sting. He rather liked the attention.

'The feeling is mutual,' he replied with a grin. 'I didn't have a good day either.'

'All right,' she said, a perplexed twist in her lips. 'I'm sorry about that.'

He beamed at her again, disproportionately happy to discover she was capable of sympathy – vindicated even, as he had some instinct telling him she was someone he could trust.

But his smile seemed to dim hers and she turned away. 'Let's just find somewhere to stay for tonight.'

'I promise not to escape,' he leaned close to say as they approached the counter of the tourist information office.

'It might be easier if you did,' she mumbled in reply.

The man behind the counter flicked his gaze from Mattia to Kira as though he were as puzzled as Mattia was about how they'd ended up here.

'Hi, we need rooms for tonight,' she said without preamble. 'Could you help us find something?' She gave Mattia a measuring glance. 'Four stars?'

'Please,' he added with a smile for the man. Leaning down to Kira, he said through the side of his mouth, 'I'm not worth five?'

She didn't even smile. 'It's a hotel, not an opera review,' she replied under her breath, and that gave him a twinge between the ribs as well.

'It's a very busy period over Christmas and New Year, but I'm sure I'll find something,' the man responded. He tapped away on his computer. 'You're in luck! There's a room showing as available at the Hotel Alpin. Premium double. It includes breakfast.'

Mattia started at the words 'premium double'. In combination with 'busy period', and the prospect was alarming.

Kira straightened. '*Two* rooms?'

'I'm sorry? I don't understand,' the man said, his smile slipping.

'We need two rooms. For two people,' she explained through gritted teeth.

'Oh, I see,' the man said stiltedly, although his puzzled gaze suggested otherwise. 'There are four of you.'

The pressure of the auditions, the performance, the impending wedding too much to hold in, Mattia burst out laughing. Leaning heavily on the counter, he shook with it, hunger and exhaustion rolling over him along with amusement.

'We're not a couple,' Kira said tightly, and laughter rose up his throat again.

'Oh, I'm—' The man behind the counter flushed. 'That makes more sense. I shouldn't have assumed— I mean, most people who come in together are— But I couldn't work out how the two of you, looking like that—'

The man realised a few seconds too late that he should have stopped talking several sentences ago. Mattia could almost see the sparks leaping from Kira's gaze.

He shrugged. 'You never know. I suppose we could have been... lovers.'

'We definitely could *not* have been!' She glowed when she was worked up. It was rather fascinating.

'Let me see if I can find a hotel with two rooms,'

the man at the desk hurriedly interrupted. 'Hotel Alpin unfortunately doesn't. Ah, if you don't mind something close to the station here, rather than in the city, then I've found—'

'That's fine. Can you book it please?'

'Eh,' Mattia interrupted, the reality of sleeping in a strange hotel room settling over him. He was too close to the edge as it was and he needed to keep a lid on his anxiety until the wedding. 'Are the windows insulated at least?'

Kira rolled her eyes and tapped her nails – bitten short and without polish – on the counter.

'I'm certain they will be,' the man assured him in an indulgent tone that convinced Mattia of the opposite.

'We can go and see, I suppose,' he said in a forlorn mutter.

When they finally walked back out into the forecourt, Mattia shuddered at the sudden cold, but Kira made no move to put her beanie back on. She ran a hand through her hair as though she wanted to tug out a tuft of it.

'High maintenance indeed,' she muttered under her breath.

He should probably tell her about his hearing, as a

warning and an excuse for his behaviour, but she kept speaking before he had the chance.

'"Lovers"? Really? Was that necessary?'

'No,' he admitted as soberly as he could, which wasn't particularly sober, as he was still tickled by the misunderstanding.

'You're not exactly my type. You're wearing more make-up than I am!'

'*And* I have more piercings,' he added, flicking the crucifix in one ear in her direction. 'Unless you have some—' He snapped his mouth shut at her indignant look. Ohi, he needed peace and quiet to calm down before he burst all of his messy intensity all over her. 'Sorry.'

'Are all Italian tenors as glossy as you?'

'If that's supposed to be a joke, I'm offended.'

'What, I thought you wouldn't mind the stereotype of the well-groomed Italian?'

He smoothed his hair as he realised he must look a mess from all the rushing. 'That's not what I meant. I'm not a *tenor*. I'm a baritone.'

'Which makes *all* the difference, I'm sure.'

'You know nothing about opera, do you?'

For a moment, he was concerned she'd respond defensively to the gentle accusation, but he shouldn't have worried. Not about Kira Watling, who swaggered and sniped and tossed her blue hair in indignation when something didn't appeal to her.

'Your performance was wasted on me,' she said. 'But you're my client and it's my job to get you *safely* to the wedding. I don't have to enjoy your singing for that.'

A little twinge at the emphasis on 'safely'. He'd quite liked that up until now, she'd charged ahead, simply expecting him to follow. Apparently, she'd worked out how useless he could be, with his sensitivities and anxieties and his sheltered existence.

'Client?' he clarified in a light tone, to shake off the momentary gloom. 'Is that what kidnappers call it these days?'

* * *

Alessandra says to look after Matty... Not sure what that means.

Kira frowned at Ginny's message as she stood in the lift of the hotel before stowing her phone in her pocket. Mattia leaned against the mirror at the back, eyes closed, hands deep in the pockets of his tailored trousers. The smallest hint of stubble shadowed his cheeks – the boy might be able to grow a beard after all.

She didn't have the faintest idea what to make of him. She was annoyed, yes. His promo performance had cost them the night here and he'd laughed far too heartily at the suggestion that they could be a couple – before using that florid term with an earnestness she had to assume wasn't genuine: *lovers*.

But despite being grumpy and annoyed and inconvenienced, she was also... a little protective. Wobbly – inside – ever since she'd heard him sing.

Look after Matty... She didn't know why the bride seemed to think he needed looking after, but she *felt* it and it wasn't entirely comfortable.

She studied his face while his eyes were closed: the pinch between his brows, soft lips tensed flat, the locks of hair tumbling over his forehead as though someone had styled him like that. He didn't give off helpless vibes exactly, although he certainly seemed to cover his eccentricities with an unnecessarily effective dose of charm.

It wasn't helplessness – it was vulnerability. He'd splashed it all over her when he'd sung from the depths of his soul that evening and made her think of idiotic turns of phrase like 'singing from the depths of his soul'. Singing was his job. He surely kept his soul out of it, for his own sake.

His eyes snapped open and he caught her watching him. She forced her gaze to remain where it was for long enough that he wouldn't get the impression she was embarrassed. She hadn't been admiring his sharp jaw or the indentation in one cheek that suggested a dimple – at least she hadn't *only* been admiring those.

'Did you call the bride?' she asked.

'I haven't had a chance yet.' His voice was gravelly and he had to clear his throat. 'I'll do it when I get into the room. I'm not sure she'll want to hear I've been kidnapped so close to her wedding day, since she needs me to sing.'

'Is that why you're getting the special treatment?'

He made a gesture that wasn't quite yes or no. 'She probably thinks I wouldn't make it on my own,' he said with a wince. 'She's not wrong. We've known each other since we were babies – well, since I was a baby and she was two. Our mothers are close friends.'

'She still thinks you're a baby?'

'Something like that,' he replied with an effortlessly stylish shrug.

Their rooms were on the top floor – a standard double and a single tucked in the far corner under the roof. Kira would naturally take that one. Just before they reached the door of Mattia's room, another one flew open, farther down the corridor.

Mattia flinched, as though he'd expected a gunman to appear and start shooting. It was a couple wrapped up in coats and scarfs, who ignored Kira and her companion; nothing unusual about the encounter, but Mattia was on edge.

Coming to a stop outside his hotel room, Kira prompted, 'This is yours,' when he stood staring at the door with a twisted frown. 'I'm at the other end of the corridor, okay?' *Matty*. The bride's nickname for him suited.

He took a deep breath as though he expected dragons on the other side of the door. 'Okay.' Fumbling with his keycard, he managed to get it open and stepped over the threshold.

Kira peered at him doubtfully, then turned for her own room. She could eat and lie down soon in her own blessed company. A quiet evening with a take-away and the spy series she was currently watching, and she'd shake off this strange opera-induced mood and gird herself for the wedding dramas to follow.

Even in the limited experience she'd gained over the past four months since the merger, she'd learned that with weddings, there could always be more drama. And that was before she added her own memories: her mortifying mistake that had to remain hidden at all costs.

Halfway down the corridor, she realised they hadn't made arrangements for the following morning, so she headed back. Just before she reached his door, he shot out of the room, his hair askew and his eyes wild. The door closed with a snick. He struggled to take a breath before opening his mouth to blurt out, 'I'm sorry. I can't stay here.'

3

Kira swallowed a groan at this new setback. She wondered what could be wrong with the room. Any hotel was the height of luxury to her: crisp sheets and an ensuite bathroom, when she was used to musty dorms with twenty other unwashed bodies up a mountain somewhere.

'I know you'll think I'm a prima donna, but I really can't sleep here. The fridge... It hums.' His throat bobbed and despite Kira's gnawing stomach and the haze of frustration, she noted the irregular rise and fall of his chest.

'Are you all right?'

His first response was a wobble on his feet and Kira kicked herself for asking. 'I— Ehm...' He rummaged in the pockets of his long coat, tugging out a pack of lozenges, a leather card purse, a ring which he slipped onto his little finger, some sweet wrappers, several receipts – and finally a small bottle. Spraying a puff into his mouth, he sucked in a purposeful breath and released it slowly, along with the scent of citrus and herbs.

With one final rummage, he frowned and peered at the door he'd just emerged through. 'I locked myself out.' His eyes slammed shut. So much drama in a single face. When his eyes blinked open again, Kira jumped. 'Can I use your shower?' he asked.

'Uh...'

Not waiting for her answer, he stalked down the hall, his coat billowing. Hurrying ahead of him, she reached her door and fumbled for her keycard, shooting a wary glance at him. There was a lick of sweat at his temple.

He all but tumbled into her room, glancing around as though he expected something to jump out at him.

'Here, I'll get you a towel,' she said, dropping her voice smoothly, purposefully.

His gaze settled on her and she knew she was right. He wasn't a prima donna. He was on the edge of an anxiety episode.

'You know, I—' she began carefully, 'I should apologise. I lied about your performance. I found it... touching.'

'You did?' A flicker of delight crossed his features and Kira stifled a sigh – of relief, of perplexity. How this man existed in the harsh realities of the human world, she had no idea.

'What piece was it?' she prompted him.

'"Dio, che nell'alma infondere".' Just saying the title, his words took on rhythm, texture – strength.

'What's it from?'

'*Don Carlo*. Giuseppe Verdi.'

'Was I imagining it, or was the other guy in love with his own mother? I thought it was Greek tragedies that were screwed up.'

The corners of his lips turned up. 'No, the woman he loved married his father. Instead of him.'

'*Shit*.' No wonder there had been so much drama. 'You're going to play a part in the performance next year?'

Wrong question. He froze up. 'I just—' He gestured wildly at the shower. 'Give me a minute.' Snatching the towel out of her hands, he bolted for the bathroom, leaving Kira blinking after him.

'I'll just go get you another keycard,' she called through the door.

The only response was the soothing splash of the water in the shower.

* * *

Kira sank onto the single bed in her room ten minutes later, a replacement keycard for Mattia on her desk, her thoughts scrambled. She'd taken it in her stride – or at least with a bit of grace – that she now had to help run weddings, as well as coaching her climbing groups and leading adventure holidays. But listening to a baby-faced operatic baritone rattle the panes of the shower stall with his powerful melodies while he recovered from a mild anxiety episode – in her bathroom – was beyond what she'd ever thought she'd have to deal with.

She should have guessed he'd sing in the shower. He spoke in such soft, measured tones, his face light, his shoulders hunched and unassuming. But his voice when he sang... She could feel the adrenaline bursting out of him. She was convinced he was in there throwing his hands up in triumph or despair, his face alive with second-hand emotions as the water sluiced over his chest. It was tempting to peek in and see if she was right, except...

The water-sluicing thing she could picture in a

little too much detail, and she wasn't supposed to be noticing these things about a client who was probably a good stretch too young for her anyway – among a host of other reasons.

She jumped when her phone rang, although it wasn't a surprise when she saw the caller ID. It was Ginny, and Kira was technically still at work, even though her work was currently twenty-four-seven and the client was naked in her shower.

'Hey,' she said, connecting the call. She liked Ginny, even though she was too optimistic about everything to be trusted. The labret piercing below her lip hinted at a streak of rebellion that Kira hadn't seen yet, but she hoped it was alive and well.

'How's everything going? Did you find a hotel? I was worried everything would be booked out at this time of year,' Ginny asked, at a mile-a-minute as usual. 'Alessandra is super protective of her friend, like you might accidentally break him or something.'

Kira smiled faintly, grateful he was only humming softly at the moment, rather than bellowing his vibrato-laden operatic vowels. 'He's a bit... particular, but you can tell her not to worry. I've got it in hand.'

As if on cue, he broke into a new melody, something drawn-out and aching, and Kira's stomach dropped.

'Is that... him singing?' Ginny asked, her voice high.

'He's in the shower.'

Ginny's spluttering would have been funny in other circumstances. 'In your room?'

She couldn't exactly explain that he'd invited himself into her room so he could have his hot, water-sluicing shower and calm down, even as Kira got worked up.

'He locked his keycard in his room.'

'Ohhh-kaaaayyyy,' came Ginny's amused response.

'It's probably best not to tell Alessandra any of this. I will have your tenor – I mean baritone – delivered in good time for the wedding and there's no need to worry.'

'What's the difference between a tenor and a baritone?' Ginny asked in a stage whisper.

'Damned if I know.'

'But the "delivery" is why I'm calling. Katy, the manager here at our cabin, told me there's a weather warning for all of Tyrol for heavy snow tomorrow.'

Unease prickled in her stomach. As a climber, she had a healthy respect for the weather, but this wasn't a climb. 'I can drive in snow. We might be delayed, but we should get through,' she assured Ginny. 'Besides, what's the other option? Holing up here for another day?'

'The wedding isn't until Wednesday,' Ginny pointed out. 'You have four days.'

'I'm supposed to take a group ski touring on Tuesday and besides, if the snow is bad enough to cause disruption on the roads, then I should try to get there as soon as possible. I'd rather be stranded with the wedding party than here—'

Another dramatic crescendo sounded from the bathroom and Kira stifled a laugh.

'Just don't take any risks,' Ginny warned her. '*You* probably have wild insurance, but if we damage his vocal chords... At the very least, Alessandra will never forgive me.'

'They're very close, apparently.'

'And the groom doesn't seem to like him much, either,' Ginny added. 'I'm wondering if he's an ex.'

'I don't think so,' Kira reassured her. *She* might have slept with a friend or two in her time, but not one she'd known that long. 'But what happened to your golden rule of weddings?'

'Meh.' Ginny gave an audible shrug. 'This isn't getting emotionally involved. It's just being nosy. You have your rock faces; I have my juicy wedding gossip. We're both thrill-seekers,' she said with a giggle.

Wedding gossip certainly wasn't Kira's idea of a thrill, especially not when it involved the surprising man booming out opera in her shower.

'Ginny, how old is Alessandra?' she asked before she could stop herself.

'Why do you want to know?'

'Just curious.' About whether she'd been checking out a guy old enough to be her... much younger brother.

'She's twenty-nine. The same age as me, actually.'

If Kira had been listening, she might have noticed Ginny's rueful tone. But instead, she was comforting herself with the knowledge that Mattia was probably twenty-seven, twenty-six at a pinch. A four or five years' age difference wasn't morally grey. She could forgive herself the ogling.

Although she shouldn't be appreciating a client that way. Andreas had done that: fallen for a woman on a two-week adventure trip. Eight years of heartache later, they'd only just sorted themselves out and got engaged, as much as the thought of her rugged mountaineer best friend getting married freaked Kira out.

Urgh, *weddings*. She couldn't think of anything worse than standing in front of a crowd in an enormous dress and a hairstyle that was a work of art, swallowing her pride and making a declaration of the most foolish and embarrassing feature of the human condition – *love*. And unfortunately, she knew what she was talking about.

'I hope you found something nice to wear, anyway,' Ginny continued, her tone cautious. 'They're super well-dressed Italians and there's a total aesthetic going on here and...'

'I've got the message, Ginny,' Kira said with a snort. 'Loud and clear. I'll make sure when I turn up tomorrow that I look vaguely presentable.' *Vaguely*.

'And *you* remember the golden rule of weddings too,' Ginny said. '*Don't get emotionally involved.*'

Kira snorted. 'Do you even know me?' But she winced, glad Ginny couldn't see her shooting a glance at the bathroom door. She was not emotionally involved. Just a little... sympathetic.

'Stay safe, anyway,' Ginny interrupted her thoughts.

'I always do. I'll see you tomorrow, although it might be late if Snowmageddon really hits.'

'Oh, please don't say the word "Snowmageddon". This chalet is cosy and gorgeous, but "Which family member would you eat first?" is not a question we ask during pre-marital counselling.'

'Don't you have a bride to fuss over or a family skeleton to shove back in the closet?'

'They haven't eaten anyone *yet!*'

'Bye!' Kira said pointedly, peering at the phone with a perplexed smile. Ginny's crooked sense of humour seemed a strange trait for a bubbly wedding planner.

Her stomach protested keenly when she stood, now so catastrophically empty that it whimpered instead of growling. Hobbling to the entry and snatching her coat from the hook, she knocked on the bathroom door.

'Mattia?'

The low, stony line he'd been singing petered out.

'I'm going to get some food. Do you have any... sensitivities?' Her word choice struck her.

The door flew open, startling a squeal out of her. And then her vocal chords – and most of her synapses – gave out entirely.

His hair formed wild, sodden curls around his face. His shoulders were even broader than they'd looked in his dapper coat, bony and glistening, the water highlighting dips and rises. A gold chain hung around his neck with a small pendant. He didn't have the sculpted torso of a climber. There was even a little softness around his middle. But half-naked, precariously covered by a towel he held bunched just below his belly button, he made Kira think of intimacy and touch – vulnerability, closeness.

Her brain was such a mess. And Mattia was cute, standing there, dripping, in the doorway, his chest rising and falling. She wondered what he would look like singing without a shirt on. She'd like to see that – as would probably a whole auditorium of opera fans.

'Why do you have blue hair?'

His blurted question snapped her out of her meandering, inappropriate thoughts. 'What?' She was too hungry to keep up.

'The colour matches your eyes.'

Heat rushed up her throat. 'What are you talking about?'

'Oh, I—' The fist gripping the towel squeezed reflexively. 'Sorry, I was just wondering – thinking about...'

Me, while you're in the shower. Kira choked back that thought. Clearing her throat, she forced her gaze up to find him regarding her with his head at an angle. He looked much better – colour in his cheeks and the brightness back in his eyes.

'I dyed my hair blue because I felt like it. Because I don't care,' she admitted.

'About your appearance?'

'What other people *think* of my appearance,' she clarified.

He gave a thoughtful nod. 'Thank you – for the shower.'

'You're welcome,' she replied with a shrug. 'Oh, I got you another keycard.' Hauling in a much-needed breath after she'd stepped away, Kira kicked herself for her slightly wobbly legs as she fetched the card.

'Would you mind getting my suitcase? The fridge —' He gestured to his ear with a grimace.

'Sure. Give me a sec.'

Escaping down the hall, she entered his dark room and immediately noticed the low hum of the mini-bar fridge. She never would have registered the sound if he hadn't mentioned it. With a deep sigh, she fumbled behind the desk until she found the plug and yanked it out. The room fell eerily silent.

Rolling his suitcase back down the hall, she knocked on the door and braced herself for the view of all that skin once more. But she hadn't prepared herself for his wide smile. He was too much – of every-thing. There wasn't enough air in this hotel.

'I'll just get dressed,' he said quickly. 'And then can we go back to the Christmas market to eat? It was so beautiful and I didn't get a chance to enjoy it. If we're stuck here, we might as well make the most of it.'

His expression was adorably earnest, but Kira was *starving*.

'Please? We can get a cab back there. I can get dressed quickly.'

She couldn't exactly say no. 'Don't you need to take your time putting your make-up on?'

'I don't wear make-up unless I'm performing,' he said with a pout, working out only belatedly that she'd been joking. 'But I could put some eyeliner on, if you like it,' he teased her back. 'I promise I'll be quick.'

'You know how good you look in eyeliner,' she grumbled as she took her coat from its hook, pausing when she realised what she'd said aloud. She risked a glance to find him biting his lip over a grin, his cheeks pink.

'I'm going to remember you said that.' His tone was light, with a breathy laugh of disbelief.

'I'll see you downstairs.' Shoving her hands in her pockets, she stomped in the direction of the lift, whirling around when she thought of one last thing. 'Oh, I heard the fridge in your room.'

His head appeared around the door-frame, a droplet of water catching the light as it fell from one of his curls. 'You did?'

'I pulled the plug out. It's switched off now.'

She didn't think she'd ever been rewarded with such a captivating smile for something so simple.

4

Mattia studied his reflection as he rode the lift to the ground floor where Kira would be waiting for him – probably tapping her foot, he thought with amusement. He'd chosen his favourite cable-knit sweater in charcoal, shoved his hands in the pockets of his slacks. His heart rate was slightly elevated, but he was inclined to think that wasn't anything to do with the panic attack he'd narrowly avoided.

He owed Kira a full explanation, but he needed some food in his stomach first, even though he was still a little queasy from hyperventilating.

His therapist would probably tell him to go easy on himself, watch a sweet movie with headphones on and get a good night's sleep, but he'd been staring out of the window off and on while he dressed, catching the glow of the fortress on the hill and the whimsical movement of the snowflakes making their muted descent.

He wanted to see more of this place with its white pillows of snow crystals and the glow of a different kind of light. Some of Kira Watling's outdoor adventure guide vigour must have rubbed off on him. The thought made him smile as the lift came to a stop with a ding.

She looked very... vigorous where she stood in the foyer with her thick coat open at the front to reveal the shirt he'd admired earlier. It was ugly and grey, designed for function and not aesthetics, but it was so tight, it outlined every curve of her athletic body. She belonged in a skintight superhero costume, except those were probably difficult to get off.

Not that he was thinking of peeling off her shirt. Or maybe he was. He gave himself a little shake to clear his head of *that* notion as he followed her out to where the cab was already waiting.

The taxi dropped them off by a little row of shops with matching green shutters, all of them decorated with bows and pine boughs, candles in the windows. The ice rink on the square was lit by a shower of fairy lights on the building behind.

Kira grimaced, but quickly tempered her expression. 'Sorry. I'm grumpy when I'm hungry and I've been hungry all day.'

He gestured her ahead and they crossed the square in the direction of the market. 'That explains a lot.'

'Oh, does it?' she responded flatly.

He opened his mouth to apologise, defend himself for the tactless statement, but his gaze snagged on the glow of the light on her cheek, showing up the scar. She was pretty – even when she scowled.

'But I don't know why *you're* so cheerful.'

A smile tugged. 'It is a bit of a surprise. I'm sure it's partly because of you.'

'Grumpy ol' me?'

The smile broke out. 'Yes, grumpy you.'

'Well, you're in luck, because I don't like crowds, either.'

'I'll protect you.'

She eyed him – a response he deserved.

'Crowds are one of the few things that don't trouble me at all. That inoffensive hum of talking in the background, it's everything and nothing.'

As soon as they approached the wooden stands under the glowing lights, Kira made a beeline for the second one along and bought an enormous glazed cookie with a smile and a polite 'Danke,' which belied how grumpy she'd been with him. Dipping her hand into the paper bag as they walked on, she lifted it to her mouth.

'You're going to eat a cookie first? Before dinner?' he teased.

His words triggered the uncomfortable memory of eating with Carla when they'd been together and he wished he'd never said anything. This wasn't a date.

'It's none of your business,' Kira stated with a lift of her chin. 'I'm starving.' She took an enormous bite for emphasis and Mattia flinched even before the noise reached his ears, but the biscuit wasn't as crunchy as he'd assumed and the sounds of the market muffled everything except the low 'Mmm' of approval in the back of her throat.

He blinked. Kira was nothing like Carla. She wasn't like anyone else he'd ever met. What a relief.

'This is so good,' she said with her mouth full. He registered the muted sound of her chewing, but he could still hear that groan echoing. Sparks crackled over his skin as he watched her. 'Gingerbread from a Christmas market is always just *better*. I don't usually like it, but this stuff, with the edible paper on the back? It's incomparable.'

The hitch in her voice sent a shiver through him.

He noticed her top lip was lush, while her lower lip was thinner. Her eyes were bright and her voice low and husky; her audible enjoyment of food was enough to give him goosebumps and she had blue hair and no make-up and a rather attractive scowl. She'd turned the fridge off for him.

He was more than halfway to a very pleasant infatuation already.

When she eyed him again, he realised he must have been staring. 'Do you want to try some?' She looked reluctant to share, but Mattia already suspected how much kindness she hid under her grumpy exterior.

'Please.' He dipped his head and opened his mouth, waiting for her to hold up the gingerbread round, but she frowned at him and drew back. Breaking off a piece, she shoved it in his direction and he had to fumble to catch it as she kept walking at her striding pace.

Of course. Any infatuation was on his side only. A woman in big boots with blue hair and no nonsense would not do *infatuation*. But he was suddenly curious about whether she had a significant other.

Also none of his business.

Besides, considering the impending reunion with Carla at the wedding and the associated stress dreams that had been assailing him for a week, it should have been easy to remember that he was terrible on dates. How fortunate that this wasn't a date – and he got an extra night to mentally prepare for the wedding.

With a puzzled smile at the strange way good fortune and bad fortune seemed to intertwine like musical motifs in an opera, he hurried to catch up with Kira as she weaved stiffly through the crowd.

He tried to glance up and enjoy the glowing ambience of the strings of lights, the luminous Christmas tree and the cosy stands with knick-knacks made of glass and wood, candles, knitwear and handicrafts, but everything was a blur as he struggled to keep Kira in sight and stay upright on the slippery flagstones.

'I don't know what you want to eat,' she called over her shoulder, 'but I'm getting chips from the Kartoffel-hütte. I saw it while I was waiting for you earlier.'

'Chips,' he repeated, already hearing the crispy potato sticks crunching in her mouth – and ringing in his ears.

She rolled her eyes. 'Are you too fancy for chips?'

'No!' he insisted. 'Oh, look, they have tramezzini,' he pointed out, but Kira didn't even stop.

'You can't have Italian sandwiches at a Christmas market in Salzburg. Get some when you go home.'

And that was how he found himself juggling a

paper cone full of skin-on chips – and a hot-dog roll with two narrow sausages, onion and some mysterious spices – as he followed Kira to a barrel table under a pine garland. He thought he'd done quite well until he lost two chips in a tricky manoeuvre around a toddler in a woollen snow-suit with tassels on the hood.

He was out of breath by the time he set his paper plate down. 'I think,' he began, 'the trick to being calm in a crowd is not to be in a hurry.'

'If I have to dawdle through a crowd, then I'm not calm,' she replied gruffly and, before Mattia had a chance to brace himself, took a bite of her sausage bun. The sound crashed in his ears and a few more chips shook onto the ground as his hand wobbled.

'Are you sure you're okay?' She shoved a chip into her mouth and that exploded through his auditory canal too. 'Are you going to eat?'

The question snapped him out of his distraction. 'Yes, of course.' He considered the messy sausage bun and lifted it gingerly to his lips. It was salty and spiced with unfamiliar flavours, but his taste buds approved.

'You remember *you* were the one who wanted to eat here,' she pointed out doubtfully.

He chewed and swallowed before saying, 'I was picturing the ambience, rather than the food – and imagined we might get knives and forks.'

She snorted a laugh, chewing with her mouth open.

He took another bite, only for a glob of sauce to fly up into his nose. Spluttering and groping for the serviette, he managed to smear a drop on his collar. 'Cazzo!' he cursed, loudly enough to turn a few heads and remind him that, while his beloved Napoli was a long, long way from Salzburg, Italy itself was just over the southern border of this small country.

'You'd like to eat your sausage with a knife and fork, but you swear? I assume that was a swear word.'

'Indeed. Swearing is an art form in Italian, although I must admit that one was unimaginative.'

'Do you want this?' She held up a water bottle.

'I think the shirt is ruined anyway. Waste of good tailoring. I seem to be a complete disaster today.'

She squashed her lips together in a manner that would have been amusing if he hadn't seen exactly what she was thinking.

'Yes, I'm a disaster every day,' he admitted.

'I didn't say that.'

'But you were thinking it. It's okay. You might be surprised to hear I have a reputation for clumsiness and melodrama. I didn't realise snow was so slippery.'

'They say there's no such thing as bad weather, only bad shoes.'

'Excuse me? These are hand-crafted Italian leather.' And his feet were growing colder by the minute.

Her sharp eyes narrowed as she studied him. 'But that wasn't melodrama before – at the hotel,' she said lightly.

'No, it wasn't,' he agreed. 'How could you tell?' He had enough experience of people assuming he was just being difficult.

She shrugged. 'I'm an outdoor guide, remember? I have some experience with anxiety and panic attacks. Does it happen often?'

He shook his head. 'I've had a few flashpoints over the years, but that's what therapy and medication are for.' His smile was a little forced, but he'd learned to trust that something would always make it better.

Even thinking about telling her exactly what had been behind his episode made the noise around him sharpen and close in on him. The brass band on the other square suddenly sounded as though they were playing a metre away. A woman in high heels made a rhythmic 'clack clack' that pounded in his skull. But the individual sounds faded back into an indistinct mass as he met her wary gaze and took a deep breath. 'It's a sound sensitivity disorder. I have exceptional hearing and that has consequences in my brain, especially if I'm already under pressure – like the audition and the wedding and all this.'

Alessandra's wedding... He wasn't in the mood to explain why the prospect of the wedding brought mixed feelings.

'I had temporary tinnitus once and since then, humming noises can be triggering, so... thank you for turning off the fridge.'

She gave a dismissive shrug and finished her sausage – wolfed it down would be a more accurate expression. She was already halfway through the little package of chips. Whether it was the sheer speed at which she ate or the cosy ambience of the surroundings, the rustle of the packet and crunch of the chips between her teeth were just sounds tonight, with no extra stress or emotional side effects.

'It might have been helpful to know in advance,' she said after she'd swallowed.

He liked the way her voice went gravelly when she was grumpy. 'You should add that question to your insurance form for our outdoor adventure, coach.'

'You could have mentioned something. I thought you were just being difficult about the double glazing.'

'With the man thinking we were a couple, I'm not sure you would have listened to me.'

She eyed him. 'Who says "lovers" anyway?' She shuddered as though the word set off some allergies.

'You're the wedding planner.'

'I told you, this isn't my usual gig. I got roped into this. I don't know anything about this stuff.'

It was the first time he'd seen her look uncertain of herself. 'No big wedding in your future, then?' he asked lightly, hoping she couldn't tell how genuinely curious he was.

She blanched, her reaction strong enough to make him regret his prying. 'No,' she answered emphatically. 'Is there anything else I should know? About you?'

What did she want to know? He kind of wanted to tell her all of his secrets, but she wouldn't be interested. 'I'm twenty-seven years old, lived my entire life in Napoli, I am an only child—'

'That's not really what I was asking.'

He couldn't keep his curious question in. 'How old are *you*?'

'Thirty-one – in the next decade from you.'

'Oh, but you meant was there anything you need to know for my safety on this dangerous expedition to Alessandra's wedding?'

Another scowl. 'Our drive tomorrow will be entirely uneventful and I'll deliver you safely in plenty of time for your musical interludes during the ceremony. Don't even suggest anything else.'

'I didn't know outdoor adventurers were just as superstitious as opera singers.'

'I don't have a lucky charm on a necklace like you,' she quipped. 'I'm assuming that's what's on your chain.'

She didn't mean anything by it, but her question brought heat up his chest and he remembered her gaze on his skin earlier.

He leaned on the barrel table, propping himself up as he brought his face close to hers. It was easy to imagine tipping her chin up and kissing her – and he had a vivid imagination. But her gaze grew sharp and he sensed a thousand little triggers. He was familiar with triggers.

'Haven't you learned anything about me yet?' he asked mildly.

'I've learned a few things.' He enjoyed it when she lifted her chin just like that. 'But not what's hanging from your necklace.'

He tugged out the gold charm on its chain, letting the soft lights reflect off the twisted horn shape. 'A curniciello, of course. To scare off the evil eye. A gift from my mother.'

'Why of course?'

'We are very serious about the evil eye in Napoli.'

She rolled her eyes. 'Lucky you're here to protect me, in case the evil eye followed you to Salzburg.'

He flashed her a smile. 'Look, you're enjoying spending time in this crowd. It must be my magic.'

'Magic? That's just what I need,' she grumbled under her breath. Her gaze snapped up to his. 'You heard that, didn't you?'

He gave an apologetic nod. 'But don't worry,' he said brightly. 'You're just what I need too.'

5

Alcohol apparently made Mattia even happier – volatile in his good mood as he swaggered unpredictably. His hand gestures threatened that he could break into song at any moment.

Kira still had her wits about her, although the fuzz surrounding her brain was thicker than she'd realised when she accepted the last ceramic mug of punch from the copper cauldron with a giant ball of flaming sugar set above it.

Perhaps she shouldn't have had anything to drink, not even punch, but she had to be off-duty sometime and it was alarmingly easy to drop her guard around Mattia.

'Foia-zahng-en-boiler?' He whirled back to face

her with a question in his eyes, pausing their progress near the bronze statue of Mozart. The muted melodies from the brass band were now behind them, as were the lights and smells of the market. 'Is that how you say it?'

'Don't look at me. You're the one who asked the woman in the dirndl to repeat the pronunciation so many times. She thought you were flirting with her.'

'I was just being an embarrassing tourist. I don't know how to flirt.'

She snorted at that.

'No, really,' he insisted. 'I don't flirt. I just fall in love.'

That earned him a perplexed glance, but he didn't elaborate. He tugged his phone out of the pocket of his sleek coat, fumbling so much, he nearly dropped it. He didn't seem to have any gloves with him and the temperature had dropped below zero while the snow created a layer of candy floss over everything.

A moment later, a pleasant voice from his phone piped up, 'Feuerzangenbowle. Feu-er-zang-en-bow-le.'

'Foia-zangen-boiler!' he tried again. 'You'd think I'd never sung operas in German,' he said with a wry smile. 'Even if it's difficult to pronounce, it was delicious. *Thank you* for taking me back to the market.' As he spoke emphatically, peering at her with his luscious eyelashes and mile-deep eyes, Kira wasn't sure whether to laugh or smack him. Even if he denied it, he was definitely flirting and there was *no way* he would ever fall in love with her.

'You dragged *me* back here. No matter what Alessandra thinks, I'm not your babysitter.'

'No,' he agreed half-heartedly. 'But I had such an awful day, and to think I'd end it here in the snow with you...' His lips broke into a smile and that was worse than the eyelashes and the hot-chocolate eyes.

She wasn't sure what point he was making by adding the 'with you'. 'What was so bad about your day? Did you fluff your audition piece?'

'I didn't... "fluff",' he said with a sigh. 'I got the part.'

'And that's not good because...?'

He paused, scraping his teeth along his bottom lip. 'It means time away from home. I'm not good with change.'

'Why not just audition in Naples?'

His shrug told her a thousand things at once, each one incomprehensible – like the other-worldly duet. 'There's not a lot of work in Napoli. I... fluffed an audition there. I've been only semi-professional up until recently, but I have an agent now. I am forced out of my comfort zone.'

The catch in his voice rippled over Kira with second-hand feelings she couldn't control. When life got too hot, she found a rock and climbed it, proved herself at each successive difficulty grade. Mattia haemorrhaged emotion all around him in beautiful puddles, enough that she wondered how he could live like that – and how much longer she had to endure it.

'At least it will be summer when I come back here,' he said with a sudden restoration of the brightness it seemed he could summon at will. It gave Kira whiplash and she didn't reply.

She kept silent in the cab, annoyed that she was hyper-conscious of his hand resting on the seat between them – and the fact that she'd climbed in next to him instead of sitting with the driver. His soft skin and neat manicure drew a disheartening comparison with her rough knuckles and bitten-down nails.

'Thank you,' he said stiltedly as the car crossed the glistening river and headed for the train station, providing glimpses of the illuminated, white fortress set above the old town. 'For earlier. The fridge.' The shadows in his expression were evident. 'Even though you didn't know what was going on, you... allora, thank you anyway.'

She waved off his gratitude with a shake of her head. 'Do you think you'll be able to go back into your room? Or is it safer to swap? The bed's a bit small for you, but you've used my towel anyway,' she added drily, hoping to lighten the moment, but the attempt backfired when her words reminded her of the view of him wrapped in that towel and standing close enough for her to see all the droplets.

He coloured, although she didn't imagine he was remembering the same thing. 'I think it'll be okay. I've got music and white-noise apps. It just caught me by surprise. I'll give you my towel.'

She avoided his gaze as they travelled up in the lift, which was difficult with all the mirrors reflecting his chaotic curls and tall figure right back at her. She'd never had a taste for expensive things, but his fine wool coat drew her eye, falling effortlessly over his form as though it had been tailored for him.

He was a creature adapted for beauty. Of course he was wonderful to look at – and listen to. He was every-thing she wasn't.

At his door, he had to rummage in his pockets for long enough that Kira regretted giving him the key-card, but he found it and got the door open. He braced himself as he entered the room, but when he crossed the threshold, the tension drained out of him and he sucked in a deep breath.

'I'll just get you a towel.'

He held the heavy door open for her and she stepped in, trying not to notice how close he was in the cramped entrance, close enough for her to pick up the scent of citrus with undertones of honey and spice. The fading notes of his cologne suited him somehow: sweet and soothing, with hints of darkness underneath.

She drew in a breath as he moved away. She needed to hold onto their differences, the fact that he was too young for her – in attitude if not in body. But he had a nice body. An even nicer face, full of life – in all its dramas. And lovely, smooth eyes – that were currently studying her with soft, dangerous curiosity as he held out the folded towel.

She hated that her breath was short with that gaze trained on her, as though he thought he could puzzle out her secrets. Goosebumps flashed to her hairline. She needed to get out of this confined space where all she could see were his hunched shoulders. She could so easily imagine stretching onto her toes and pressing her lips to his. The kiss would be so soft, full of uncertainty and surprise.

She hated surprises. She really didn't need this

right now, just before a wedding that would drag her worst failures back out into the light – that enormous mistake that meant there would definitely be no big wedding in her future.

Straightening, she realised with a jolt that her back was squashed into the door, which was trying its best to shut on her. 'I, uh... I should go get some sleep.'

Mattia drew back so quickly that he knocked his head on the shelves behind him with an 'Ahia!' Kira made for the corridor, but the heavy door landed against her back and she stumbled right into him, her face pressed into the fragrant collar of his shirt – her body colliding with the full length of his.

She registered the pressure of his hands on her back – and the desire to stay where she was. She wasn't usually a hugger, but the softness of his coat, the heat of his lean body, created a pleasant fog over her skin and in her mind.

It had been a while since she'd been close to anyone – scratched that itch. That wasn't what this was about. He wasn't her usual type – not even close. But something flared – something that definitely shouldn't have right now.

'Scusa.' He cleared his throat, shoving at the door that was still trying to close on them. He managed to prop it open, but trapped Kira against him. 'Oh, I'm—'

He fumbled with the door again, straining to hold the heavy thing open, and Kira ducked out under one of his arms, slipping awkwardly away with heat in her cheeks.

'G'night!' she called over her shoulder without looking back, hoping he wouldn't think anything of her wobbly tone.

'Buonanotte!'

As she fumbled with her keycard, she couldn't resist one last quick glance along the hall. She found him leaning heavily in his doorway with one hand propping him up against the frame, curls tumbling over his forehead as his coat made a cape around his dramatic figure.

When her own door closed behind her with a thump, she leaned against it and took an enormous breath in the pitch-dark room.

She needed to deliver this baritone into the safe hands of his friends as quickly as possible.

* * *

Kira got up early for a run the following morning, grateful for the diligent efforts of the municipal authorities in clearing the footpaths after the substantial snowfall overnight. Flakes were still floating in front of her as she jogged, but not enough to impede their progress into the mountains for the wedding. Pounding the pavement cleared her head – and the frigid air cleared her lungs – and she felt herself again.

These weddings were to blame, forcing her into something she wasn't good at, adding variables she didn't know how to calculate – variables like quirky singers with magnetic smiles.

She knew the best ways to minimise the dangers of rockfalls, could plot an off-piste ski route across terrain and even teach sullen teenagers to scale the indoor wall. But emotional high points? She couldn't shake off a sense of impending doom, even though she told herself it was her own experiences clouding her judgement. Just because she'd been part of one disastrous wedding a long time ago didn't mean there was a rational basis for her belief that she was going to ruin this one.

Kira with her blue hair and her big mouth and stubbornly not-pretty face would be well out of her depth and she was looking forward to none of it – well, perhaps the skiing day.

Today, she would be herself again: no heart-pounding, breath-stealing *anything*. Whatever had been wrong with her yesterday would be gone today. She did *not* have a little crush on the hopeless baritone with the baby face and she didn't have to be grumpy about that. She only hoped he wouldn't want to listen to opera for the entirety of the three-hour drive.

Marching along the corridor when she got back to the hotel, she rapped on his door. 'I'm going to have a quick shower and grab some breakfast. Then we need to go.'

The door flew open and she jumped back, startled. 'Good morning.'

How quickly the optimism of the jog could drain away. He'd looked good in a collared shirt and tailored trousers, but in supple tracksuit bottoms and nothing else, his bare feet flexing appealingly on the hotel carpet, he made her mouth dry. And that was before she got to his sleepy-eyed, tousle-haired morning face. Oh dear.

'Don't you ever think about putting a shirt on before you open the door?'

His smile dimmed, his hand resting self-consciously on his chest, which only drew Kira's eyes there. 'Do you always wake up in a bad mood?'

'When there are weddings involved, yes,' she muttered.

'And me? When *I'm* involved?' He ducked his head to catch her eye.

'I'm sure we'll get on okay when you're properly dressed.' *And my hormones don't scream at me so loudly.*

'I was just finishing my yoga.'

Her gaze drifted behind him to where a mat was set up at the foot of the bed. She was rather curious to see his yoga.

'I'll meet you in the breakfast room,' she said, backing away. 'Don't take too long with your eyeliner!'

'I only wear it on stage!' he called after her. 'Sorry to disappoint you!'

6

'Yes, it looks like we'll be a little delayed, but I'll be there soon, cara mia,' Mattia said to Alessandra, his phone pressed to his ear. He hoped it was true. Traffic was moving, finally, which was more than he could say for their slow trip out of the city and onto the Autobahn. At least the heat was blasting from the vents on the dashboard of the minivan.

'I can't believe you had to go to an audition so close to my wedding!' It wasn't her wedding for another three days, but he wouldn't dare mention that.

'You haven't even asked how the audition went.'

'I know it went well. Nobody can resist you when you sing and I can hear it in your voice that you got the part.' There were no secrets from Alessandra –

and she would never accept anything but the highest praise for his musical ability, even though she was biased. 'But three months away from home? It's a long time.'

'It's only ten weeks, actually. And I'll be able to go home at least once.'

She continued as though he hadn't said anything. 'How are you doing after the auditions – and the delay last night? I was *worried*.'

He smiled faintly. Alessandra was his biggest cheerleader, but she did *worry*. 'It was fine. I'm fine, Ale. Focus on the wedding.' Her marriage – to a guy who barely gave Mattia the time of day, but each to their own.

'That's what Carla keeps telling me.'

There was no way he could stop his insides seizing up at the mention of her name, so he let it happen and then waited for his muscles to relax again. 'She's right,' he replied mildly.

'Yes, something you have in common,' Alessandra responded brightly – too brightly, considering she was discussing her two best friends who had dated each other and then broken up in sticky circumstances. 'We'll be all together soon,' she said softly, making him glad she couldn't see his scrunched-up grimace. 'That's what I wanted for my wedding – to celebrate it with everyone important to me.'

He dropped his head back against the seat and tried not to imagine she meant bringing him together again with Carla. 'I'll see you this afternoon, hmm?'

'It's so beautiful here – and so quiet in the snow. I can't wait to show you.'

The thought of all the snow didn't exactly soothe him. 'I'm glad it's everything you wanted. Ciao, cara.'

He felt Kira's curious glance as he disconnected the call, but he waited to see if she'd ask – *what* she'd ask. He suspected she wouldn't be able to wait long. The hum of the unfamiliar car engine drilled at the back of his mind, but the swish of Kira's technical trousers sounded somehow louder. She moved around a lot.

'What were you arguing about?'

'We weren't arguing,' he insisted. 'Perhaps Italian conversation is more animated than you're used to.'

'But you did this *thing* with your face. You looked like someone just killed your cat.'

He smacked a hand to his chest in horror. 'Don't even suggest something like that!'

'Yikes, you actually have a cat? Sorry.'

'I don't have a cat, but that's terrible.'

The gaze she flicked him was pleasantly warm. 'I'll choose my metaphors more carefully from now on.'

'Thank you,' he said with a pointed nod and flung himself back against the seat with a sigh. 'Do you know the happy couple?' he asked after a moment's pause.

'I've met them once. Ginny – my colleague – did most of the planning. I just help out when needed, thank God. Why? Are you secretly in love with the bride?'

He choked. 'No! Alessandra is like a sister to me. But perhaps that makes it worse. She's always been my biggest supporter and she's moving on in life... without me.'

Kira's only reaction was a brief, assessing glance. 'Maybe you shouldn't hang onto her.'

He couldn't help laughing, even though that earned him another doubtful look. 'That's your advice? Don't be attached to anyone because they might leave you?'

She made a low, disgruntled sound in her throat. 'I didn't really mean it like that, but it's good advice anyway, isn't it?'

'You don't have friends, then?' he asked, provoking her on purpose.

'I just choose my friends carefully,' she said, her

mouth tight, and because he wasn't wise the way she was, he was immediately thinking about earning the right to be called her friend. 'So all of this makes you less than happy about the wedding? Does the singing make you nervous?'

'No,' he said with a shake of his head. 'I want to do that for her. It's a sort of... blessing. It's the one thing I do very well.'

Her non-committal nod amused him. 'You still sound about as excited as I am – which is not very much.'

He nodded. 'For one, I don't get on very well with Joe, as much as that upsets Alessandra, and worse...' He belatedly realised he could be opening Pandora's box by bringing this up. But he didn't think he could hold it in anyway. 'I... dated the bridesmaid.'

'Mattia, you sly dog.'

It took him a second to understand what she'd said and her teasing tone registered before anything else – and the way she slightly mispronounced his name that he rather liked. But he managed a mock-peevish scowl.

'Is it going to be awkward?'

'You have to ask?' he replied, his voice high. 'We got together because of Alessandra and now...' Even Alessandra couldn't always bend the world to her will.

'She dumped you, then?'

'Yes, but it was my fault,' he mumbled. The more time passed, the more he was convinced of that.

'What, you couldn't keep it in your pants?'

'I did *not*. How could you even think—?'

'Chill out, opera boy. You basically apologised for her dumping you. Unless you cheated, maybe you should give her some of the blame and not beat yourself up?'

She spoke so casually, dropped that drawled nickname – which he chose to interpret as an endearment – and seemed to defuse all his wound-up emotions with a single word. But the situation was more complicated than she made out.

'I offended her.'

'Like, you insulted her taste in music or you denied the holocaust?' Kira asked warily.

'Neither! I would never do either of those! I just...' Again, Kira's outrageous turn of phrase made it easier to get the next part out. 'She bites her fork when she eats,' he explained, flinching inwardly at the memory.

'Is that a euphemism for something?' Kira asked quizzically.

'No! Her spoon too. It was like fingernails scraping on the blackboard! Every meal!'

She nodded slowly in dawning comprehen-

sion, her lips compressing in thought. He wondered if she realised how expressive her lips were,
given the cardboard face she put on for the
world. 'And you told her this.' It was a guess, not
a question. 'Does she know about your... sensitivity?'

'The official name is misophonia and yes, she
knew. We knew each other for a long time before we
dated. It just never bothered me that way before.'

'Did you ask her to try to stop?'

'I told her it seemed to be getting worse the longer
we were together. She interpreted it as a way to break
up with her. She was really hurt.'

'Did you intend it that way?'

'Of course not! We'd been together nearly a year. I
thought... I thought that was it; we were together.'
That sounded naive now he had to admit that to Kira,
but she'd probably already worked out he was a little
naive.

'No offence to the bridesmaid, but that sounds like
her problem, not yours.'

That took the wind out of him for a moment. 'I
should have told her sooner – should have brought it
up with my therapist straight away,' he insisted. 'By
the time I mentioned it to Carla, I was quite stressed
about it. But breaking up with someone because of an

eating habit is the stupidest reason in history and what if...?'

'What if you missed out on something good, something important to you because of your hearing?'

He'd been about to say, '*What if love isn't enough to make a relationship work?*' Kira's sentence was close enough for the moment, despite missing the mark.

'You're going to see her this afternoon, eat dinner with her tonight. Are you going to be okay?'

He shifted uncomfortably. 'Maybe there'll be a snowstorm and we'll have to stay another night.'

She chuckled, low and rough, and he had the fleeting thought that he'd rarely heard a sound so raw and wonderful. 'You'd rather brave another fridge?'

'You're here to turn all the fridges off for me,' he pointed out with a pout. 'But I listened to you crunching on chips last night without thinking I was about to have a heart attack, so I think I'll be okay.'

'Oh, God, my mum is always on at me for eating with no manners,' she said with a wince. 'But for you, I would have tried.'

Mattia had to bite his lip against the thought that that was one of the nicest things he'd ever heard.

'If we don't show up today, the bride will think *she's* having a heart attack, right?' she continued. 'I think we both have to just face the problem.'

'You're annoyingly right. But what's the worst that could happen?'

'Um, a hell of a lot of things.'

He sank further into the passenger seat. 'I do want everything to work out for Alessandra.'

'But?'

'There's no "but",' he insisted. 'She'll marry him and be happy. Why do you think there's a "but"?'

She opened her mouth, probably to defend herself, but snapped it shut again, squirming in her seat. 'A good friend of mine got engaged recently,' she said in such a rush that he suspected she'd surprised herself with the confession. 'I understand the thing about moving on without you. Maybe I'm a little salty he's going ahead and doing this, changing things.'

He threw her question back at her. 'He? Are you secretly in love with him?'

'Pfft,' was her only reply at first, lifting her chin. 'Definitely not in love with him.'

'But?'

'There is no "but"!'

'Ah, there definitely is.' He loved that she was so tough, he could unapologetically rib her like this. 'What? He's an ex?' He turned in his seat to face her, shifting the seat belt.

'Are you a gossip?'

'I'm naturally curious.' *Especially about you.* 'Will you have to go to his wedding? Are you over him or do you hold a torch?' *What kind of guy is he?*

'There was nothing to get over. I suppose I'll have to go to his wedding, but they're not rushing anything. I just never thought he'd agree to get married at all. We were kind of kindred spirits like that: nothing in life is certain and we shouldn't make promises we can't keep.'

He couldn't decide if her words were sensible or bleak – and whether she truly believed them or simply used these opinions to keep people away. 'So we just shouldn't make promises?'

'Not in relationships, anyway,' she said flatly. 'Another reason I hate that I now have to work on weddings.'

'You and this friend, you were just casual,' he guessed.

'You can't dump friends, right?'

'No,' he agreed emphatically. 'One of the reasons I don't really understand bed friends – not that I'm judging you, if you can manage that.'

'Bed friends?' she repeated with a sidelong smile. 'I like that expression. But I wouldn't even go that far. Andreas and I... we just let off steam occasionally – or used to, before he was with Sophie.'

The idea stuck in his throat uncomfortably. 'Maybe that was too much information – the steam, the...' No words came to finish the sentence, so he used his hands to communicate the images that had formed in his head at her statement.

She snorted a laugh. 'Sounds like you have too many inhibitions to manage a bed friendship.'

Inhibitions probably wasn't the word he'd use. 'It just doesn't make sense to me,' he continued. 'If you find someone attractive and you get on well, isn't that a relationship anyway, even if you're telling yourself you're just friends? You don't think you might be secretly heartbroken that your friend is getting married?'

'I'm not secretly heartbroken,' she said curtly. 'And you can find someone attractive and still not want to share your life with them.'

She had a point, especially if he considered that she apparently didn't want to share her life with anyone.

'Are you the kind of guy who's looking for his soulmate?' Her tone was strained.

Failing to stifle a slow smile, he watched her as he said, 'I appreciate all that effort to swallow your sarcasm.'

Her nostrils flared. 'It's clear we don't have a lot in common, but that's no reason for me to judge you.'

Mattia wanted to insist they had more in common than it appeared, but he couldn't articulate what that was. An affinity. Vibes. All the stuff she would dismiss anyway, even if she felt it too. 'I suppose I am looking for a soulmate – with little success so far. But that's not what I was talking about. It's more that the feelings are different, between friends or lovers – before and after. You don't have to share your life with a lover, but you share... *something*. You change each other.'

A twinge of discomfort tugged in his chest as he thought about Carla – her body warm against his at night, the soft conversations they'd had after sex. He'd bet Kira was already pulling her big boots on a minute after an orgasm, while her partner lay stupefied on the bed and helplessly watched her go.

When Kira spoke, it was obvious she had no idea of the absurd turn his thoughts had taken. 'I try not to let anyone change me.'

The catch in her voice echoed in his ears. There was something here – something important she wasn't saying. He could feel it, a hazy suggestion of hurt that made his chest ice up.

Kira swallowed and straightened. 'I'm sorry she hurt you and that you have to go through seeing her again like this. Another reason weddings are hell.' End of topic.

'It is hell when we have to see people,' he agreed sagely, steering the conversation back into familiar territory.

It took a moment for her to pick up on his tone. 'Are you teasing me, opera boy?'

'Opera boy chooses not to answer that question.'

'You are wise beyond your years,' she quipped.

Flicking on the indicator, she peered over her shoulder before changing lanes, skirting the traffic with smooth, expert manoeuvres. But it wasn't long before she gripped the wheel with a pent-up huff, stomping on the brake.

'I hope you told Alessandra we wouldn't get in until this evening,' she bit out.

When he turned to look ahead, the source of her frustration was obvious. 'Eh, not exactly.' Snow hit the windscreen in little explosions of powder and one lane ahead was completely blocked, lorries backed up nose to tail. 'We're not *actually* going to get stuck in this, are we?'

She shrugged. 'I've been in worse.'

'That doesn't reassure *me*. The highest mountain I've climbed is Monte Vesuvio and the only other time

I've seen snow, it was in a performance of *La Traviata* and made of soap bubbles.'

'The snow won't hurt you, but if you keep sighing like that, you might use up all the air in the car,' she said drily.

He scrubbed his hands over his face and through his hair, watching her gaze dart away from him when he opened his eyes again. 'Could we listen to music?'

'Sure, as long as it's not opera. That's not really my thing.'

He smiled faintly, fiddling with the stereo system until he had the Bluetooth connected. 'I do listen to a variety of musical styles, even if I'm only trained in one.'

Feeling her curious anticipation in the way she held her taut, compact body, he scrolled through his library, taking his time to decide on the best music mix for the journey. When he saw the song title in one of his playlists, he knew in an instant it was right.

With a lift of his eyebrows for Kira, he pressed play and the funky, lively guitar riff from 'Snow (Hey Oh)' from the Red Hot Chili Peppers filled the van.

7

For a seven-hour drive that should only have taken three, the trip passed surprisingly pleasantly – not that Kira would admit that, even to herself. Mattia was an excruciatingly congenial travel companion.

The road narrowed after Mayrhofen and she was now navigating through a white valley, the windscreen wipers on full against continued flurries. Chalets with wooden balconies dotted the meadows to her right and on their left, the mountainside rose steeply, rock-fall barriers groaning under the weight of snow.

And her baritone companion was singing along with some Italian crooner, complete with air guitar, as though he were on stage in front of a crowd of adoring fans, his voice in a hundred colours, from lively and smooth to rough and aching. He made people *feel* things and while Kira didn't want him to turn his magic onto her, she was a little in awe of it.

Ginny and Sophie and the others from I Do Destinations would probably want to keep him on their books for future events. He could probably make the pettiest jealous ex cry at a wedding.

'I would applaud, except I think you'd prefer I kept my hands on the wheel,' she said when the song finished.

'What did you think? Honestly,' he asked. She could almost hear him batting his eyelids hopefully at her.

'I think your calling in life was opera after all. Too many wrong notes on the guitar,' she joked.

He laughed, a deep sound from his stomach that reminded her of the powerful vibrations of his serious singing voice. 'I meant of the song. It's Eros Ramazzotti, a national treasure. Have you heard of him?'

'I have to admit, there's only one person I think of when you mention Italian singers.'

'Ah, yes. The incomparable tenor. You know he couldn't read music?'

'Can you?'

'Of course! I spent years of my life studying music.'

It was about as far as you could get from climbing

crags. For a man who smelled like designer cologne, wore a gold chain and silky, patterned shirts that were nicer than anything she owned, and used his powerful, refined voice for a living, he was surprisingly sympathetic.

When the opening synthesiser of the next song filled the van, he grinned at her for long enough that she was forced to meet his gaze. Then the iconic opening chords came in and Kira recognised the song with a stifled smile. Not that it helped. Mattia could tell.

He beat his hands against the dashboard, bobbing his head as though it wasn't the most embarrassing thing Kira had ever seen.

'You know this, right?'

'Of course,' she mumbled in reply.

'Can you sing along?'

'No!'

'It's more fun if you do, I promise. Just the chorus!'

'I'm concentrating on the road,' she said, jerking her chin at the windscreen.

But she had no hope against his pout. He sang the section just before the chorus and it took some effort for Kira not to join in, although she needed a moment to gather her pride. But her fingertips tapped on the steering wheel.

At the first words of the chorus, he tossed his head and increased the volume of his singing, arms flailing. Kira snorted a laugh, but there was no way she could resist leaning towards him and singing, 'Woah-oh, livin' on a prayer!'

With a delighted smile, Mattia turned to her and they sang the rest of the chorus together, her voice rusty and barely in tune – not that that seemed to matter to him. Her chest was light and she laughed at him when he continued singing into a pretend microphone like Jon Bon Jovi in the music video.

'Key change!' he announced just before the final chorus and Kira could imagine him turning in a dramatic spin on stage. She was laughing so hard, she almost missed the navigation system telling her to turn left.

'Whoops!' She made the sharp turn, skidding slightly, but she resisted applying the brakes and the winter tyres quickly regained traction. Mattia had flung his arms out, bracing himself against the dashboard with his eyes squeezed shut.

'We're alive,' she said drily.

He pried one eye open and released a breath. Then he peered out of the windscreen, ducking forward. 'Are you sure? This place doesn't look real.'

Kira followed the instructions Ginny had sent her

towards the parking lot, ignoring Mattia and his dramatic gasps while she manoeuvred the van into a narrow space, her lip tucked into her teeth in concentration. When she'd pressed the park brake and sat back in her seat, she asked, 'What?'

'Look! At that!' he said, his voice high.

She blinked. Lush pine forest rose to one side, powdered with snow as thick as the icing on a wedding cake. On the other was the village of Lanersbach, a cluster of peaked roofs with carved, wooden eaves.

'What?' she asked again, as he rolled his eyes. All around the isolated valley rose mountain summits, dappled with snow on their steep slopes.

'The landscape is... extraordinary. Did you drive us into a different world?'

'No,' she said quizzically. 'This is Tyrol.'

Groping for the door-handle, he tumbled outside, his neck bent backwards as he spun in a slow circle, taking it all in. Raising his arms, he marvelled at the snow showering around him, glistening in the glow from the street lamps as the sky darkened with early dusk.

'Evviva! Woohoo!' he cried out, taking a step – right into a snowdrift. 'Ahi!' Stumbling out of the icy, wet pile, he grasped the door for balance, throwing her a wry smile that caught Kira in the ribs.

She was used to finding men attractive when they had overdeveloped muscles in their backs and big, blunt hands for grasping rocks and tying knots. Patterned shirts with too many buttons undone, bright smiles and clumsiness were not supposed to inspire this fluttering in her gut.

But there it was. Her throat thickened and her chest tightened and maybe she was ill? If she had a virus, that might explain why her insides were goop just from looking at him. She couldn't help thinking that his friend Alessandra was right about one thing at least: there was something special about Mattia that needed protecting – mostly from himself, she added, as he lifted one foot to inspect his sodden shoe with a grimace.

'Cazzo!' he cursed.

'Get back inside!' Kira called. 'I have to phone Ginny to send the shuttle for us and I don't know how long we'll be waiting here.'

Swinging himself back into the seat, he gave a violent shiver and pulled the door closed. 'Maybe I should just look at the beautiful snow and not touch it.'

Shooting him a tolerant smile, Kira held her phone to her ear and climbed over the centre console into the rear of the minivan.

'Finally! Please tell me you've arrived! Alessandra is beside herself.'

'We've arrived!' Kira was glad to declare, amused by Ginny's effusive relief. After her colleague promised to send the shuttle for them, Kira hauled her rucksack upright and popped the snaps as she signed off, 'I'll see you soon.'

'Kira,' Ginny continued tentatively before Kira could disconnect the call. 'You remember what I said about... being presentable?'

'For fuck's sake, it's minus five degrees out there and even the rich people will be wearing technical boots,' she grumbled. 'But I remember, which is why I'm going through my stuff right now to find a... *blouse*.'

Kira's nose wrinkled. She wasn't sure she'd ever used the word before. It sounded like something used for blowing her nose.

'You're the absolute *best*. You won't believe this group. The bride is gorgeous and super sweet, but holy shit, this lot use their silver spoons to check their reflections! London finance types with money to burn – or freeze, in this case. You have to manage them carefully and part of that is earning their respect early on.'

'I'm sure I'll earn their respect on the slopes,' Kira pointed out, 'but putting on a nice shirt won't kill me.'

'And... some make-up? Did you get that stuff I recommended?'

When Kira had determined that every last item of make-up she owned was so old, it was unhygienic, she'd asked Ginny for advice. 'I brought some make-up. I won't embarrass you.'

'Fuck, I wish that didn't make me sound like such a bitch.'

Kira grinned, remembering the first time she'd discovered Ginny was a terrible potty mouth, as bad as any mountaineer, although she kept up a perfect facade for her clients – a skill Kira wasn't sure she would ever master.

'See you soon. But you owe me a drink after this.' She stilled, her brow pulling down. Since when did she *want* to hang out with the staff of I Do Destinations? The two very different travel companies found themselves in a marriage of convenience, which Kira had assumed would never be anything other than merely convenient. Ginny surely wouldn't want to hang out.

But her colleague answered, 'I'm going to need a big one too!' with a smile in her voice. 'It's a deal.'

After disconnecting the call, Kira rummaged in

her stuffed rucksack, tugging out her toiletry pouch and a rather crushed cream blouse she'd only ever worn once. It had a sort of scarf thing attached that she had no idea how to tie, but other people made it look so effortless, she was certain she'd work it out somehow.

Ducking to avoid whacking the roof as she flailed, she unzipped the collar of her merino base layer and whipped it off. That was when she caught sight of Mattia, wide-eyed and turned in his seat, frozen and staring.

Her skin flushed with heat. His look was difficult to misinterpret – especially after their conversation about attraction and friendship – and if she'd wanted to misunderstand on purpose, the strangled sound of surprise in the back of his throat would have under-mined the attempt. His gaze drifted along her shoulders and down her arms, then back up, snagging on her breasts before snapping up to her face as his cheeks blossomed pink.

'Sorry,' he said tightly, whipping around to face forward – about thirty seconds too late. His chest rose and fell heavily.

Kira slipped the blouse over her head and stuffed her arms into the silky sleeves, grimacing at the skip in her heartbeat and the tightness of breath that she really didn't want to be feeling right now.

'Don't worry,' she said peevishly. 'I'm used to sharing dorms and tents and close quarters. It doesn't matter to me if you saw my bra.'

His breath hitched audibly again and he mumbled something inarticulate. It might have been fun toying with him, teasing him for making a big deal out of attraction, but in truth, she was frustrated.

These vibes had nowhere to go except the bedroom and she couldn't exactly drag opera boy to the room she was sharing with Ginny and work these feelings out of their systems while she was supposed to be assisting with the wedding.

Even if an improbable opportunity presented itself, she didn't particularly want to educate Mattia about attraction and sex without affection – leaving out that 'something' that he'd obviously shared with his ex, that Kira wasn't interested in.

But just thinking about his liquid eyes on her made her skin sensitive and started a warm heat inside her – a pleasant, smooth, gratifying heat – and the wedding suddenly felt a lot more complicated.

8

Mattia couldn't look at her without remembering, even though he felt faintly impolite every time he did.

She asked him if he was warm enough and instead of answering, he caught a glimpse of the strap of her white bra and then his brain populated the full image: no-nonsense cotton cups, plunging low.

'Mmm-hmm,' he managed, forcing his gaze away again.

'The shuttle will be here within twenty minutes. The hotel is up in the hills and the road is inaccessible to normal traffic in the winter.'

'Ah,' he replied. Manners were too ingrained in him to keep conversing with her while he stared pointedly away and he turned back to her instinctively, this time catching the view of her collarbone in her gaping neckline. She was tanned, with a handful of freckles, and his eyes traced up along her neck before he'd realised what he was doing and choked.

She didn't notice. A grimace darkened her features as she fiddled with the ends of material at the neckline of her blouse, eventually twisting them into an elaborate knot that made her look as though someone were keeping her captive and did not achieve the careless chic the design was made for.

He opened his mouth to say something, but she turned away, grumbling under her breath as she grabbed a toiletry bag and climbed back into the driver's seat. He felt every swish of material over her body as strongly as the repetitive drip from a leaky faucet, except with a different set of overwhelming feelings.

Was this what happened to him when a strong woman was a little bit kind to him while they were stuck together for twenty-four hours? She thought he was a pain in the arse and he saw sunshine glowing out of her tanned skin.

She'd tipped down the rear-view mirror and swiped on some lipstick before he even realised what she was doing. The shade was too pale for her colouring. Taking a stick of mascara, he flinched when she carelessly applied it.

'What?' she asked, her voice short.

'Nothing.'

'You're a terrible liar, opera boy.'

That's what he was afraid of. He might blurt out how much he liked it when she called him 'opera boy'.

'I realise I'm doing a bad job with my make-up, but unless you're willing to apply it for me, you can keep your opinion to yourself.'

'I didn't say anything!'

'You're *vibing* at me.'

He forced himself back in his seat, rubbing a hand over his face. 'I *could* do your make-up if you—'

'No! I realise you'd do a better job, but you'd also kill off my pride, so leave it.'

Forgetting he wasn't supposed to, he stared at her as she slapped on some beige eyeshadow that was so offensive to his aesthetics, it hurt. 'I like your pride,' he said without thinking.

'You'd better get your coat on,' was all she said in response. Of course she wasn't suffering from the same strange affliction he was, unable to take his eyes off her in the confined space, enjoying every sharp comment she made. She snapped the lid of her make-up case shut and zipped the toiletry bag violently closed. She didn't look at him.

'Can I at least—' He'd raised his hands before the thought had fully formed in his mind.

She turned to him doubtfully, her brows drawing together as she took in his hands, hovering at the level of her shoulders. 'What?'

He quickly unfastened the fabric at her neck, ordering himself to keep his touch light and his eyes up. The complex knot took some undoing, which tugged a smile onto his lips.

He was successfully ignoring his own lolloping heartbeat and the tight air around them until he caught sight of her swallowing – with some effort. His gaze slid to the movement of her pulse just below her jaw. *Huh.*

The backs of his fingers grazed her skin and he wished they hadn't shared so much at the beginning of the journey about intimacy and sex. It was too easy to imagine drifting closer, twisting his fingers with hers.

But even though her chest rose and fell with unsteady breaths, she kept her gaze averted. She probably didn't even want to be friends. He wasn't the type to 'let off steam' the way she did. He just liked her eye-rolls, strong hands helping him and steady words keeping him grounded. He could live with it, if that's all he'd ever receive from Kira Watling. It was a nice diversion at the wedding.

A little infatuation – that's all it was.

A distant buzz suddenly sounded in his ears, growing quickly louder, and Kira tore away as soon as she heard it too. Shoving her arms back into her coat and tugging a neck warmer over her head – smudging her eyeshadow, he noticed with chagrin – she jumped out of the van to flag down the driver of a rapidly approaching snowmobile.

He frowned. A friend of hers?

His confusion only increased a moment later when the gruff, solid man with weathered skin and a plush moustache hauled open the door of the minivan and hefted Mattia's suitcase out of the back. Dumping it onto the aluminium trailer attached to the snowmobile, he returned for Kira's rucksack and proceeded to tie them down with straps.

'Who is this?' he asked Kira, stepping gingerly out of the car and grimacing at how cold his feet were, since they'd got damp during his stupid frolic in the icy stuff.

She eyed him as though he had a wheel out of place. 'That's Norbert, the concierge from the chalet.'

'Is he taking our luggage ahead for us while we wait for the shuttle?'

Kira patted him condescendingly on the arm. 'Norbert *is* the shuttle.' She locked the van and stalked to the snowmobile, her boots crunching snow. 'Are you coming? You'd better do your coat up tight.'

Her voice travelled in a muted fashion through the thick snow, threatening to disappear and leave him stranded in this strange, white land. Even when he'd toured Japan years ago with a youth opera company, he'd never felt as far from Naples as he did in that moment.

Hurrying after her, his lifeline in this over-whelming – beautiful – place, he stopped short when he saw her throw her leg over the leather seat and settle behind the driver.

'Eh...' he said stupidly.

'Come on!'

Fumbling to close the buttons on his coat – it was double-breasted – he hoisted himself awkwardly onto the back of the machine. His shoes slipped on the footrest as the driver revved the high-pitched engine, the noise roaring in his ears. Mattia squeezed his eyes shut, hoping the sound would be the worst part of this journey.

When the snowmobile leaped forward in a shower of ice particles, Mattia unfortunately did not travel with it, flailing his arms as he fell. A moment later, he was swallowed up by a snowdrift, his hip smarting as he hit the pavement.

'Porca miseria e cazzo di merda!' he bit out, snow sliding down the back of his neck.

Kira's footsteps sounded and then her hands were fisted in his coat, helping him rise and regain his balance. 'Whoops,' she said, brushing snow off his shoulders. Pulling off one of her thick gloves, she reached up to his head.

It was worth the sacrifice of his dignity have her fingers sweeping through his hair. He ducked his head in a silent plea for her to keep going.

'Thank you for not laughing,' he said softly when she finished, lifting his gaze tentatively to her.

She bit her lip. 'It's taken a lot of effort.' She gave a sigh. 'I don't know what I'm going to do with you.'

As long as she did *something*.

Mattia grimaced as she led him back to the snow-mobile where Norbert was grinning beneath his moustache, no qualms about tearing down his pride.

'Festhalten, hmm? Hold,' he said, miming with his fists.

'You could have told me,' he muttered, not sure if he was talking to Norbert or Kira.

When he took his place behind her, he didn't find anywhere to hold on, so he slung his arms around her

– and then leaned in and tightened them. It was nice to have an excuse. This time, when the machine took off, he yelped – but stayed in place.

After crossing a narrow bridge over the rushing creek, its banks piled with snow, Norbert bore them up into the pine forest, eerie contrasts of dark branches powdered with white in the fading dusk. The light from the snowmobile's headlamps created the impression of hurtling through a tunnel.

The world was bigger here – or people were smaller. The steep slopes were wild because they were unconquerable except by ambitious and expensive feats of human engineering that nevertheless felt precarious in comparison to the stalwart mountains.

The familiar bustle of Naples – blinding colours, crammed balconies, fast-talking locals, palms and fresh fruit, puttering motorini and the ghosts of a thousand generations – was a world away. Here, the rugged land changed the people and not the other way around.

But right now, a human invention was bringing them through the deep forest, throwing him around hairpin curves and chewing up the altitude with a thunderous growl from the engine. The speed stole his breath. Yes, he was besieged by noise, flooded with anxiety, but he had his hands clutched in Kira's jacket and the icy wind in his face, a sparkling, foreign world around him and... he was enjoying himself?

A glow of light ahead signalled the end of their journey and when the trees gave way to a clearing, a wooden chalet came into view, tucked under the mountain, a marshmallow cap of snow on its peaked roof. It was something out of a dream: carved wood, pale-green shutters and wrought-iron detailing, big enough to house their small group for the wedding week, as well as a few luxuries, he guessed. And beyond the cabin, a valley opened up, flawless under a covering of snow, with jagged, stony peaks rising in the distance beneath a smouldering moon.

The scene was dramatic, breath-taking, yet also inviting, and it suited Alessandra perfectly.

When Norbert cut the engine of the snowmobile, Mattia was swallowed up by the silence. Distant hints of sound – dripping snow, scurrying animals, wings flapping – were so muted, he couldn't tell if they were real.

'Uh, Mattia?' Kira's voice cut through the dampened quiet. 'You can let go now.'

'Oh!' He pried his fingers open – with some difficulty, as the cold had penetrated to his bones. Unlike his awkward hop, Kira swung her leg over in a graceful dismount and eyed him.

'You'd better go inside before you get frostbite. Please tell me you have gloves – and some better shoes – in your suitcase.'

'I have gloves,' he confirmed, 'and... other shoes.' He hesitated, wishing for a debrief or a shared look or some acknowledgement of the end of their strange twenty-four hours together – some gesture of friendship.

But she didn't even look at him as she said, 'Go! I'll see you at dinner.'

9

The Kitzingalm Hütte was not the kind of mountain cabin Kira usually found herself in.

She glanced doubtfully around the twin room she would share with Ginny for the duration of the wedding celebrations, all her insecurities roaring back to life. Usually, when she stayed in Berghütten, as they were known in the German-speaking parts of the Alps, it was in a dorm room with ten strangers, sleeping on bunks, with the faint smell of stale socks in the air. This cosy room with wood accents, soft wall sconces and the subtle scent of fresh air and dried lavender was making her nervous about breaking things or getting the floor dirty. It even had an ensuite, rather than septic communal toilets and a chronic shortage of water.

The beds were both immaculately made, with crisp sheets, a fluffy duvet and a throw blanket, but the far bed had a small pile of jewellery on the bedside table and a fluffy toy on the pillows, so Kira guessed that was Ginny's, although why a grown woman brought her plush dog to work, she didn't know.

Placing her tattered, dusty rucksack down next to the nearer bed, she lamented that a lick of make-up and a soft blouse she couldn't tie herself weren't enough to make her belong.

A prickle rushed to her hairline at the thought of tying her blouse, and the past twenty-four hours washed over her. If this place – full of luxury and for-ever happiness – seemed foreign to her, then Mattia was even more so. But he'd *felt* real – as real as grippy limestone under her fingertips and nothing but air at her back. The buzz of adrenaline when he looked at her was certainly similar.

Gargh, she needed to get her head out of her own butt, try to forget her reservations about this stupid occasion – and the disturbing intimacy of the past day – and do her job. If there had been a climbing gym nearby, she would have done a few quick 7c problems just to clear her mind. Her main comfort was knowing she was taking the groom and his friends up the mountain in two days. Hurtling down a slope on skis was almost as good as hanging off a sheer cliff.

The door of the room burst open and Ginny appeared, looking more frazzled than Kira had ever seen her.

'Boy, am I glad to see you!' Giving Kira no time to brace herself, Ginny wrapped her in a tight, clinging hug.

'What's up?'

'Oh, just every wedding party pitfall all at once – with added cabin fever! We have to get ready for dinner.' She marched into the ensuite and rummaged in an enormous toiletry bag.

'I am ready,' Kira said, holding out her hands to show off her blouse.

Ginny's only reaction was a wide-eyed look, full of reservations. Kira grumbled under her breath and her shoulders slumped.

'This is still only my second wedding,' she pointed out as Ginny patted her forehead with a sponge, leaving behind some residue that Kira couldn't name. Foundation? Concealer? Face dust? 'Dare I ask what the usual pitfalls are?'

'Well,' she began with an eager smile, 'we have the

heartbroken bridesmaid, the big group of inconsiderate lads who should have organised their own bachelor party, a bride with *very* specific ideas and – my least favourite – a dickhead groom.'

'How can there be so many dickheads getting married?'

Ginny shrugged. 'A lot of dickheads in the world, I suppose.'

Kira wasn't sure whether to laugh or groan, although with Ginny, the answer was usually laughing.

'But I've been doing this job for long enough to have learned that personal taste is an amazingly diverse thing,' she nattered, tugging down the skin under her eye until her reflection looked like something out of a horror film and applying dark-brown eyeliner that complemented her auburn hair.

Mattia must wear pure-black eyeliner. And Kira was still not supposed to be thinking about him.

'And maybe not everyone is as picky as we are,' Ginny added after she'd finished one eye, giving Kira a wink.

'Or maybe we aren't to most people's tastes.'

Ginny turned to her in indignation. 'I can't believe you just said— Actually, I can. But you make yourself that way on purpose, whereas I...'

Kira stilled, her thoughts stalling on Ginny's suggestion. All this introspection was making her stomach churn. One odd evening with a soft-eyed opera singer should not make her outlook shift and Ginny didn't know what she was talking about. No one knew the mistake she'd made all those years ago and she had to keep it that way.

'But don't tell me you haven't had a crush on your share of dickheads,' Ginny continued with a grin.

'A crush? How old are you?' Kira had certainly slept with a dickhead or two, but she hadn't had crushes since she was a teenager. She was all or nothing and since 'all' would never work, she was left with 'nothing'.

'But the biggest problem is the bride, and not in the usual way.'

Kira pricked up her ears. 'What's she like? Mattia made her sound like a saint.'

Ginny dropped her lipstick and the case made a clack against the sink. 'Oh, my God.'

'What?'

'I just realised you spent a whole day with the opera singer. Alessandra talks about him like he doesn't really function in normal life. I hope he wasn't an arse – or a diva.'

'That's a stereotype,' Kira grumbled. 'It was fine. He's normal.' It wasn't quite true, but she was unreasonably annoyed with the bride for underestimating him. She held her breath, waiting to see if Ginny would pick up on her carefully blank tone.

But Kira was saved by the wedding drama. 'You'll be able to help me.'

Beckoning for Kira to sit on her bed while Ginny took up the opposite position on her own, she gave a wriggle like a dog settling into its blanket and leaned conspiratorially close.

'Get this: the bridesmaid is the opera singer's ex!'

Kira hesitated, tempted to pretend she didn't know but struggling to produce an appropriately false reaction. Luckily, Ginny ploughed on.

'Alessandra set up Carla and Mattia and she's heartbroken that they split. You know how brides think everyone else should be happy too?'

'No.'

Ginny laughed as though she'd made a joke. 'Well, Alessandra said she also feels guilty about moving permanently to London after the wedding and she wishes her friends still had each other. I suppose it's a cliché: weddings are the best place for new love to bloom.'

That statement made Kira want to barf.

'Anyway, she asked me today – in this lovely, gracious way she has where you don't feel imposed on even though she's totally imposing on me – if there was a way we could get them together – like make them spend time together, alone if possible.'

Kira's skin was suddenly cold. Stupid fine blouse. She should have kept her thermal shirt on.

'Alessandra says they're sure to get back together because it was a misunderstanding, the reason they broke up, and they're both such lovely people who can't hold a grudge.'

Nostrils flaring, Kira bit the insides of her cheeks so she wouldn't say anything.

'She says it's her dearest wish that her friends re-capture the love they had,' Ginny said with a mock swoon.

Images of Mattia's face as he'd told her about Carla flashed in Kira's memory. *It was my fault.* His tone had been pained – with misplaced guilt, she'd assumed. But he must have felt something strong for Carla at one stage, enough that he'd mentioned finding a solution to the problem with therapy. What he'd described also *was* a kind of misunderstanding: Carla had thought *he* wanted to break up. Lashing out because of wounded pride wasn't something Kira could blame the woman for.

'I thought you were a wedding planner and not a

matchmaker,' she said, managing an even tone with some effort.

'I did wonder whether to point that out, especially since she told me all of this while I was busy tying up the wrapping on the wedding favours.'

'What the hell is a wedding favour?'

Ginny blinked at her. 'That's a conversation for another time. The point is, the bride is always right.'

Kira couldn't resist. 'I think I'm beginning to get this: the bride is always right and the groom is often a dickhead.'

'Ha ha, Kira. But the point is, all we need to do is to try to seat them together, get them into a snowball fight – that sort of thing. It shouldn't be too much extra work and it's for a good cause, but I *need* your help, because I have a thousand other things on my mind.'

'We can't seat them together, not for dinner,' she insisted, earning a surprised glance from Ginny.

'Why not?'

She wasn't sure she could explain his discomfort to Ginny without revealing confidences that suddenly felt too intimate.

'There's no seating plan tonight anyway,' Ginny continued. 'And I really hope we don't have to make any more changes for the reception. I've spent *hours* on it!'

'On a seating plan?'

'Just wait until you have to help me with the bower and the place settings!' Ginny seemed genuinely excited, but Kira's stomach was churning. Her awkward wedding memories were from a long time ago and there hadn't been a bower or any fuss with place settings, but she still had a bad taste in her mouth.

First, she had to get through dinner with the fancy guests at the fancy cabin – and face the fancy opera boy who shouldn't feel like a friend already.

Adjusting the scarf part of her blouse as she followed Ginny down the hall towards the dining room, she accidentally undid the knot Mattia had tied. Swallowing a curse, she quickly tied a water knot and tried to forget about the stupid thing.

As she stepped into the dining room, she suddenly understood why Ginny had been so concerned about Kira's appearance. While the traditional construction of rough-hewn wood was hinted at here and there, the white walls with grey accents, natural stone fixtures and jacquard tablecloths turned the room into a fine restaurant – and the guests were even finer.

Kira picked out Alessandra straight away. She was a vivacious woman with black hair in careless curls that had probably taken an hour to style, standing by the window talking to man with his back turned. Her make-up was flawless; her blouse with its edgy collar had not a wrinkle, which Kira considered to be some kind of dark magic. Instead of the felt cabin slippers that Kira had shoved her stocking feet into, Alessandra wore some shiny black designer things with a low heel.

The men weren't wearing ties, but they were otherwise dressed for a business meeting – at least that's what it looked like to Kira – in navy or camel jackets and leather loafers, their hair subtly styled.

Suddenly feeling out of touch with normal people, Kira smoothed her black hiking trousers that she'd hoped wouldn't be noticeable as such. The wedding party *weren't* normal people, she reminded herself. They were top earners, probably descended from other top earners, but the knowledge didn't stop the tide of self-consciousness up her throat.

'Oh hi, Kira!'

Uh oh, the bride had caught sight of her. Alessandra beckoned her over and then wrapped her arms around her in a hug that was far too familiar, punctuating the action with a kiss on each cheek. Kira wouldn't have been surprised to find matching lip marks on her face.

'Thank you *so much* for taking care of Mattia. He has such a delicate artistic spirit and I was so worried about him getting here safe.'

Kira wouldn't argue about the 'delicate artistic spirit', but Alessandra seemed a little too caught up in her honorary big sister role. Mattia was all grown up.

She was gathering her thoughts in search of something appropriate to say – and drawing a blank – when she finally glanced at Alessandra's companion. She'd assumed it was Joe, the groom, but when she saw the face above the navy jacket, she stopped breathing altogether.

What's the worst that could happen?

Seeing her old friend Aarav Grewal again came pretty close. He'd been there that day twelve years ago – also a groomsman – giving her a pitying look as she'd slowly realised the enormity of the mistake she'd made. He *knew*.

No. Now was not the time to see Rav again. The memories she'd been keeping at bay pulled loose, freezing in her chest and rushing up her throat. It was a long time ago; she'd been young and stupid. But the feelings were still with her, damn it: mortification mainly, as she came face to face with the past she'd successfully avoided for all her years at Great Heart.

Rav glanced at her. Kira held her breath, waiting

for her final defences to fall and reveal her to be the misfit who wasn't worth the effort, but Rav said nothing, eventually wandering away to speak to the groom who was standing by the fire with a tumbler of something.

Kira blinked, unsure whether to be relieved or offended. Rav hadn't recognised her.

She could barely think, let alone manage any small talk and it was a relief when they sat down to dinner – until she noticed that, in her distraction, she hadn't been able to stop Ginny from ushering Mattia to the end of the table to sit with a woman who had to be the bridesmaid – Carla.

10

Soft jazz music played through subtle speakers set behind the lighting throughout the room. Mattia liked jazz. Not quite as much as the Red Hot Chili Peppers, but he enjoyed the syncopation and the rawness of the melodies.

He could focus on that. For the sake of Alessandra's happiness, he had to get through this dinner without drawing attention to himself. The clink of cutlery and the murmur of voices in the room would at least mask the sounds from Carla, seated opposite him, that he'd allowed to balloon into a stress trigger. One day, he was confident, he'd be able to eat with her and feel nothing – but unfortunately not today.

After an awkward greeting – pressing his lips to

her cheek had been a vertigo-inducing mix of familiarity and tension – she'd been watching him closely
ever since.

Alessandra's parents, who he called Zia Francesca
and Zio Giorgio – his honorary uncle and aunt – sat
nearby, but after a delighted welcome, they'd largely
left him in Carla's clutches. A wink from Zia Francesca
made him think that might have been on purpose.

His ex had a narrow face, striking, dark features
and rich, brown hair with subtle highlights. She was
wearing some kind of gloss that made her lips look
moist. It reminded Mattia of kissing her – another
awkward thought, when they weren't together any
more.

There had been a time when he'd enjoyed being
close to her, but now her presence made him recoil.
He must be broken in some way, to both long for affection and then physically despise it afterwards, but that
was his oversensitive existence in a nutshell. He
wished he could undo the year they'd been together.

He couldn't help thinking of Kira and *her* friend
who was also getting married – her friend-with-for-
mer-benefits. It was a strange boundary to have drawn
– physical intimacy but no emotional intimacy. Usually, a friend was the other way around.

His gaze was drawn continually to the other table,

to her quiet, stoic presence. He wondered whether the drive had tired her out, even though she'd seemed incapable of growing tired. Her expression was pinched.

But she refused to meet his gaze. She'd tied another complex knot at her throat. She was probably just uncomfortable in the blouse – and the company.

It was just like Alessandra to insist that the two planners join them for dinner, rather than leaving them to eat in the staff quarters, but Kira looked as though she would have preferred cooking her own beans over a gas stove in the harsh cold outdoors to sitting at this elegant table, repeatedly picking up the fork, fiddling with it and then putting it down again. Her body moved slightly, suggesting her knee was bouncing under the table.

Alessandra had fussed over him for twenty minutes when he'd arrived, seeing him settled into his room herself as though the chalet belonged to her and exclaiming in horror at his wet socks. But now she had her head bent towards the other wedding planner – an energetic woman with dark-red hair in a stylish cut and a piercing just below her lip – undoubtedly sorting last-minute details.

Joe had a glass of local beer in front of him and was conversing loudly with his identical friends, less interested in the practical arrangements.

'Aren't you hungry?' Carla asked, giving him a nudge with the back of her hand that dragged his attention back to his own dinner.

His stomach growled as if on cue, the strange day of extremes catching up with him: the warm van and the freezing snow; sitting still for hours and then careening up the hill on the snowmobile; a drooping service station sandwich for lunch followed by a three-course meal at a luxury cabin for dinner. Taking up his spoon, he took a sip of warm broth, savoury and tangy with fresh chives – and thought of Kira and her enthusiasm for her sausage the night before.

'Good?' Carla prompted him.

He glanced up to find her watching him intently and the goosebumps came up again. When she was certain she had his attention, she dipped her spoon into her broth, moving it carefully towards the far edge of the bowl and then to her lips, into her mouth and back out again.

Soundlessly.

Mattia stilled as the difference became apparent. Cutting off a small piece of the bready dumpling floating in the soup, she placed that in her mouth as well, chewing slowly with her lips closed. She accidentally tapped the metal on the ceramic bowl, wincing as she took her next spoonful, but the implement never touched her teeth.

Mattia stared at his own dumpling, his stomach churning. Did this mean he truly was a horrible person telling how much the sounds had stressed him out?

Then a more worrying thought: did Carla want something from him? He flattered himself they'd been tolerably good in bed. Could that be it? He'd heard weddings made people think about jumping into bed together – a thought that only made his gaze swerve to Kira again. He probably wasn't supposed to be contemplating the wedding planner like that, but he could still remember the skin of her chest, just below her collarbone, brushing the backs of his fingers as he tied her scarf.

He enjoyed physical intimacy – a lot – but he doubted he would be able to switch off everything else that had happened in their relationship for it. Kira might manage that somehow, but he couldn't.

'I hope you'll be done with all this stuff about the flowers and the personalised gold cards to come skiing on Tuesday,' Joe spoke up, a little too loudly. Mattia suspected his glass had been filled several times already.

Alessandra was still and collected. 'I'm not coming

skiing, amore. We only have two more days before the wedding and there's still the chapel to decorate. I told you, I had a dream of how it would all look when we got married.'

She was full of dreams of the very best of everything – and she had the unique backbone to make her dreams a reality.

'But this is what the wedding planner is for,' Joe insisted. 'I thought we were combining this wedding craziness with a skiing holiday.'

Mattia's hackles went up on Alessandra's behalf.

'Joe,' Alessandra purred, 'we'll have time afterwards, when we head to Switzerland for our honeymoon. You have fun with your lads on the slopes and I'll work with Ginny to make everything perfect for the day. We'll both be happy, hmm?'

One of the groomsmen slapped Joe on the back. 'You're only a bachelor for two more days, man. You don't need to spend them with your ball and chain.'

The red-headed wedding planner – Ginny? – spoke up. 'Plus, we've got a qualified guide and ski instructor, now that our agency has merged with an adventure travel company. I'm sure you've got an amazing day ahead of you with Kira.'

'Kira?' one of the groomsmen repeated, as though Kira had been invisible up until that moment.

She looked as though she wished she were invisible, her posture stiff and her expression blank. It gave Mattia a shiver of misgiving.

'Oh, did I forget to introduce you all?' Ginny said brightly. 'Anton and Rav are the groomsmen – and Joe is the groom, of course. Guys, this is Kira Watling from Great Heart Adventures. She's a climbing instructor and guide in real life, but we nab her for help with weddings occasionally.'

Ginny seemed genuinely warm, but her introduction had done nothing to ease the tension that was pouring off Kira like melting snow.

The groomsman – Rav, apparently – was staring at her as she staunchly avoided his gaze, her cheeks turning pink. If Mattia had understood what was going on, he might have interfered, she looked so brittle.

'My God, Kira,' Rav said, his voice high. 'I didn't recognise you. How long has it been?'

Mattia was desperate for context, his mind ringing with the stand-offish opinions she'd expressed that morning. *Choose your friends carefully; don't make promises.* The flash of conviction in him was strong. Someone had hurt her. *This groomsman?* Surely even she couldn't be so collected if he was an ex. It was someone else.

Kira spoke casually. 'It's been a very long time,' she said to Rav. Glancing from Ginny to Alessandra, she explained, 'We went to school together. Bournemouth College. I did not have blue hair back then.' She chuckled, but Mattia wasn't convinced.

The moment at the hotel, when he'd made her tell him about her hair, there'd been something in her voice.

'You're an adventure guide. That's so cool,' Rav said. 'You always were sportier than all of us. We'll have to catch up.'

'Does that mean she knows—?'

Before the groom could finish his question, the servers entered with the main course – schnitzel or a fried potato dish with a side of pickled red cabbage – and snagged Joe's attention away from Kira. She released a long breath through pursed lips, her expression blank.

'It's sweet that Joe wants to spend so much time with Alessandra, don't you think?'

Mattia wrenched his eyes from Kira to find Carla watching him brightly. He didn't want to talk to Carla. He wanted to bustle Kira down the hallway and into a cupboard and ask her what was going on. Hopefully, they'd get locked in the cupboard for a few hours at least. Maybe he could redo the knot of her blouse for her.

But he wasn't locked in a cupboard with Kira. He was stranded with Carla who cut a piece of her schnitzel carefully, placing it into her mouth with as much care as she'd taken with the soup.

'I can't believe she's getting married in three days.' Carla's eyes were misty. 'It's going to be *such* a beautiful wedding.'

With one more glance at the *not*-wedding planner with her shadowed eyes, full of secrets, he imagined Kira did not agree.

11

Kira would have much preferred to be trapped literally between a rock and a hard place. The groom's talkative mother was relating in some detail her recent group tour on the Camino de Santiago. Rav's curious looks warned her not to stray from her current conversational partner, so she was stuck racking her brain for polite responses when she knew nothing about the topic, but Nadine assumed she knew every turn and waymarker.

Dessert was finally over and Kira only needed to hold out for another few minutes, she guessed, before she could escape back to her room and hope Ginny didn't ask too many questions. She'd got through an excruciating dinner. Another few minutes wouldn't kill her.

'In the first half, it rained and rained all day – my God. Luckily, they don't advertise this route as a walk in the park, because it was such a challenge, we weren't certain we wanted to go on. But you must have done the route a hundred times, in your job!'

Between the squeeze in her chest at how out of place she felt, the panic about Rav letting slip something she'd rather the wedding party – and especially Ginny – didn't know, and the lingering tenderness Mattia had inflicted on her, Kira wasn't sure she wanted to go on either. Thinking of a response was almost impossible.

'Erm, I've never done it actually.'

'You *haven't*? Oh my! You absolutely must! Such a challenge, and so spiritual.'

'My spiritual challenges involve a helmet and ropes and vertical camping. I'm not really a pilgrimage type.'

Nadine's expression suggested Kira had punched her in the face. Shit, she hadn't meant to insult anybody. People outside the climbing community rarely appreciated the scale of the challenges. How she wished she could escape this dinner and climb something instead.

'I mean, the Camino is great, if that's what you—'

'Kira!' Ginny's slightly panicked voice rose over the sound of Kira digging herself into a very deep hole. 'We were just talking about confetti.'

She suspected her confused grimace wasn't helping the situation, but her game face was slipping. 'That's just littering. Why is it even a thing?'

Complete silence greeted that statement. Kira should just wander farther into this valley until she found an actually isolated cabin, and spend the rest of her days there. It would be better than attending *any* more weddings. Better for everyone.

'It's Italian tradition,' the bride eventually spluttered.

'Well, in that case...' Kira didn't quite manage to keep her sarcastic comment under her breath.

'Um, we have biodegradable confetti. Don't worry,' Ginny said with a laugh that no one would believe was natural. 'We're all glad the old tradition of rice was adapted so it's not dangerous for pigeons.'

More silence. By the look on her face, Ginny would hyperventilate in about ten seconds.

'These traditions really need to be updated sometimes. Like that garter one, where the groom takes it off with his teeth. Urgh.' Kira shuddered, only to notice Ginny's face going from white to red.

'Oh God, you're not planning to do *that* one, are you?'

'It symbolises... fertility,' Alessandra said, her expression pinched with dismay.

Crawling out of her skin at this table of people from another planet, Kira struggled to sit still, her gaze darting around the room – and finding Mattia, his eyes trained on her. Warmth rushed up her chest, but it squeezed too, knowing she shouldn't be feeling anything when she looked at him.

'At least Kira will be lucky for the wedding,' Ginny said, shooting her a tight look that clearly said *Shut the fuck up, now*. 'She's our "something blue".'

'Lucky, hmmm,' was all Alessandra could manage in reply. 'Who else wants hot chocolate? Maybe we can go sit by the fire,' she suggested suddenly, her voice strained. 'I'll have mine with vodka.'

That was Kira's cue to get the hell out of there.

* * *

Dinner and dessert were delicious, but interminable when Mattia's thoughts were torn between guilt about Carla, and curiosity about Kira – as well as those cupboard fantasies that wouldn't go away When Alessandra proposed moving to the den, Mattia paused in indecision, Carla's eyes hanging off him as though she were actually holding his arm, when Kira quietly excused herself and headed for the door.

'Ehm, I need to get my... sweater,' he mumbled, making for the exit after her.

Closing the wooden door to the dining room behind him, he scoured the hallway for signs of her, just catching the swish of her slippers and creak of the floorboards. He was hurrying after her, determined to find out what had upset her – because he was certain she was upset – when the door behind him opened.

'Matty, can we talk for a minute?'

Hearing his nickname in her voice sent a wash of memories through him – stricken ones from the end of their relationship as well as deep, immersive ones from the beginning. Maybe Kira had a point: it was better never to let anyone close enough to hurt.

'Sure,' he said, making no move to take the conversation to a more comfortable location.

'How have you been?' Carla began.

He paused for barely a moment, before his experiences of the past two days galvanised something inside him and he spoke more openly than he'd expected. 'We've had all dinner to talk, Carla. What do you really want to say to me?'

He already knew, as much as he'd been telling himself he didn't.

'Did you notice anything... different tonight?'

'Yes, I did. I appreciate the effort you went to.'

She seemed to take his stiff words as encouragement. 'I understand now, that I wasn't fair to you, and I'm really sorry.'

He sent a forlorn glance along the hall. 'I accept the apology.'

'You do?'

Her delighted expression unnerved him. 'I'm sorry too. Most people wouldn't even hear those sounds.'

She took a step closer and he resisted the urge to move an equal distance away. 'But *you* can,' she said gently, her gaze growing soft. 'I shouldn't have let something like that come between us. I know you're sensitive and I love that. I shouldn't have taken it personally.'

He paused, waiting for relief to flood him at her words. The hurts, the worries about whether he'd ever find someone he could be himself with could all go away again. He could go back to the way things were before.

Except, that didn't work.

'It's okay, Carla. You can let it go.' He hoped she would.

'We're still friends, right?'

An uneasy prickle crept up his neck. 'Mmph,' he agreed non-committally.

With a dull thud, his heels hit the skirting board and he realised he'd backed himself up as far as he could go, but Carla was still coming closer, her brown eyes luminous in the gentle lighting. *Ohhhh no.*

He experienced a flash of something warm as she approached, an echo of intimacy that tugged at him. His conversation with Kira from that morning was fresh in his memory. Friends, lovers, soulmates, blowing off steam. Her straightforward conversation and expressive lips. Mattia couldn't do this.

He slipped out from where she'd caged him against the wall and ran an agitated hand through his curls. 'I'm really sorry,' was all he said. He needed to find Kira and ask her why she'd been upset – and hear her claims that she *wasn't* upset and gently wheedle her until she told him.

'Matty, wait!' Carla called after him when he made for the corner where he'd last heard Kira. 'Is that all you're going to say?'

'Ehm... Right now? Yes. I have to—' He stumbled as he whirled around to make his escape.

Safely out of Carla's sight, he took a panting breath. Kira was nowhere to be seen and he didn't know which one was her room – or whether she'd tolerate him knocking on her door. Whether he could do any good even if she did.

He was dreaming if he imagined Kira Watling needed anything from him. But it was a rather pleasant dream.

* * *

'You certainly know how to make an exit!'

Kira barely lifted her head from her pillow to acknowledge Ginny's wry comment when her colleague returned to their room an hour later. Kira had already had a quick shower, brushed her teeth and slipped into her tracksuit; she was an expert at efficient use of a bathroom. Now she lay sprawled on her bed with her earbuds in, watching climbing videos on YouTube to forget about the entire rotten day.

Of course Ginny wouldn't let her. She perched on the edge of Kira's single. Kira knew Ginny would never tell her off with strong words, but her gentle disappointment would be worse, which was why she was surprised when Ginny's actual words were, 'The thing with the garter really should be retired, even if it symbolises fertility.' She shot Kira a cheeky smile.

'It's not really symbolism. It's a pretty clear allusion to sex.'

Ginny snorted. 'In some places, they nail a pair of the bride's shoes to a tree to "stop her running away".'

'Urgh, seriously?' Kira sneaked a glance at Ginny, trying to work out if her colleague truly wasn't mad at her. 'I am sorry I said that stuff out loud in front of the bride, though. And Joe's mother is going to hate me for eternity.'

'Maybe not quite eternity,' Ginny responded, which did nothing to ease Kira's mind. 'But it's okay. I know this is hard for you and I also know you're trying.'

Just not succeeding. But she was stupidly touched by Ginny's understanding. She'd thought the advice about not getting emotionally involved had been entirely unnecessary, but she seemed to react to everything emotionally right now.

'I hope they put an extra shot of vodka in Alessandra's hot chocolate,' she mumbled.

Ginny laughed, but then moved onto the other subject Kira would rather have avoided. 'That was an interesting coincidence, that you know one of the groomsmen. Is he a real dick?'

'He's fine,' she said carefully. 'A nice guy – at least

he was in school.' It was the truth. All Rav had done was witness her lowest moment.

'Apparently, the group of them – Joe and the groomsmen – met at university in Exeter.'

The *University of Exeter.* Kira pressed her lips together and hoped Ginny would change the subject. She wasn't the same person she'd been when she'd seen Rav last, and it wasn't only her blue hair.

Ginny moved to her bed and slipped out of her court shoes, peeling her stocking socks off. 'The opera singer is a sweetie,' she commented, looking away from Kira as she tugged the tie from her curly hair.

Kira progressed from pressing her lips together to grinding her teeth.

'I didn't expect him to be tall and handsome. No wonder the bridesmaid regrets letting him slip through her fingers. Oh, and you'll never guess what I saw!'

'I don't particularly want to guess,' Kira said.

'It's working! Throwing them together! I think maybe I would enjoy a side business in matchmaking.'

'What do you mean by, "It's working"?'

'I saw them together in the hallway, talking intently – standing really close.'

Kira hated the taste of acid in her mouth and the

way Ginny's words made her want to throw something and yell at Carla that she hadn't appreciated him.

'If it's worked so quickly, I don't think you can give your spurious matchmaking attempts much credit. They must have both regretted breaking up.' She refused to be miserable about that fact.

Ginny scrunched her nose at Kira. 'Don't quote facts at me. I'm a hopeless romantic and I think it would be wonderful if the bride's friends found their way back to each other.'

'Does this mean we don't have to worry about Alessandra's matchmaking request any more?'

'I suppose I could ask the staff if they slept tog—'

'Ginny! No!'

'Maybe *you* could ask him how it's going, since you seem to have got on okay.'

Kira's stomach swooped. 'Do you really think that means I have an "in" with the opera singer?' she asked, hoping Ginny didn't notice her voice wobbling.

'Good point. But until we're certain they're back together, I think we need to keep setting them up. Surely there'll be opportunities tomorrow on the glacier tour. Maybe we can strand them in a gondola alone.'

'These gondolas are big enough for thirty people,' Kira pointed out grumpily.

'I'm sure we'll think of something. Maybe a snow-ball fight, where they'll clear the snow off each other and then stare, obviously thinking about kissing. I wish someone would matchmake *me*. I always have to go out and ask people to date me.'

'I think most people don't matchmake because they respect the free will of the couple involved,' Kira grumbled. 'There is a chance they don't want to be pushed together.'

'It's harmless,' Ginny insisted.

'Have you ever had a long-term boyfriend – with a messy break-up?' Kira asked with a sigh.

'Depends what you mean by long-term. Six months I managed once, but I scared him off as usual. Why do you ask?'

'It's just complicated when there's a break-up in-volved – pride and hurt feelings. I wouldn't want it to explode at the wrong time during the wedding.'

'Past relationships are like a bomb?' Ginny joked, but Kira wasn't laughing. She hoped old break-ups weren't bombs that could still explode at any time. Then Ginny asked the worst possible question. 'You've experienced this? A big break-up?'

Kira froze, the awfulness of that moment washing over her again as though it had happened yesterday. If she wanted to explain to Ginny, now was the time.

After twelve years, countless summits and crags and a life rebuilt on her own terms, it shouldn't have bothered her. She'd told Mattia they both needed to face their problems, but she didn't want to face hers.

'Of course not,' she replied as smoothly as she could, letting her head fall to the too-soft pillow and starting another video on her phone.

Ginny thankfully let the subject drop.

12

'You'd think he'd never seen a mountain before,' Kira muttered the following day as she led the group through the snowdrifts to the cable car station. That day was their excursion to the ice cave with a photo shoot. As the famous wedding photographer would only arrive for the ceremony, Kira's boss Willard had convinced Great Heart's regular nature photographer Rhys Bowen to take the pictures in the cave, which meant there was one person even grumpier about being here than Kira herself – although that knowledge was little comfort to her.

The fact that she was muttering to herself about Mattia should have bothered her, but she had enough other things bothering her that she barely noticed.

Foremost among them the fact that Rav was trying to talk to her, so she couldn't keep checking back to make sure Mattia made it safely across the ice in his terrible shoes. Or he might trip because he couldn't seem to stop craning his neck to gawk at the ragged, snowy peaks just visible above the forested slopes.

Keeping ahead of where Rav was following too close for her liking, she led the way across a small bridge over a creek that was flowing sluggishly. Both banks were piled with snow hardened to ice.

'It's ice in that part! And look at the layer of snow on the twigs. It looks like someone put it there on purpose.'

Kira supposed she should be satisfied that Mattia was cheerful and not miserably cold.

'You sound like Alessandra the first time I took her skiing,' Joe said drily. 'It's not a fantasy world.'

'But it looks like one.' His voice was soft, as though he were singing one of those quiet parts of an opera scene that sounded like speech.

He spoiled the reverent moment by slipping on a patch of ice with the flair of a slapstick performer, landing heavily on the seat of his tailored trousers. He yelped and hissed in pain, especially when his bare hand landed in a snowdrift. The boy wasn't even wearing gloves.

Carla and Alessandra rushed to help him up and he at least looked sheepish and brushed off their clutching hands to push himself to his feet. He slipped and slid a few more times before he'd cleared the black ice, like a lanky baby animal learning to walk.

Rav caught up with Kira while she was distracted and she couldn't come up with an excuse to stop him falling into step beside her. He obviously wasn't put off by the thunder in her expression.

'How've you been, then?' he asked. 'You dropped off the face of the earth after—'

'I just really got into climbing – holding onto the face of the earth.'

He laughed more loudly than her joke deserved. 'I'm glad things worked out for you. It wasn't—'

'Rav, I'm really sorry, but now isn't a good time to talk about this.' There, another guest insulted. Kira should tick them off a bingo card and at least win a prize for her rudeness.

Rav's expression was pinched. 'I just wanted to ask if Christian knows you're here.'

Just hearing his name was enough to make her skin crawl.

'I haven't spoken to Christian since... then.' She swallowed a grimace. Did that sound as though she was still hurt by what had happened? She hated how weak all of this made her.

'Should I... tell him?'

'What? Why?'

'I just wondered whether it would be less awkward than a surprise at the ceremony on Wednesday.'

Kira stilled as the shock ricocheted through her. Wednesday. *Oh, shit*. Christian was coming to the wedding. He must be one of the guests staying down in the valley, not close enough to join the wedding party at the chalet. She hadn't believed this occasion could get any worse for her, but it just did.

'I'm sorry. I thought you'd know.'

I'm sorry... She was pretty sure Rav had said those words to her twelve years ago, when it had become clear that Christian had screwed her over.

'No, I... Well, um... I need to go and sort out our booking,' she said, approximating what she hoped was a halfway normal facial expression as she gestured at the ticket booth. Taking one step away, she turned back when a disturbing thought echoed in her head. 'Please don't say anything... about that – to Alessandra or the others. I'm here to do a job and...'

More pity crossed his features and Kira's stomach turned. She bolted for the ticket booth, angry and annoyed that she had feelings that wouldn't stay stuffed

down where she put them. She was officially the worst
wedding planner in the history of the profession and
if she wasn't careful, she'd ruin everything.

After confirming their group booking, she trudged
back through the snow to where Carla was handing
out tiny bottles of something alcoholic. Either it
would be sickly sweet or so strong it would numb your
vocal chords and Kira really could have done with
knocking something like that back right now.

'Is everything all right?'

Mattia's low voice behind her, surprisingly close,
made her pause. 'I should be asking you that,' she
mumbled. Glancing over her shoulder – bad idea, he
looked like a fallen angel with his shoulders hunched,
curls over his forehead, his hands stuffed into the
pockets of his long coat and a silver cross dangling
from one earlobe – she waited for him to respond.

'Is that groomsman—'

She cut him off. 'Look, it's fine and not your concern. Go enjoy the views – with Carla. You're not going
to get any smiles out of me today.'

He was quiet for a long moment while Kira's curiosity got the better of her once more. That she noticed – and appreciated – the strong cut of his jaw and
the contrast with his lips, pouting in thought – was
even more concerning.

Turning away, he said, 'Why do I want to turn that into a challenge?'

*   *   *

Go enjoy the views – with Carla.

If Mattia hadn't known better, he might have thought he detected a ring of jealousy in her tone – a prospect that made his heart leap quite inappropriately. But he was also put out at the suggestion that he'd enjoy the company of his ex-girlfriend, after everything he'd told Kira the day before.

'You two stand right at the glass,' Alessandra said, nudging him so hard as they filed onto the cable car that he nearly stepped on Carla's toe. Alessandra had the strong hands of a bossy, Italian nonna – and the same built-in urge to matchmake, it seemed.

The background hum of quiet machinery was unfamiliar, unlike the drone of traffic and occasional blare from the engine of a motorino that characterised the soundscape of home. Alessandra's wedding party was hushed as they crowded into the little gondola making its way slowly around the turning.

Carla shot him an apologetic glance as she was squished next to him at the front, but he was still a little buzzed from the morning – his second snowmobile ride, the landscape that burned beauty onto his retinas everywhere he looked, the short exchange with Kira.

He knew exactly where she stood behind him: in the middle, casually holding the metal stand for balance. It felt as though he would have known that with his eyes closed, the way he knew she wasn't comfortable around that groomsman, even though she wouldn't tell him why.

But he couldn't close his eyes now, not when the world was so enormous around him. The sheer scale of the place made him uneasy, but still, the landscape drew him in and none of his reservations could dull the thrill of anticipation zipping to his toes.

Another gondola rushed into the station, braking gently, and then it was their turn. With a surge of acceleration, the little car whooshed upwards, pressing gravity down onto its occupants.

The breath was squeezed out of Mattia's lungs as they lifted high off the snowy ground. The mechanical hum was replaced with cotton wool silence. While inside the gondola, he heard muted whispers, the shuffling of feet and swishing coats; outside, the utter quiet seemed to push against the glass.

Apprehension swelled in his chest, not because of the gravity-defying gondola swinging gently high above the ground, but because of the oppressive quiet. He'd experienced the feeling before in sound-proofed recording studios and performance spaces with engineered acoustics. It would start with a distant buzz, as though someone had let a single fly into the space. Gradually amplified between his eardrums, it would become a persistent drone and then a tense vibration, filling his head until the world didn't exist – only his own spiralling senses.

Sucking in a deep breath through his nose, he pressed a hand to the cool glass in front of him and braced himself. The landscape that had appeared one enormous wall of rock and snow and pines stretched and opened as they travelled higher, a rocky outcropping on one side, a snowy saddle and a steep ravine on the other.

They reached the first pylon and passed it with a deep whir. Winter cloud cover painted everything grey, but as they rose and rose, the sun fought to shine through until the sky was a glowing blanket of mother-of-pearl. There were no straight lines, only rounded lumps of snow, miniature pines and jagged protrusions of rock half-covered in powder.

The town below disappeared; the valley looked tiny. Peaks and ridges emerged before them, rolling out a new world where life was insignificant and yet every breath precious. He could feel his world expanding.

No, wait, that was the pressure in his head. He swallowed discomfort as a light ringing threatened his eardrums. With a pop, the pressure normalised and he took a deep, shaky breath.

A breeze swept along the ridge, showering the gondola with tiny particles of ice and sending the little cabin into a swing. His other hand gripped the railing tightly and his gaze was dragged down – and down.

'Hold onto him, Carla. He looks like he's going to keel over.'

He managed to shoot Alessandra a scowl at the hint of satisfaction in her comment, but he had to convulsively swallow again to equalise the pressure.

'I'm fine,' he grated out, shocked at the reedy quality of his own voice.

'Hasn't he ridden the cable car in Sorrento?' Joe asked.

'Not since I was a child,' Mattia replied as the gondola clattered over the wheels of the next pylon. 'I vomited,' he added with a tilt of his head that he regretted a moment later when he noticed spots at the sides of his vision.

Skiers criss-crossed below them as the station came into view and the hum of the giant wheels moving the cables droned more loudly. One down, only two more cable car rides to go until they reached their ridiculously high altitude destination.

Another curse of his sensitive hearing was that he caught every word when Joe murmured to one of the groomsmen, 'At least he's one of the girls and isn't coming skiing with us tomorrow.'

A sharp intake of breath behind him. It was Kira, he knew it was Kira and he could *hear* her bristling in his defence. Whatever scratch to his pride he'd experienced at Joe's words was nothing compared to the satisfaction bubbling in his stomach now.

The gondola braked suddenly and inched around the turning, the doors bouncing open. He stepped out on wobbly legs and *whoosh*, the air was forced from his lungs again, this time by the bitter cold. His hands iced up instantly – at least, that's how it felt.

'Do you need a second?' Alessandra's hand on his back was gentle. 'Carla can stay with you. Just take your time and come up when you're ready. We can enjoy the view at the top while we wait for you both.'

He shot Carla an alarmed gaze, but she only responded with a close-lipped shrug. Perhaps he did need a moment – away from Alessandra and her machinations, and definitely away from Carla. 'There's no need for Carla to stay behind. You all go ahead. I'll catch up – *please*,' he insisted. 'I'm fine,' he assured Alessandra who was studying him doubtfully.

For one of the first times in his life, her attention chafed.

He waved them off with a sigh of relief, glad to send them on ahead without him. In the concrete courtyard between the two gondola stations, fog swirled, thick in one place and wispy in another, skiers and pylons and rocks appearing and disappearing in the distance. His breath crystallised as soon as it left his lungs.

Even if he had taken the cable car near Sorrento recently, he was *not* in Campania any more. Piles of snow lined the courtyard, with pillows of it clinging to the roofs and more floating down to form a fine layer at his feet. He noticed icicles clinging to the eaves of the station buildings.

Icicles!

Fascinated, he took swift steps to the lowest part of a pitched roof and stepped up onto a metal ski stand, stretching onto his toes and—

'What the *hell* are you doing?'

13

Kira watched with a sense of inevitability as his foot slipped. What else had she expected when she'd decided at the last minute to wait for him? Those shoes had zero tread and this man attracted mishaps like the sun in the solar system. That might also explain that blinding smile he could produce at the drop of a hat.

Before she could reach him, he landed heavily with his stomach against the ski stand, his head dashing against the wood cladding on the wall.

'Yikes! Mattia!'

'Icicles,' he said weakly when she reached him.

'*Icicles?*'

'I wanted to touch the icicles.'

Of course he'd wanted to touch the icicles. He went to rub a hand over his face, but she snagged his wrist before he could.

'Careful, you're bleeding.' She'd never struggled to keep a straight face while saying those words.

'I always wanted to play the Phantom of the Opera. It's a baritone part,' he murmured in reply. His gaze snagged hers. 'I made you smile – laugh, even.'

Her straight face slipped entirely. 'I'm laughing *at* you, not *with* you.' But boy, this was so much better than brooding about seeing Christian again. Maybe she could just lean into this... *thing* between them, even if it didn't make sense.

It was his turn to chuckle. '*Joe* was laughing at me. You are too kind for that.'

Her smile dimmed as she remembered the groom's callous words. She opened her mouth to say something, but Mattia beat her to it. He was developing a habit of doing that.

'It's nice that you wanted to defend me.'

'You seem to have plenty of women lining up to defend you,' she said, aiming for a dry tone to cover her peevishness as she peered up at the trickle of blood on his forehead.

'Jealous?'

With any other person, she'd have given him a shove and a glare, but his tone was so light and... hopeful. Instead of telling him off, she blushed – she actually blushed.

'How am I supposed to tell Alessandra you scratched up your face trying to reach an icicle?'

'Spoken like a true wedding planner.'

That earned him a shove – lightly, on the shoulder. 'Oh, shut up!' Unfortunately, the rough touch still reminded her of a bathroom door flying open to give her a more intimate view of an opera singer than she'd ever imagined.

She wasn't supposed to be remembering that. Not only was she the world's worst wedding planner, there was the side gig as a matchmaker – which she was also screwing up spectacularly.

'Come on. Let's get you cleaned up. I have a first aid kit in my bag.'

A violent shiver racked him and he fumbled in his pockets, retrieving a pair of fine leather gloves that belonged on the catwalk in Milan and not at 2150m of altitude. His scarf looked to be made of wool, with an intricate pattern in grey and blue, but it was far too thin.

'Didn't you bring any snow gear?' she asked.

'I don't own any. I didn't realise...'

When he trailed off, she turned to find his gaze turned up again, taking in the ever-changing panorama of the peaks in the fog. They were only at the first station and the views would get so much better, but he appeared to run out of words anyway.

'I didn't realise any of this,' he said when he'd regained his balance. 'I didn't know what it would be like up here.'

'That's fair enough,' she replied, leading him into the men's toilets without hesitation and propping her pack on the sink to find her first aid kit. 'Were you feeling sick in the gondola?'

He shook his head and then shrugged with less certainty. 'A little. It was more—'

'The sounds?' she guessed. 'But it's quiet.'

'That's worse sometimes,' he admitted. 'I can feel tinnitus closing in on me.'

'What about the pressure in your ears? Is it painful? You have something to suck on in your pocket, right? Might help for the next one.'

He appeared surprised for a moment that she knew what was in his pockets, but he had been quite strung out when he'd emptied them in front of her two nights ago. 'You're right. I'm sure that'll help.'

She moistened a swab and approached carefully,

trying to focus on his words and not the intimate position she'd found herself in with him once more. He clutched the sink with his fine hands and she could imagine he was resisting reaching for her to steady himself. That probably wasn't the case. More likely, she was misreading his gaze and imagining the air between them growing thin.

When she dabbed at the scratch, he hissed in shock.

'It's not deep,' she reassured him.

'I don't think I'd cope if something actually happened to me – blood spurting and all of that. I'd pass out.' Another smile threatened, but it was preferable to that nonsense about the air between them.

'Sometimes, that makes people easier to treat,' she said evenly, cleaning the last of the blood. It was a minor abrasion, but it would probably scab over into a dark, dappled patch on his forehead that would show up in photos. 'You know,' she continued with a sigh, 'I've worked on two weddings so far and in both of them, we've had to patch up a bridesmaid.'

He laughed, full and rich, like his singing voice, and it showered down Kira's spine. 'I'm not strictly speaking a bridesmaid, although I'll allow it, since I am on Alessandra's side. Bridesman, perhaps?'

'"Bridesman" sounds like a spy code name or a

mythical creature. You're definitely rather the mythical creature.' She mumbled the last part, forgetting he would hear every word.

But if his expression was anything to go by, he enjoyed what he heard. 'Does Alessandra know this is the experience you bring? Patching up mythical creatures?'

She stuck her chin out. 'First aid training is always an asset.'

The next thing she felt, to her utter shock, was his finger under her chin, the smooth tip of his thumb moving along her jaw, and his face close enough to feel a gust of his breath. Oh, shit, there was no universe she'd imagined where he touched her like this, as though stage lights shone right on them.

'Mattia,' she began, meaning to put him off, but not quite managing to form any more words, her breath short.

His gaze dipped, roaming her face from under his lashes. 'Mmm?'

His voice should have come with a warning label: *Do not listen unless you wish your heart to leap out of your chest.* Her thoughts were well ahead of her actions, wondering how it would feel to kiss him, if it would be above average because it had been a while for her or because he trained his lips as part of his job.

The above average part was not in question, despite the fact that he was clueless in the snow, as bright as the bloody sun and probably still hung up on his ex.

Her phone peeped, making him jump. The half a second of distraction was enough time for Kira to tear herself away. She tugged the device out of her pocket to find a message from Ginny:

> Well that didn't work out as planned.

Ginny had no idea.

Kira's skin felt tight and jitters tempted her hands as she washed them and then packed up the first aid kit. She didn't want to think about what had just happened – or *nearly* happened – but her mind wouldn't stop replaying the firm pressure of his fingers on her face. Falling into bed with someone, scratching an itch, would be unwise in the circumstances, but understandable. Touching her face, a prelude to a kiss that wouldn't go anywhere, however...

The sensation of being out of control, at the mercy of her own feelings, shook her. She had to see Christian again in a few days. She had to prove – if only to herself – that she wasn't the fool she'd been twelve years ago. It wasn't a great time to discover she could still be susceptible to these idiotic flutters.

Part of her still wished he'd kissed her.

Angry with herself for succumbing to weakness – if only in her own head – she wrenched her rucksack closed and stomped for the exit.

'Kira!'

She heard the curiosity in his voice and ignored it.

The queue for the second gondola was mercifully short and she hoped he'd let the subject drop by the time they'd got through the turnstiles and into the cabin, but as soon as he settled next to her on the leather bench seat, he said, 'I'm sorry if I did something wrong.'

'It was just a scratch. No harm done. Next time, choose a low-hanging icicle,' she insisted, purposefully misunderstanding.

'I wasn't talking about the icicle.'

Goosebumps raced up her arms.

'I am glad it's you who stayed back to babysit me.'

That was too much. 'You know what? You shouldn't be glad. Alessandra wanted to give you and Carla a moment alone. You have unfinished business with her.' She tugged off her beanie and ran a hand through her hair.

'I told you what happened with Carla.'

The cable whisked the gondola up at sudden speed and Mattia cut himself off with a startled choke, falling back against the seat. His shoulder pressed into hers; it was no touch at all, but Kira felt it in the whoosh of her stomach.

'You told me you regretted how it ended. Looks like she's keen for a do-over.'

He was so close to her, she heard the deep, disgruntled noise in his throat at her comment. 'That doesn't mean I can just go back.'

'Urgh, you said you were afraid you'd missed out on something amazing! Here's your chance.'

Tension was rolling off his tall frame as he leaned his head back against the Plexiglas. 'Why do you want me to give Carla another chance?' he asked, his tone strained.

'Alessandra wants romance at her wedding.'

The honey and citrus scent of him reached her nose. His throat bobbed as he swallowed.

'I asked why *you* want me to give Carla a chance?'

She froze, her gaze fixed on his face as he stared blankly past her. She did want him to get back together with Carla so she could forget all of the ways he imposed on her emotions – and she vehemently didn't.

'You want a partner – commitment, love.' She

flapped a hand dismissively. He wanted all those things that had given her hives for... oh, about as long as it had been since she'd last seen Christian. 'You thought you'd found all that with her. Why not try to fix it?'

'Because I don't think she's the right person for me after all,' he said, sounding far more rational than he should have, making a pronouncement like that.

'People aren't "right" and "wrong",' she insisted, tearing her gaze away from him. If that were true, then she was always 'wrong'.

Gazing out at the mix of manicured ski slopes and wild rocks and cliffs, the sharp dips and sudden rises of a landscape that was too big to be tamed, the view called to her, as always. In the physical challenge of a climb or a difficult descent, life appeared simple: breath, muscle, fuel, sleep.

Survival, she could do. Anything more complex and she was out of her depth.

'I'm assuming she's learned to eat without clinking her cutlery now,' she pushed, shifting to give herself an inch of breathing room. But he stretched in response, his knee knocking hers. If he kept touching her, she'd... start to think it felt easy and natural. 'You two looked cosy last night. Ginny said you had an intimate discussion after dinner.'

He sat up straight, shooting her a disapproving look that was several notches too dramatic. 'We did not look "cosy", and do you want to know why I was out in the corridor last night?'

She didn't really, but he continued before she could stop him.

'I was looking for *you!*'

14

Kira looked alarmed at his admission, sending his stomach dropping rapidly into the valley as it became clear that his crush on her was one-sided. If she felt any attraction to him, she wasn't interested in dwelling on it, whereas he could barely think of anything else.

He liked the way she moved: more practical than graceful and always with purpose. He liked that she rarely smiled, making those occasions all the more arresting. He wanted to trust her and lean on her and let her tend all of his wounds.

But she was pushing him back to Carla.

The gondola shuddered into the next station and he scrambled to follow her, groping for her arm and finding her hand. For a single, startling moment, he held her rough one in his and his mind raced with images of that simple action: holding hers under the table while she struggled through dinner conversation; Kira clutching his before an audition; strolling hand in hand along the lungomare in Naples as the sun set.

She pulled her hand back as they walked out into the stunning sunshine, dissolving the images in his brain. Mattia threw his forearm over his eyes at the sudden glare. 'Ah, this place is *violent!*'

'I don't think that's a description I've heard before.'

He peeked to find her looking up at something. When he followed her gaze, he was confronted with a landscape he could never have imagined. Protrusions of jagged rock erupted from the pillowy cushion of snow. Directly before him, the ground zoomed up, impossibly steep, to distant peaks he could barely see. Carefree skiers zigzagged down the slopes, giving him heart failure just watching.

She ushered him to the next station and through the turnstiles as he cricked his neck and bobbed his head to keep his eyes fixed on the mind-altering, high altitude environment.

Taking a seat in the gondola – Kira only scooting closer when someone else piled onto the bench after them – she avoided his gaze, but he wasn't sensible enough to take her hint.

'Are you going to ask me why I was looking for you?'

The gondola whooshed off at that moment, making his stomach swoop for what felt like the fiftieth time that day. The pressure in his ears built and he rummaged for his lozenges.

'These are usually for my voice, but they're working well for my ears today,' he commented, hoping to disarm her again. 'I noticed something was bothering you at dinner.'

Her nostrils flared and that was all he needed to confirm his suspicion that she was upset about something – something to do with the groomsman who seemed to know her. He waited for her to deny it.

When she didn't respond, he proceeded cautiously. 'After you saved me from a fridge and patched me up after the icicle incident, I'm the last person who'll judge you. Let me help, if I can.'

A flicker of dismay was her only discernible reaction. 'You can't help,' she insisted. 'And I wouldn't want you to anyway.'

He released a slow breath. Her answer couldn't have been clearer. He should leave her alone, forget about this bubble he imagined forming around them when they were together.

His mind raced for a way to stop her slipping away, but he was distracted by his own disappointment, by the confounding strength of his desire to be close to her. Perhaps he was starved for affection, but he'd have to have a screw loose to look for it with her. Except... deep down, he suspected she was starved for affection too – even more profoundly than he was.

'All right,' he said gently – a strategic retreat, for now at least. 'I just wondered whether it might help to talk about it.'

She glanced at him, unsettled, a blue strand of hair on her cheek.

After a few intense minutes of seeing nothing but her turbulent eyes and crooked lips, the gondola rattled over a pylon with a clunk-clunk, making him jump. The cabin, swinging through the air above the ski slopes, came back into focus.

He glanced out of the window to his right and choked. 'C-cavolo. Oh my fucking God.'

They were hanging over a deep void on one side, a jagged wall of rock and on the other: nothing. Everything. The whole world. The ground slipped away – far, far away – beneath them as they dangled from the wires.

The pylons they'd just passed were bolted precariously below one rocky peak and the rapidly approaching station perched at the edge of the drop. One false move and...

Right at that moment, the cable car jerked and came to a standstill. Although it wasn't still; residual momentum rocked the gondola back and forth on the cables. His gaze locked in horror on the impossible drop, his ears filled with the muted whistle of the wind and the thick silence, his throat closed until he wasn't sure he could breathe.

Kira's shoulder connected with his chest, hard enough to wind him – and then force him to inhale deeply. Opening his mouth to protest her rough action, he stalled when she didn't move away again. She didn't meet his gaze. Her arms were crossed. But she *leaned*. Tight. He sat stockstill, eyes up, and let her press him into the corner of the gondola, wedged safely amidst the violent beauty of the landscape and the terrifying silence.

'You could look away if it's making you panic,' Kira pointed out softly.

'No, I can't. It's powerful... Don't you feel it? You *have* to feel it.'

Her breath slipped from her mouth on a soft sigh.

'You *feel* everything. It's exhausting.' She mumbled the last part, but he heard every word.

'It's not as exhausting as pretending I don't.'

* * *

When the cable car started moving again and they finally got out at the top, making their way to where the others were waiting, Kira's heart was pounding as though she'd just climbed a new crag at her highest level of difficulty. Riding a gondola with Mattia Bentivoglio was an extreme sport.

How a person could be so jolly after a head injury, while slipping backwards down a snow-covered slope in a pair of silly shoes, Kira had no idea.

'I am *so* glad you're here,' Ginny mumbled out of the side of her mouth as she tramped after the rest of the group. 'I can't imagine being responsible for all of this. I'm starting to think we should always have adventure guides with us!'

Kira swallowed a sharp retort about not being allowed to do her job because she had to play nice instead. She felt out of her depth and was infinitely annoyed about it. She couldn't stop Mattia bumbling into disaster, she couldn't get him to keep a lid on his feelings – for her sake or anyone else's – and every conversation seemed to skim topics she didn't want to touch on. She wished she'd been able to come up with an excuse for her behaviour at dinner last night. Mattia might have accepted it and left her alone.

Rav himself might stumble into a taboo topic at any moment and that would be the kind of disaster she couldn't prepare for. Physical danger would have been preferable, but they were only touring an ice cave on prepared paths and she didn't even have any risks to keep her mind busy.

The biggest disaster she could picture was her friend Rhys, the photographer, finding out about that time in her past that Rav had been part of. The team at Great Heart Adventures was her family, but they wouldn't recognise the idiot she'd been twelve years ago and she didn't want the embarrassment of them finding out. At least Ginny kept Rhys busy with unnecessary instructions. He might never usually photograph people, but this was an ice cave and he was incredibly talented at landscapes.

From the harsh sunlight and blinding snowdrifts above ground, their group of ten – plus the two wedding planners and Rhys – followed their tour guide through a narrow gap in the snow, down wooden steps dug into the ice and into the dim, blue world thirty metres below the ski slopes.

Kira had seen crevasses before – and seracs, ancient ice shaped into fantastical structures by physics and the passage of time. But she's never actually been *inside* a glacier. On an expedition, it was too dangerous. She didn't want to imagine the long list of safety measures this place would have to implement to keep the environment stable.

As she shuffled slowly through the warren of tunnels with the group, her mood and her sceptical tendencies led her to lament the taming of this great glacier – for all of five minutes. Between the ice walls that held millions of cubic metres of water, the air was hushed and still, but heavy with the immensity of the structure.

She couldn't help asking Mattia, 'What do you hear?'

He cocked his head like a bird, which was an interesting simile. He'd be one of those colourful males with fancy plumage. 'Scratching, groaning – lots of echoes. It's *enormous*.'

'Really?' Kira strained her ears, but all she got were the muted footsteps all around her.

A frown etched onto his brow. 'I feel like I can hear it moving – a long way away. But this part is still.'

'That's right!' their tour guide piped up. 'Glaciers are ice rivers, constantly moving, but here it is static, frozen solid to the rocks. It's unusual, but we wouldn't be able to visit if this weren't the case. You can hear the ice cracking in summer, even though the terminus is nearly four kilometres away.'

Mattia stayed close to her as they ambled through the tunnels. 'Did you know sound travels faster in ice than in water? And faster in water than in air?' he asked, shoving his hands in his pockets. 'I learned about that when I was a teenager. My mother thought I was making things up.' How he managed to say that with a fond smile, Kira didn't know. 'I could hear things, particularly if I put my ear to it. I told her our neighbours wanted to divorce and when she found out it was true, she was worried I had some supernatural gift. I had to research the speed of sound in different substances to convince her.'

'So you really can hear four kilometres away in here?'

'If the icicles would stop dripping, I might hear more. There are cracks everywhere. Instabilities. It's quite terrifying,' he finished with a wary glance around him.

There was no adrenaline kick here, no physical challenge, but Kira's heart beat loudly anyway. What did the mountain care whether she lived or died – whether Mattia held her hand or not? Whether Rav said something that poked the scars on her heart? In here, her life was like a drip of water.

As they waited to descend a ladder, she hung back and tugged off her glove, smoothing her fingers over the wall of ice. At the entrance, the tunnel had been white: *névé* and firn, the two stages of transition from snow to ice. But here, it was a deep blue, the lamplight showing up the colour as it penetrated a few feet. Air bubbles were trapped in the ice, along with particles of rock and dirt.

Spreading her fingers over the frozen surface, she *felt* it.

Quickly checking that no one was looking, she pressed her ear to the ice – and heard an immediate *pop* that sounded close enough to make her jump. Distant white noise, like waves, created a background symphony, punctuated regularly by clatters and creaks, and Kira suspected she would think differently every time she visited a glacier in the future.

She felt a little light-headed, which made her uneasy.

'Kira? You coming?'

She jerked her head away from the ice wall at Ginny's summons, giving her cold ear a vigorous rub. Hurrying down the ladder, she tried to clear her head, but Mattia had waited for her and followed close behind her once they reached flat ground again and her wobbly emotions were all his fault.

'Is it warmer in here than out there?' he asked, his brow knit.

She nodded. 'If there's ice melting, it must be around zero. You'd survive in here, if you got stranded overnight.'

He shuddered. 'I don't know what would be left of me with this incessant drip. You'd have to talk to me all night.' He winked and the hairs on the back of her neck stood up. He had no right to flirt with her when she was out of her depth. He especially had no right to look so adorable while he did so.

After the first crevasse, they climbed the ladder again and the path opened out on one side with lights illuminating a shimmering, rippling surface.

'Is that water?' Mattia gripped the rope strung along the side and leaned out, his jaw hanging open.

Kira's lips twitched in amusement. 'What do you think is all around us?'

He eyed her and even that was cute. 'All around us is ice, while that is liquid. It's some kind of miracle.'

'Don't call your saints too quickly. It's thermodynamics.'

'It's *amazing*,' he said softly.

Her chest full and tight with pressure – and not

the kind of pressure that kept the water a liquid rather than a solid – Kira grinned, a laugh rising from her stomach. 'It is amazing,' she agreed.

A group of tourists in a rubber boat floated past and waved, the flash of a camera penetrating the eerie thickness of the ice.

He bit his lip thoughtfully. 'You feel it,' he said, a hint of *I told you so* in his tone. 'The power of this place.'

'Unfortunately,' she quipped.

Moving slowly, as though he didn't want to alarm her, Mattia came close enough to whisper in her ear, 'Don't worry. Your feelings are safe with me.'

With a dazzling smile that was far too cocky for someone who'd slipped while trying to grab an icicle, he inclined his head in an invitation to continue after the others. Kira realised with a start that they'd dropped behind and that was all his fault too.

Up ahead, Alessandra's exclamations of wonder and delight reached a new crescendo and Kira hurried to catch up with Mattia, peering around his tall frame when he slowed his steps. Her heart rate kicked up again.

She felt his deep gasp at the same time as her own breath caught.

15

Fingers of ice grew in front of Kira's eyes, twists and swirls and little waterfalls, as though a stream had been snap frozen. The cavern was high and wide and full of ice formations more beautiful than anything a sculptor could create. Occasional protrusions of rock hinted at the summits that ranged above.

'Up there would be the *randkluft*,' she whispered, 'the place where the glacial ice pulls away from the rock. It's one of the most dangerous parts of a mountain for climbers, but I've never seen it from... underneath.'

'Oh my God, I am bringing every couple here from now on!' Ginny squealed, interrupting the hushed awe. 'Alessandra, you and Joe go stand on that platform and Rhys – camera! We only have half an hour in here. Kira, can you take them around to that cave there and I'll call instructions. These photos are going to be *epic*!'

'Urgh, weddings,' Kira said through gritted teeth, although she appreciated the reminder that she was not here to gaze in wonder at the natural phenomenon – or let the baritone bridesman get to her. 'Will you be all right?' she asked Mattia warily. 'Don't touch anything and watch your step in those shoes.'

'Of course. I'm not going to lick the icicles.'

That comment made her eye him in alarm.

She had no choice but to follow Ginny's instructions and moments later, found herself juggling Alessandra's handbag while trying to stay out of the background of the photos. The ice formations created angles that Rhys would be certain to enjoy capturing, despite the bride and groom also in the frame. At least he was snapping wide shots and didn't have to capture Joe and Alessandra's facial expressions in detail. She knew how much he would loathe that, given his perfectionist streak.

Ginny obviously found Rhys frustrating, but Kira couldn't exactly take her friend aside and explain why he was so surly. Ginny should have learned by now that everyone associated with Great Heart had a tough outer shell.

Kira was restless – itchy – from the slow day. If she were honest, she was restless from the day of emotions with no outlet, plus the way weddings inevitably made her face her own life choices. She wanted to climb something and these frozen waterfalls were looking pretty good.

A burst of loud Italian broke into her ruminations, booming and ricocheting off the rock in eerie waves. Only one person in the wedding party had such a rich, powerful voice. Kira peeked around the curl of ice in front of her to see him making Alessandra's mother laugh with his dramatic tone, trying out the acoustics of the ice cave.

'Yes!' came Alessandra's enthusiastic response to whatever he'd said. 'You *must* sing something for us in here!'

'Are you sure it won't break the ice and bring the whole cave down on our heads?' Joe joked under his breath.

Kira's chin jerked up. She wanted to break some ice over *his* head!

'Go ahead,' their guide said with a smile. 'The sound properties in here are very unusual.'

'Opera is unusual enough in normal conditions,' Joe continued.

Kira's gaze settled on Mattia, standing across the cavern from where she stood, half a smile on his face. There was no way he hadn't heard, but he didn't lash out in reply; he straightened, planted his feet and cast a gentle spell into the space.

It was almost no sound at all at first. A low rumble that slowly grew into a melody. From his stance, the way he seemed to tense every muscle in his torso, she'd expected an explosion of sound, but instead it was a shimmer, a disembodied tune that seemed to come from every corner separately.

She barely noticed his voice growing louder, shaking every molecule of air – and rock and ice. The music seemed to have colour and shades of dark and light. Mattia was only a conduit, as though the song came to him from another realm.

Kira heard it through her veins. She wanted to ask him if he did it on purpose, playing his audience's emotions like an instrument. The quality of his voice, so unassuming when he spoke, transformed into an act of nature when he sang the heavy climax of the song. She hoped someone had their ear to the ice kilometres away and could hear the swell and resonance.

He held the final note for long enough that a

slight tremor entered his voice and then cut off the sound with a suddenness that made the silence feel violent.

Take *that*, Joe.

Rhys and Ginny stood frozen, dumbfounded. Alessandra and Carla called out, 'Bravo!' and their applause created a high-pitched din that was painful after the shine and colour of the past few minutes.

Mattia propped his hands on his hips and took deep, even breaths, flicking Alessandra's mother a quick grin when she patted him fondly on the arm.

'I did not expect that,' Kira heard Joe commenting behind her.

Kira hadn't expected Mattia either and she didn't know what she was going to do with him.

* * *

'When I pointed out I hadn't spent much time with Joe, I did not mean I wanted to sweat naked with him in a sauna.'

After lunch at over 3,000 metres at the restaurant – with transport by snow groomer – the wedding party had made it back down in the cable car and returned to the relative calm of the Kitzingalm Hütte with a couple of hours until dinner.

Alessandra slapped his arm. 'I didn't mean naked! Do you really think *Joe* would go into a sauna naked?'

'Good point,' Mattia grumbled.

'You can keep your towel on.'

Darn, that was one excuse not to join Joe and the groomsmen in the sauna shot down. Mattia couldn't imagine he'd enjoy it, even without his intimate parts on show. The groom and his mates would laugh deeply and make inappropriate jokes. With nothing else to do but talk, they'd be deeply uncomfortable.

'Aren't I one of the bridesmaids, rather than a groomsman?' That made him think of Kira again with a sizzle of satisfaction.

'But you don't want to get a manicure with us.'

'Remember at school when I went through that black nail polish phase? I could do that again.'

Then Alessandra brought out the heavy artillery – a pout so pronounced in her wine-coloured lipstick, she reminded him of the Neapolitan ghost stories where a single look could condemn a man to die. 'For me, Matty? It's my dearest wish that you and Joe should get to know each other and be friends.'

Mattia thought perhaps the two were rather mutually exclusive, but he couldn't voice that worry.

'I'm *marrying* him and you're my best friend.'

That reminded him of Kira again and their conversation in the van. He *was* a little resentful of the change that would take Alessandra away from him, and perhaps that was part of the reason he'd never imagined getting along with Joe.

'Fine,' he said with a sigh, giving her a kiss on the cheek in farewell before trudging back to his room to change.

The sauna was a small, wooden hut built onto the far side of the chalet, technically outdoors, which made Mattia grimace as he'd only just warmed up from the trip on the snow groomer. There were also no changing facilities attached, so he had to slap down the stairs in the complimentary felt slippers, clutching his towel.

But when he stepped inside, he understood why it had been constructed that way. One corner of the sauna was made entirely of glass, framing the glistening, white valley and pine forest groaning under a heavy layer of snow.

'Shut the door, mate, yeah?'

Shuffling inside and closing the door, Mattia noticed that there was only one person sitting on the wooden slats – someone he rather wanted to talk to, which meant *not* Joe.

'Rav, isn't it?'

'Yeah.'

'I won't offer my hand, because... well, you know.' He grimaced inwardly, the fug of warmth in the room spreading out his presence of mind like gas particles. Great, now Rav would either think he had sweaty hands after two seconds in a sauna or that he was scared of dropping his towel. Both were unfortunately true.

He chose a spot that he hoped was a polite distance away and racked his brain for something to say that wasn't *Why was Kira upset with you last night?*

To his surprise, Rav brought it up. 'Are you a friend of Kira's? I didn't know she liked opera.' He gave a halting chuckle at his own joke.

'She doesn't,' he replied curtly, propping himself up with his elbows on his knees and hanging his head as sweat gathered on the back of his neck. 'We bonded over Bon Jovi and the Red Hot Chili Peppers. She's an old rock soul.'

To his surprise, Rav laughed – properly this time. 'She's still the same as she was at school, then.'

Mattia peered at him out of the corner of his eye. He wasn't sure he liked the fondness in the other man's tone. He certainly didn't like that he didn't understand it. 'You knew her when she was a teenager?'

Rav nodded. 'We were a close bunch of friends all through secondary school.'

That certainly sounded like 'just friends' rather than anything else, but he remembered the catch in her voice when she'd told him she didn't like to let other people change her.

'But I haven't seen her in... oh, it must be more than ten years. We went off to university and she...' His expression tightened, reminding Mattia of the emotion strung taut on her face whenever he'd seen her speaking to Rav.

'You left her behind?'

Rav's eyebrows shot up. Perhaps that question had been too belligerent, but Mattia was desperate to understand the subtext.

'No— well kind of, yes,' Rav answered with a frown. 'To be honest, I was pissed off at Christian for ending it so badly. She's good value, Kira. It would have been nice to stay friends even though they broke up.'

Mattia sat up straight, rubbing a dollop of sweat out of the corner of his eye. His chest was tight – both from the bubble of pressurised heat and from that hint of what had happened. *Christian.* Having a name was enough to set him off. His stomach twisted, remembering everything Kira had said about relationships.

Rav kept speaking, as though the intimacy of the

sauna had given him permission to get this off his chest. 'Maybe he shouldn't have gone out with her at all. Friendships between men and women can be complicated, you know? Then you add in a history like that – and the way he broke up with her was rotten—' Ravi looked away with a grimace.

Mattia filled in the rest of the picture: a young, less jaded Kira (just as sporty and hot) wouldn't have been prepared for the sudden end of the relationship, because she was loyal in every cell of her body. It would have crushed her.

'Well, you know Kira,' Rav was saying, making Mattia belatedly tune in again.

'Hmm?'

'She gave him one. Not that what he did wasn't shitty, but she got mad and then he got mad and I think they both said things they might not have with a clear head.'

'I've seen her grumpy, but to make her truly mad – he must have really deserved it.' Mattia had to snap his mouth shut before he said anything further. Rav's uneasy look suggested he'd growled rather than speaking those words in a normal voice.

'Maybe, but I thought we were all friends and after that, she just... I didn't hear a thing from her. She cut herself off.'

That *did* sound like Kira 'I don't like people to change me' Watling.

'I'm a bit worried about the wedding, to be honest,' Rav continued. 'I don't think Joe knows. It happened before we met him.'

What happened? What did it have to do with the wedding?

The door swung open. 'Hey, mate! You got started without us. Hi, Matty. I didn't bring you a beer.' Joe swung a beer into Rav's hand, tapping his own against the bottle and taking a swig as he sat down between Mattia and Rav, hitching his towel up. The other groomsman, Hugh, followed him in.

'Hi, eh, don't worry about it,' Mattia responded, eying the beer. Given his pores were weeping in the heat, he couldn't imagine alcohol was a good idea. He'd heard Britons did enjoy warm beer, although perhaps that was only in *Asterix*.

Mattia leaned forward, trying to catch Rav's eye to continue their previous discussion. What was worrying Rav about the wedding?

He was uneasy, his heart beating strangely, although he'd lost track of how long he'd been sweltering in the sauna, so that could have been the reason.

'You coming skiing tomorrow?' Joe asked him casually, although Mattia was either oversensitive or he detected a hint of competitiveness in the groom's tone.

He shook his head. 'I've never tried it before. I wouldn't want to hold you back.'

'Or cause more problems for the wedding planner,' Joe teased, making Mattia wonder what Alessandra had said and whether they'd all realised he was following her around like a lost puppy. He swiped another stream of sweat off his brow.

'Speaking of the wedding planner,' Rav continued, leaning forward to catch Mattia's eye. 'Is she single? Kira?'

Before Mattia could swallow his distaste at the question, Joe and Hugh were wolf-whistling and slapping Rav on the back.

'You're going to have a go at that one?' Hugh teased.

'You're just jealous you brought your girlfriend and you can't try it yourself,' Joe ribbed Hugh.

Mattia ground his teeth, wanting to leap up and remind Joe with a very stern index finger that this was his *wedding* and he shouldn't be suggesting his friend would cheat on his girlfriend – let alone objectifying their wedding planner and ski instructor.

'Her?' Hugh scoffed. 'I've seen prettier racehorses, but she does have nice t—'

'*Hugh*! Cut it out!'

It was even more distressing that Rav was the one defending her and not Mattia himself. He was struggling for air, discomfort seeping up his spine.

'I was just wondering if she was single because of the wedding.' Rav met Mattia's eye meaningfully. 'Because Christian and his girlfriend are coming.'

Christian. Coming to the ceremony. Kira's ex. Did she know? What if she didn't!

Mattia leapt to his feet, tottering alarmingly. His vision blurred, but he could still see the door. His whole body felt as out of focus as the little wooden hut.

'E-e-excuse me,' he stammered and hurtled for the door, even though his head swam. He had to find her.

16

She wasn't in her room, but after an astonished Ginny had opened the door and finished making a decent impression of a fish, she'd told him about the makeshift climbing wall in the chalet loft. Taking the stairs with one hand fisted in his towel and the other clinging to the banister, his head felt out of synch with the rest of his body and sparks exploded at the edge of his vision.

But when he imagined Kira turning up at the wedding to be confronted by her ex, the man who had most likely broken her heart and turned her off relationships for more than a decade, another shot of panic fizzed through his chest.

Finding the chipboard door at the top of the stairs in the dim loft, he wrenched it open and tumbled in, faltering when he was confronted with an image he would never have expected.

Kira hung from the ceiling.

If she'd been hanging the way gymnasts did at the Olympics, he might not have been so dumbfounded. But her hands were not fisted around rings or a bar and her body was not falling straight, at the mercy of gravity. Her knees were bent, holding her lower body tight to the slope of the roof. Her hands and feet were anchored by little plastic grips. The only part of her body that appeared to be obeying the laws of physics was her hair, spraying out from her head in pale-blue strands.

With an expert shift of her legs and arms – and a ripple of muscle through her torso – she swung to the next holds. Her body stretched and strained, the movements not graceful, but effortless. Mattia watched her and felt as though he could see all the beauty and utility of the human frame captured in her.

If he'd been an artist, he would have imagined drawing her in pencil, shading the curves of muscle in her arms and back, the arc of her bottom. As he wasn't an artist, his brain fired in a much less helpful direction. He could trace those lines with his hands – his lips. In his fantasy, he imagined making her feel good – *feel* everything, including her own stark beauty.

But Kira didn't want to feel anything so radical. And she probably wouldn't let him kiss her. Especially not after she heard what he had to say.

Which was what, again? Something about a turd of an ex-boyfriend.

His vision flicked in and out of focus and his mouth was suddenly as dry as terracotta. He managed to feel grateful for the rubber mats lining the floor under the climbing wall as his legs finally buckled.

* * *

When a muffled thump dragged Kira out of her haze of concentration, she did not expect to find Mattia – naked, except for a bunched towel – crumpled on his knees on the landing mats.

The loft room that had been converted into a bouldering wall had a low ceiling, so she relaxed her toes and swung out, hanging from her arms for a moment before dropping to the floor. He blinked up at her as she approached, as though he were the surprised one.

'What's the matter?' She peered into his face, checking pupil dilation out of first-aid habit, noting no signs of injury. The dressing on his forehead was coming off, but there was no fresh bleeding.

He plonked into a sitting position, belatedly remembering the towel and arranging it hastily, a flush spreading up his chest.

'Don't worry, I'm getting used to the sight of you in a towel,' she joked, willing her gaze to stay where it was and not undermine her words by taking a trip down his chest. It slipped to his big, bony shoulders, making a daring slide along his collarbone, but she pulled up just in time.

He opened his mouth to speak, pausing to lick his lips and swallow heavily, as though he'd seen in her gaze how much she wanted to skim her fingers over him. But when he managed to get some words out, she realised she'd misinterpreted. 'Do you have any water?'

When she handed him her bottle, he drank half of it without stopping and sighed with relief.

'Grazie, carissima.' He leaned back on his arms, which unfortunately showcased the great expanse of skin. 'I don't think I like saunas.'

That at least explained the towel and his state of undress.

'You have to keep your fluids up.'

Confident he'd recovered, she stood to fetch her hoodie and slip it on, now the strain of climbing was no longer keeping her warm. Mattia's eyes followed the action intently enough to make the hairs on her arms stand on end. As though realising too late what he was doing, his gaze snapped away again as she joined him, cross-legged on the mat.

'Did you run up all those stairs just to drink my water?'

He straightened so quickly, the towel shifted. 'I have to warn you about the wedding!'

'What? Is there an assassin? Or even worse: a lack of canapés? Ginny seems to think that would be a disaster.'

'No.' His hesitation and pained look made her uneasy. 'There are other guests who are only coming to the ceremony and not staying here with us.'

She nodded. 'I think Ginny said there will be about thirty at the ceremony. She's got it all under control. What are you so worked up about?' It was killing the buzz she'd just achieved on the bouldering wall.

'You know Rav met Joe at university?'

'Mattia! Can you get to the point?'

'Sorry,' he muttered, giving himself a shake. 'I just wanted to tell you gently.'

'Tell me *what*?'

'It's Christian. He's coming. He's here – in the valley.'

The exact information she'd been trying to process by shoving it out of her mind with physical strain. She gritted her teeth.

'You were talking about me with Rav.'

He drew back, obviously surprised by her bitter accusation. 'I'm sorry? I was worried about you.'

She didn't want to be touched, but everything he did seemed to dig too deep. 'Worried about *me*? You're the one who required first aid on two occasions today!'

'I know, but I could see something was bothering you.'

'Nothing is... bothering me,' she lied, stubbornly ignoring the fact that Mattia obviously knew she was lying. 'And I already knew he was coming.'

He winced. 'Ah, I probably should have assumed... that you would have everything under control and you wouldn't need my help.'

Her throat was thick when she belatedly appreciated that he'd rushed up here half-dressed for her sake. 'Why do you even care?' she blurted out.

A rueful smile touched his lips. 'I didn't think it

was such a mystery that I *like* you!' He punctuated his sentence with a loose hand gesture full of frustration and discouragement.

A hot blush rose to the surface of her skin, even though it was only attraction, this hugging-kissing-closeness kind of 'like' that she was also resisting.

With that glint in his eye, he reminded her of a cheeky sprite – a faun or an elf – that lived on a slightly different plane where the world was more colourful. Certainly, he was so beautiful, he seemed to glisten in and out of focus in her world of rock and dirt and violent nature.

As though he sensed he'd disarmed her, he continued in a smooth voice. 'This guy Christian hurt you when you were still young enough to feel it.'

'That's ridiculous,' she insisted, more out of habit than anything else. 'I was only seventeen when we got together – too young to feel much of anything except confusion.'

'Is he the reason you choose your friends carefully now?'

'That's simplistic.'

'But not untrue?'

Kira couldn't bring herself to outright deny it, but she also couldn't afford to dwell on the memories of that time – her gullible optimism, misplaced loyalty.

The realisation that if even her best friend couldn't love her, how could anyone?

'What happened?'

There was no way she would admit the whole, sorry story – not at a damn wedding. 'Relationships end – mine do, at least.'

'But what do you mean by "relationships"? You don't have relationships,' he pointed out, far too insightful for Kira's good.

She fidgeted, uncomfortable with how much she'd already shared with him. 'I just meant Christian only wanted one thing from me and that seems to be the way it goes. I've always been one of the boys. I didn't like to be indoors as a kid and I gravitated towards the boys, no matter how much my mum tried to steer me towards make-up and movies. Then Christian was the first one to discover his mate had boobs and might be good for a f—'

'All right, I get it,' Mattia said with a grimace.

'But I'm not going to change the way I am just so I'm not alone.' She lifted her chin.

'Of course you shouldn't,' he agreed hotly. 'Especially when you're...'

'What? What am I?' she asked with a snort. She'd spent adult life determined never to care what men thought of her, but here she was, desperate for his answer. Mattia broke her established rules just by breathing and she still wasn't sure why she was sitting here allowing her skin to prickle, rather than running a mile.

'So... vigorous.' He gave his arms a shake for emphasis.

She drew back and eyed him. 'Is that supposed to be a compliment?'

He dropped his forehead into his hand. 'Of course! You are stronger than these bed friends of yours. You can do everything they can – better. They're scared of you. Their egos won't allow them to commit to you because their fragile masculinity needs reinforcement and you have more important things to do.'

Her jaw dropped and it took her several seconds to find her voice. Her knee-jerk reaction was to dismiss him, but what he said rang in her head, like the bell struck in the Christmas market during that first performance when he'd thawed the edges of her heart. He was building her up – possibly too far – not knocking her down. She hadn't expected it.

'Perhaps that might be part of the reason,' she acknowledged. 'But there's also the fact that the only thing I can cook is beans on a single gas burner, I leave clothes all over the floor and while I know some guys like the climbing physique, it's my face they'd have to love.'

'And why wouldn't they?' he responded belligerently. 'Did Christian make you think you aren't beautiful?'

'A mirror tells me every morning! Don't try to convince me I'm pretty, Mattia. We both know that would be a load of shit and I'd rather respect you.'

He sucked in a breath through his nose, his sharp jaw working. His gaze dropped to her mouth and he swallowed, giving his head a little shake. 'It's a difficult choice.' His voice was so deep and smooth, he could speak to her on another level – a deeply physical one, that distracted her from the task of puzzling out his convoluted meaning. 'I do want your respect – quite a lot.'

His pained tone dug right under her skin. The way he pinned her to the spot with just a hot gaze. He should have been a stranger – a client. But even as she'd tried to clear her thoughts on the wall, she hadn't been able to stop thinking about his hand clasping hers – and what it would be like to kiss him.

She could lean in just a little and her mouth would be on his. He'd kiss her back, those long fingers curling into her hair, holding her still as he slowed it down. But Kira had momentum and she could tackle him to the mats. She could touch him, work out whether he was made of flesh and blood or something non-corporeal, like his music.

Except, it wasn't only her professional obligations that got in the way. Mattia was looking for his fairy soulmate and didn't do casual. She wished he'd stop looking at her with such raw intensity if there was nowhere for the attraction to go.

'Thanks for running up here naked to save me, but I'll be fine. It was a long time ago. I'm not a starry-eyed teenager any more. I've learned not to let people get to me.' She hoped that was true.

'I suppose that is a real skill – another one I've certainly never mastered,' he said, glancing away. 'I always wondered if it's about learning not to feel anything or simply learning not to show it.'

Kira scrambled to her feet, her rubber climbing shoes tripping her up in her hurry to get to the door and put some space between her and those confronting words. He fed off emotion, swam confidently through it, enjoying getting wet. Kira couldn't swim and didn't want to dip in more than her toe. Another reason getting closer to him would be a bad idea.

'Hey,' he began as he caught up to her in the hallway, 'I didn't mean to upset you.'

'I—' Denying it would only prove his point. 'We just bounce off each other strangely.'

Walking next to her down the narrow steps, his shoulder nudged hers over and over again. 'I noticed that too. I like it.'

He *would*.

'If people find me intimidating, why aren't *you* frightened of me?' she asked, slowing to let him consider his answer and bump his arm against hers a few more times.

They came to a stop outside the door of her room before he'd formed a response. 'I think it's because—' Dramatic pause. He dipped his head and dropped his voice. 'I've discovered your weakness.'

There was a smile in his voice, but his words still sent a bolt of unease through her. Her alarm must have shown on her face, because he shook his head and lifted a hand, stretching his fingers under her ear, his thumb on her cheek, and she froze. This was certainly one weakness he'd discovered. She liked to be touched. Perhaps she needed it. Perhaps that was why she'd been feeling restless.

'Shh,' he said softly. 'Don't worry. I won't tell anyone.'

She wrenched her eyes open to scowl at him. 'What are you talking about? What weakness?'

Swiping a strand of hair off her forehead, he drew back to smile at her in all his dark, elven glory. 'You, Kira Watling, are one of the kindest people I've ever met.'

It could have been a platitude. From anyone else, it definitely would have been, but spoken in Mattia's deep, other-worldly voice, punctuated by a brush of his thumb over the scar on her cheek, she couldn't dismiss it.

'I don't... "Kind" isn't an obvious choice to describe me. You said "vigorous" first.' She extricated herself from the touch, immediately feeling the loss of it.

'That too, but it's not a weakness.' His smile was amused now, as though he knew something she didn't. 'You are also one of the grumpiest people I've ever met, but despite everything, you are always kind, even taking fault on yourself when you shouldn't.'

The lump in her throat was too big to swallow. 'You should go and take a shower. You'll get cold and I can see the salt on your skin from here.'

His cheeks were pink again when she looked into his face. He gave her an awkward smile. 'See you at dinner.'

Just before she managed to escape, he leaned close, hesitating for a breath before pressing his lips to her cheek. It was nothing – a throwaway gesture. He'd kissed Carla's cheek in greeting despite everything unpleasant between them. But he was too close, with all his warm skin and soft words. He *liked* her, which was strange, but stranger still was how much she liked him, drama and all.

Kira couldn't breathe – she couldn't think. She could only react.

17

The floor beneath Mattia's bare feet was suddenly unstable. The hallway had fallen silent, the air still. The world might have stopped turning, because Kira's – slightly sweaty – hand was on the back of his neck and her breath was on his lips. She wouldn't—

She did. And it was wonderful.

With just the right amount of pressure to make the contact zing to his toes, she kissed him, mouth hot and slightly open, full of frustration and surprise and... recognition. There was that soft upper lip, followed by a brush of her firm lower one – and then a little swipe of her tongue. A hitch in the back of her throat – a tiny sound of delight that wormed its way under his skin.

Ohi, it was more than he could take.

It was hesitant, a first discovery of warmth and pressure, underscored by the tug of need he knew she felt too. It was too fast for him, too deep for her. But kissing Kira, teasing her lips with his, was raw and clumsy and utterly perfect.

Until she pulled away.

'Sorry,' she said, her voice all breath. 'I didn't mean — I know you wouldn't—'

'What? No, don't—' He was still seeing stars behind his eyes and the world was moving too quickly for him.

'Okay, right. Bye!' Licking her lips, she gave him a quick smile and disappeared behind her bedroom door with a soft snick – making her sudden escape.

He had to prop himself up on the door-frame until he got his breath back.

'Matty?'

He jerked back from the door at the shrill sound of his name, groping frantically for the towel that was miraculously still slung around his waist. Alessandra was stalking in his direction, her eyes wide, her gaze taking him in from head to toe. He hurried to intercept her.

'What are you doing here?' Her voice was high,

strained. 'Outside Ginny's door. Naked. My *wedding planner*!'

His stomach swooped and his expression hardened. He opened his mouth, probably to blurt out that Alessandra should have known it was *Kira*, not Ginny, but Carla emerged up the steps from the ground floor. He groaned inwardly. Had she heard Alessandra's assumption?

'Nothing. I'm not doing anything,' he insisted.

But Alessandra was on a roll. She dropped her voice so only he could hear. 'I know you don't like Joe and you're still recovering from the break-up with Carla, but I did not expect you to act out like this.'

'You've got the wrong idea.'

'I know Carla hurt you,' Alessandra continued, glancing between Mattia and his ex, 'but she didn't mean to. I'm going to be living full-time in London now and I just want the two of you to have what I—'

She burst into tears. Carla met his gaze with a grimace of her own and slipped an arm around their friend.

'Shh, cara,' Carla crooned. 'It's your time. We're here for you and happy for *you*. You don't have to solve our problems too.'

Alessandra gave a sniff. 'What problems? Have I

been so focused on the wedding that you haven't been able to talk to me?'

Mattia was beginning to think Kira was right about weddings.

'No,' Carla lied with some accomplishment, flicking him an amused look. 'Maybe we should go and find some herbal tea to calm you down and let Mattia get dressed. He looks freezing.'

* * *

Outside the wide – thankfully triple-glazed – windows of the chalet sitting room, the cosy evening had darkened into night, plump flakes of snow catching the light from the lamps. A new, unspoilt layer had gathered after Norbert had performed his twice-daily clearing, perfection in the stark, wild landscape.

Inside, the fire was loudly consuming a handful of logs behind glass, the wine was hot and spiced and the scent of pine completed the intimate setting. It was all of Alessandra's dreams come true, a winter wedding to remember for the rest of their lives. Except the woman herself was busy whispering urgently in Mattia's ear.

'You could have at least told me you were flirting

with Ginny, so I didn't get a shock – or get my hopes up about Carla!'

Mattia fisted a hand on his thigh, not sure what to say to his best friend to fix this, and frankly unwilling to discuss it right now, with everyone else in the same room – and the lingering effects of the kiss still in his bloodstream.

Kira hadn't joined them in the den, which should have been a relief, since his gaze had found its way to her too many times over dinner, but he felt her absence just as keenly as he'd felt her presence. She'd ignored him anyway, so he was alone in the fixation regardless of whether she was in the room or not.

'There's no reason to be shocked. Nothing happened. I was on my way back from the sauna and I realised I wasn't sure about plans for tomorrow, so I thought I'd ask.' He hoped the lie flowed more smoothly than he usually managed, now he'd had an hour to practise it.

'It *really* looked as though you'd just come out of the room,' Alessandra said slowly. 'You were leaning as though you'd just kissed someone.'

'I was never in the room,' he said gently, disputing the part of the sentence where he didn't have to lie. 'But I understand why you'd be upset. Nothing should overshadow your wedding and nothing *will*.'

She frowned at him. 'You know what I want most is to share the happiness with all of you.'

He wasn't certain she was going about it the right way, but he couldn't fault her heart.

'That's why I was so alarmed,' she said earnestly, turning to him. 'You're not the type to... you know.'

'Eh?' He wasn't the type for a lot of things: ice, saunas, snowmobiles – cable cars.

'Casual sex!' she hissed.

Either Alessandra had unhappily spoken into a natural lull in conversation or everyone in the room had heard and frozen in shock.

'Mamma mia, Alessandra,' he mumbled, glad that only her parents and Carla understood Italian. 'Since I was in the sauna with your fiancé until just before you saw me, it wouldn't say much for my skills in the bedroom if that's what I had been doing,' he said through his teeth.

Finally, Alessandra seemed to take a breath and some of the tension drained from her body. 'Right. I'm sorry. Of course you weren't... doing that. Not that you couldn't talk to me about it if you were.'

He obviously *couldn't* talk to her about his love life right now, but that was fair enough. And since when did he think about having a 'love life'? He'd stumbled into the relationship with Carla and now had an infantile crush on someone with whom he'd only shared a quick kiss – probably out of pity, because he was making a fool of himself.

A kiss that hadn't stopped replaying in his mind.

'But I suppose it was silly on my part to think you'd jump into bed with someone you've only just met.' Her sharp giggle made him wonder how much of the sweet, spiced wine she'd drunk. 'I know you're too sensitive for that and I love you that way.'

She sighed and rested her head on his shoulder, her hair tickling his jaw. How often had they sat like this over the years? He was so much taller than she was, but she'd always been the 'big sister', the older, wiser one.

But in that moment, Mattia was uneasy, deep in his stomach. The wedding was in two days. Between Kira's ex problem and his own, the event felt like a mess and despite the awe-inspiring location and all her best efforts to create the wedding of her dreams, Alessandra had just burst into tears right in front of him.

He was about to ask her if everything was all right, if she wanted to go somewhere to talk – although where they'd go when outside was a frozen wasteland that could give them hypothermia – when she lifted her head and brightened.

Dropping her voice to a whisper so soft he barely heard it, she said, 'I suppose there's hope for you and Carla, yet.'

Before he could protest, Alessandra set down her mug and stood, making her way to where Carla was talking to Ginny. Inwardly groaning, Mattia braced himself. Whatever Alessandra had to say to either of them, he wasn't sure he wanted to hear it. He only hoped she'd believed his excuses. He didn't want to land the other wedding planner in trouble because the bride was determined to see her friends settled before she permanently left Naples. Perhaps he should have told her the truth.

Urgh, no, after the strange conversation he'd just had with Alessandra, he couldn't backtrack and admit he'd kissed the *other* wedding planner, especially when he could barely believe it himself. Only two more days and they'd have made it through the wedding alive. He only had to keep Alessandra calm for another two days.

'Ginny,' Alessandra interrupted gently, 'I've just had the most wonderful idea and I'm certain it can't be too difficult to arrange.'

Mattia held his breath.

With her bottomless patience, Ginny smiled en-
thusiastically and waited for her to continue.

'You know how important kisses are at Italian
weddings. And this is an Italian *winter* wedding. We're
going to need a lot more mistletoe.'

18

'She finally beat you, huh?'

Ginny looked up from where she'd been scowling at her laptop, propped on the bed in front of her. 'What do you mean?'

'You've been muttering to yourself about kissing for the past ten minutes. Will you finally admit you're annoyed about all the special requirements for this wedding?'

'I'm not annoyed,' she insisted, making Kira laugh, 'as much as it feels like a personal affront to be sourcing a heap of mistletoe when I haven't been kissed in...' She counted on her fingers, but quickly gave up. 'Anyway, getting enough mistletoe at such short notice won't be easy. I had already ordered a couple of bunches for the church, because it's always nice for a winter wedding, but I'm not sure how much more I'm going to be able to get my hands on. I don't suppose you have a sickle and know a grove of oak trees nearby?'

'No. Which is what you should tell Alessandra.'

Ginny glanced at her with another smile. 'You're probably right. Can you teach me how to say that?'

'N-o,' Kira repeated.

'It really is the magic I need in my life,' Ginny said drily.

'But to be honest, I'd rather be out there collecting mistletoe for you than stuck with this group much longer,' Kira grumbled. She'd been in a better mood before dinner, probably because her own kissing clock had been put back to zero – her whole love life had been put back to zero after that halting, exploratory kiss.

But then she'd spent dinner listening to Rav defending Christian until she wanted to hit him – or hit Christian, since Rav stammered half-heartedly through his friend's excuses.

She couldn't shake the feeling she was going to ruin this wedding – in a more serious manner than through a lack of mistletoe.

'Aren't you usually stuck with groups in your job?'

Ginny asked. 'I assume you can't escape to a nice hotel room after a day with them either.'

'No, but people are nicer when they're expecting challenge and hardship. For a wedding, the challenges and hardships are a nasty surprise.'

Ginny chuckled, always so bright, even when Alessandra was pushing her to her limit.

'Do you want me to help?' Kira offered.

Ginny shook her head. 'You've got an important job tomorrow, getting Joe to ski away his jitters.'

'He has jitters?' Kira asked doubtfully. She'd only seen his confident swagger and superior taunts.

'Oh, yeah,' Ginny said with a roll of her eyes. 'This is why it's good to get to know the couple before the big day. Alessandra is actually really sweet and Joe dotes on her, he just thinks he needs to pretend he's certain.'

'Shouldn't he *be* certain at this point? It's kind of difficult to back out now.' Unease dug in and made itself comfortable in her stomach. If Joe backed out now... He might need a good kick up the arse tomorrow, not a ski tour. Alessandra would be mortified – crushed.

'Everyone's uncertain about their wedding two days before,' Ginny said with a shrug. 'You just learn to accept it and make an attempt anyway.'

Kira frowned. 'That's not very romantic of you. What about all the true love and soulmate crap?'

'That'll come, don't worry. But doubts are normal – healthy even. Ignoring doubts is where couples tend to hit problems.'

Kira fell silent, further conversation crowded out by her own thoughts. She'd always hoped her healthy scepticism would save her from any further romantic mishaps that would crush her heart – and decimate her pride. But if doubts were normal, then hers were nothing special.

She blinked back the twinge of feelings she'd been pushing away since Mattia had found her at the bouldering wall that afternoon. She shouldn't have kissed him to distract herself from the messy situation with old memories and present challenges. But he was a lovely distraction, her fallen angel.

'Ginny, do you think men find me intimidating?' she asked before she'd thought the question through.

'Definitely,' Ginny replied without even looking up from her screen. 'I'm a little jealous. It must be so handy on a night out – no losers trying out their cheesy pick-up lines when you just want to drink and dance.'

Kira stared at her colleague – her friend? – uncomprehendingly. 'You're jealous? I thought you wanted a boyfriend.'

'I do, but not a dude asking if I have a map because he got lost in my eyes,' she said in a mock male voice, all while tapping at her keyboard and squinting at the screen.

'Someone seriously said that to you?'

'God, it happens all the time. Such losers.'

Kira chuckled. 'I think your complaints about being single are a little feeble. Sounds like you have guys falling over themselves to go out with you.'

'Oh, I go on dates, don't you worry. But after two or three, they just never call, or they send me a polite text or something. *You* wouldn't have to waste your time with those losers. Only brave ones approach you.'

Brave ones and... Mattia with his self-destructive tendencies and sensitive hearing for her weaknesses.

'You have a point,' Kira said, resisting a smile. 'If the other option is two or three boring dates for nothing, I'd rather skip to the sex.'

Ginny's response was a peal of laughter. 'Is that your motto: "skip to the sex"? I like it. That way, I'd at least get something out of it.'

'Do you mean you go on all of these dates without making it that far?'

'More times than you'd think,' she groaned.

'They're all so nice – until they're not interested any more.'

Kira snorted. 'Well, the only people brave enough to come near me only want sex, so I don't think there's hope for either of us.' Except that Mattia had come close. And she needed to stop thinking about how he went against everything she understood about relationships – and about *herself*.

Ginny was quiet for long enough that curiosity dragged Kira up out of her brooding. The wedding planner was watching her.

'Hope? For what? I didn't think you wanted... all this: love, commitment.'

'I don't want *this*: a wedding with more manoeuvres than a military exercise. These gestures don't mean anything anyway.' Even that time when she thought she *did* want love and commitment, the wedding fanfare hadn't featured.

'But you do want to fall in love?' There was a hint of *I was* right*!* in Ginny's tone that made Kira uncomfortable.

'I don't know,' Kira replied irritably. 'Maybe it's not always great being alone, but I can't imagine someone...'

'Was it a big shock for you when Andreas proposed to Sophie?'

Where had *that* come from?

'Wait, don't get prickly,' Ginny back-pedalled. 'I'm just annoyed Sophie's out of the singles club too. I wasn't insinuating anything else.'

Kira eyed her. 'But you know—'

'I gather you have a history with Andreas, yes.'

'A *casual* history. God knows I did not want anything more with *him*. Sophie's got her work cut out for her.'

'But they're so wonderful together,' Ginny said with a sigh. 'Imagine pining for each other for *eight years!*'

'It explains why he was a miserable git for eight years,' Kira quipped. Flopping back against her pillow, she blew a strand of hair out of her eyes, noticing absently that the colour was fading back to the bleached dirty blonde under the blue. So many layers... Her throat tight, she continued before she could talk herself out of it. 'But you're right. Andreas was supposed to be like me. Relationships weren't for us. Then Sophie comes in and everything changes. Now they're getting *married*. I'll be left with Laurie the cock-up, misanthropic Rhys, poor old Willard and the eternally grieving Toni.'

'How horrible,' Ginny said drily. 'There's still five of you. I've only got Reshma left – and she's the big boss. Our admin support, Tita, is happily married and now Sophie... All of my friends are loved up. Just not me.'

Listening to Ginny, she couldn't help thinking it was infinitely better to not want love, especially since Kira wasn't certain she was still capable of it anyway, she'd spent so long denying the emotion existed.

'But I'm fine alone,' Kira insisted. 'I don't know why this stuff is suddenly getting to me. Too many weddings!' Too many reminders of her biggest mistake.

'Maybe I'm in the wrong job,' Ginny moaned.

Kira glanced at her with an indulgent smile. 'You are in exactly the right job.' Considering all Ginny's hard work to make everything perfect, Kira thought it might be wise to warn her about her slip-up with Mattia. 'I should probably tell you about something that happened today. I have this irrational fear I'm going to ruin the wedding, when you are so amazing at this and you've put in so much effort.'

Ginny's grin was back in an instant, giving Kira the strangest urge to hug her. She really was under the influence of this wedding drug, thinking about hugging and kissing and handsome, clumsy opera singers.

Before Kira had a chance to continue, Ginny said, 'It's just frustrating that I go to so many weddings, but

I can't even get drunk and snog the groomsman!' Her laugh echoed through the room once more. 'Reshma would kill me!'

Kira's smile faded. What would the head of I Do Destinations have to say about Kira's lack of professionalism over the past two days? Mattia wasn't technically a groomsman, but she had snogged him, as much as using that word for that kiss made her wince.

She would just have to make sure it didn't happen again.

'What did you want to tell me?' Ginny asked when she'd recovered from her fit of laughter.

'Uh—' Kira's mind raced. 'Mattia nearly collapsed in the sauna and I saw him naked.'

'Oh, my God, is *nowhere* safe for that man? Was he at least naked with Carla?'

'No such luck,' Kira said flatly.

'How am I going to look after him tomorrow while you're off razing the slopes?'

Kira eyed her. 'Razing the slopes?'

'Isn't that what you cool kids say?'

'No.'

Ginny shrugged. 'Oh well, have fun anyway. Maybe you'll get *your* jitters out of your system too.'

Kira opened her mouth to protest, but she did feel kind of jittery. Maybe that was why she'd kissed Mattia. Wedding stress. Nothing more. Nothing to lose her job over.

'But don't worry,' Ginny continued. 'You can't ruin the wedding. The only people who can do that are the bride and groom – and maybe the weather, but that's not a person.'

19

Kira's frustration awoke in full force the following morning as she drank a coffee and scrolled through various weather reports, while pretending she wasn't urgently looking out for Mattia.

She wished Ginny had never said anything about the weather. While it was possible the wedding planner had been right that Kira couldn't ruin the wedding – even if she was awkward around the guests and had kissed the singer – the spectre of heavy snowfall hung over her consciousness as profoundly as the guilt at kissing Mattia.

No matter which way she looked at the reports, taking the group off-piste for a more adventurous tour was too dangerous today.

Managing risks, planning contingencies and dealing with sudden changes in conditions were part of her professional skill set, but the knowledge that she was heading for the slopes with a man who was supposed to get married tomorrow weighed on her.

With a pent-up sigh, she closed down the browser, tapped on the green telephone icon and scrolled to Andreas's number.

'Hello?'

Tugging the phone from her ear in surprise, Kira bit back a grumble before forcing herself to respond. 'Uh, hi Sophie.'

'Is everything okay with the Lee-Martinelli wedding?'

'Yes, for Christ's sake!' she snapped. Kira could almost hear Sophie blinking on the other end of the phone call. 'This isn't about the wedding. It's about skiing, which is why I called Andreas.'

'Oh, I— Of course. Sorry, Kira. I'm just nervous about this one. We haven't used this venue before and winter weddings have a few more variables – even before we add skiing.' Kira could hear the grimace in Sophie's voice.

'Ginny is working on the wedding variables and I'm in charge of the snow-related ones. Can I talk to Andreas? I assume he's there with you.'

There was a rustling sound and Kira had the uncomfortable thought that Sophie might have still been in bed – his bed. It irritated her that his new happiness with Sophie brought into stark contrast her own isolation.

'Yes, just a sec,' Sophie said. 'He went to get more wood for the stove. Andreas?' She heard a muffled, 'It's Kira.'

'What's up?'

I have a really bad feeling about this wedding. 'Have you seen the avalanche reports this morning?'

'Not yet. But the warning level must be high where you are.'

'They've raised it to level four. We won't be leaving the prepared slopes.' Unfortunately.

'Good call.' In typical Andreas fashion, that was all he said initially. 'Was there something else?'

'No,' she replied, equally sparse with words.

'Is... everything okay with you? With the wedding?' he asked warily.

She'd never been more relieved that Andreas didn't know about *that day* twelve years ago. He assumed she had the same opposition to weddings in principle that he'd had – until Sophie. Andreas had been even more upset by the merger between Great Heart and I Do, but admitting he loved Sophie – and finding that love returned – had mellowed him much more than she'd expected.

She sighed. 'They're getting married tomorrow. It shouldn't, but it's changing my approach to risk management.'

'That makes sense,' he agreed evenly. 'But you know Toni's gone over our insurance arrangements carefully. You're covered. The client decided on this.'

'I know, it's more the feeling,' she grumbled. 'A *wedding*. A once-in-a-lifetime thing, full of wild superstitions.'

'I thought you didn't buy into all that?'

'It doesn't matter what I think. I'm responsible for getting the groom to the altar tomorrow.' As well as not losing it when she saw her ex and definitely not kissing any more members of the wedding party. Not that there was anyone else she wanted to kiss. 'It's a nightmare. I'd rather be taking clients across the Grand Couloir right now.' She wouldn't. The avalanche warning for Mont Blanc must be through the roof, but he should see through her hyperbole to the truth of her discomfort.

'I understand but remember, on the mountain, you're in charge. If you're not comfortable with the risk, don't let them take the risk.'

'Right,' she agreed, trying to muster his confidence. 'But I reserve the right to kill Willard later for creating this wedding monster.'

Andreas chuckled and there was a soft click over the line that Kira realised belatedly – in horror – was a smacking kiss, probably against Sophie's forehead.

'Good luck surviving the wedding, Watling.'

'Thanks,' she said drily, ending the call. It had better not come down to a matter of survival. Although if she died before the wedding, she'd never have to see Christian again.

Speaking of survival, she noticed Mattia striding into the dining room, headed straight for the coffee machine. With a quick glance to check that, of the two other people in the room, neither was paying attention, she hurried up to him, placing a hand on his back to get his attention.

He jumped, knocking over the wire rack holding the coffee pods. 'Ahi!' He also studied the room with a furtive glance as he popped the pods back into the rack. Kira helped him, both of them pausing when her fingers brushed his hand. 'Is this what Austrians call coffee?' he said, clearing his throat and drawing his hand away slowly.

'It's what George Clooney calls coffee,' she quipped weakly.

'Ah, he's not Italian. That explains it.' He managed

to press the pod into the machine and looked around for a cup. Finding only a mug, he set it underneath and pressed the espresso button, his frown deepening as he watched the coffee emerge from the spout.

'I need to talk to you,' she said under her breath.

When he looked up to meet her gaze, her muscles turned the consistency of the froth. One look at his sharp jaw, the silver cross dangling from his ear and his dark eyes under impossible lashes seemed to turn her into a liquid.

'Now?'

'Yes, now,' she said, annoyed that the bright glint in his eye was making her thoughts veer off course. She beckoned for him to follow her out of the room.

'Bene,' he said with a nod and knocked back the espresso before trailing after her.

It quickly became apparent to Kira that the hallway would not be an appropriate place to discuss *not* kissing. Footsteps sounded on the floor above and the staircase creaked. Grasping the front of Mattia's shirt – another silky button-down with a fussy, paisley pattern that had no right looking so good on him – she tugged him towards the end of the hallway, searching for somewhere out of sight where they could talk.

One door led to the kitchen and another to an

extra set of bathrooms, but there was one more door. With the creaking getting louder behind them, she grasped for the door-handle, expecting it to be locked. But the door swung open. Without thought, she dragged Mattia inside with her.

She vaguely registered a storage cupboard with a small window, dimly lit shelves and wooden crates. But before she could even gather her thoughts, her brain shut down and her body came to life.

Because Mattia's palms had settled on her cheeks, his fingers in her hair, and his face was so close, his gaze on her mouth. And then he was kissing her.

Oh... boy. She hadn't imagined it. The man could kiss. If yesterday's had been a rehearsal, this one was the main performance. His mouth was hot and tasted of coffee, his lips drawing her out while the pressure built to an irresistible level.

The wanting, the adamant brush of his lips over hers, sent Kira reeling, her brain running after her in confusion. With a hitched groan, he deepened the kiss and all of her nerve endings stood at attention.

She felt his soft hair under her fingers, although she didn't remember lifting her hands to his head. His arm curled around her waist, which she was grateful for, as she was struggling to remain upright. The shelf behind her dug into her back, but she ignored the slight pain, urging Mattia closer. He was leaned over her, his mouth hot and open and firm on hers, his chest heaving against her.

Breaking the kiss audibly, he dropped his mouth to her neck and she couldn't hold in a breathy squeak of shock. Letting her head fall back, she lost her footing and shot out a hand, knocking over an empty crate with a thud.

The sound startled Mattia and he reared back, catching her on the chin with the top of his head. She yelped and fell against the shelf when his hold on her loosened. He fumbled to catch her.

'Aaaccidenti!'

Kira shot out a hand to press over his mouth, glancing at the door with alarm. She heaved in several deep breaths, gathering her scattered wits.

'What was that for?'

He peered down at her with adorable earnestness. 'For?'

She licked her lips, still seeing stars. 'Why did you kiss me?'

'Why... Wasn't that why...?' He flushed, his cheeks turning bright pink and his neck bobbing as he swallowed. 'That wasn't why you brought me in here?' he asked in a small voice.

Kira snorted as she swallowed a laugh. 'No.'

'Ah.' Even that short syllable, his voice thrumming with embarrassment, had baritone intensity to it. 'I didn't quite mean for it to— I shouldn't have assumed — Anyway, what did you need to talk about?'

His brow was pinched and she wished she could reassure him. *Don't apologise for one of the hottest kisses of my life. You had a much better idea for what to do in this cupboard.*

But she had a job to do. 'Actually, I needed to explain about yesterday – that it was a mistake. I shouldn't be... We shouldn't... I could get in trouble for kissing you. I'm here in a professional capacity. Your friend is my client. I know I'm not very good at this wedding stuff, but kissing a member of the wedding party is really against the rules.'

His expression sobered. 'That makes sense.'

'And besides,' Kira continued, 'we're only here for another two days and you told me you don't do casual, so...'

He nodded firmly. 'Yes,' he said with a nod for emphasis that seemed to be for his own benefit.

'I was also hoping you maybe wouldn't mention it to Alessandra?'

He laughed, loudly enough that she considered pressing her hand to his mouth again, except that he looked so inviting with that wry smile on his face, the feel of his mouth on her fingers wouldn't have helped her focus on her job.

'Don't worry. Alessandra has enough on her mind right now. There is no way I'd add to her stress.'

'Right,' Kira responded, suddenly glum. 'I should get going.'

'Yes, right,' he repeated, not meeting her gaze.

She wanted to kiss him goodbye, even if it was just on his cheek, but it had never been clearer that kissing was a bad idea. 'I'll go out first. You wait a few minutes in case someone sees us.'

His only answer was a nod and a pained grunt. He must have been imagining being caught with his tongue down her throat too.

Slipping out and closing the door quietly behind her, she was relieved to find no one in the hallway. Pausing for a few breaths to let the adrenaline and endorphins rushing through her system circulate a few times, she gave herself a shake and headed for the stairs.

20

Mattia concluded later that morning that people who lived in cold climates couldn't be very religious. First, he had to fight his way from the car park where that hellish snowmobile had dropped him off, through biting wind and ice particles as sharp as his nonna's tongue. After slipping and sliding across the treacherous road – where cars were inexplicably still zooming along, leaving zigzags in the snow from the deep tread – he then had to trudge through a foot of the white stuff to reach the little chapel made of dark slats and wooden roof tiles, a little bell tower on one end.

Once he'd finally stumbled up the steps, throwing the door closed behind him and leaning on it against the wind, his relief lasted only a moment, until he noticed the chapel was also freezing. If the priest intoned for too long, parishioners would get frostbite. They'd better hope he'd managed to save their souls first.

Alessandra and Ginny were hard at work, tying bows and unrolling white gauze. Carla had a pair of tiny scissors, performing keyhole surgery on the enormous floral bower that barely fit in front of the modest wooden altar, and the other member of their party at the chalet, Hugh's girlfriend Tonya, sloshed wine into glasses and appeared to be speaking without the necessity of breathing.

'...such a great idea. The hydrangeas give it a boho touch and I love the ivy and the pine cones. Oh look! Your friend is standing under the mistletoe!'

He scooted out from under the little bunch of leaves before anyone got ideas. He'd had enough of kissing today. Well, not enough of the action of kissing, but certainly enough of talking about it.

After flying so high, his thoughts mush and his heart pounding as Kira tugged him into the privacy of the storage room with her, he'd crashed and shattered just as quickly when he'd realised he'd misunderstood. She could have stopped him before he'd made a complete fool of himself. Instead, she'd kissed him back just enough to make him question everything, before calmly explaining that it shouldn't have happened.

The worst part was, she was right; it shouldn't have happened. His heart simply disagreed – strongly. He was used to listening to his heart.

'Don't talk to me about mistletoe,' Ginny mumbled. 'I have to go in a minute and collect our haul from Mayrhofen.'

'You *can* never have enough mistletoe at a wedding,' Tonya continued, taking a sip of wine – a large sip.

'I only wonder that I thought three bunches would be enough,' Ginny continued. Mattia thought perhaps she was being sarcastic, but her tone was so even, he couldn't tell. 'But don't worry,' she said brightly, brushing a strand of hair out of her face with one gloved hand. 'The church and the chalet will be *dripping* with it when I'm finished.' Definitely sarcastic.

'Good,' Alessandra said breezily, 'since I want to get lots of photos of all the guests kissing under it.'

'I'll make sure the photographer knows,' Ginny said as she eyed the enormous bow of gauze tied around the chair in front of the altar, making minute adjustments. 'Her flight is delayed, but she's due in this evening.'

'Oh? I thought the photographer was that grunting

mountain man who came to the ice cave with us?' Tonya asked, with emphasis on 'grunting mountain man' as though it were a compliment.

Ginny laughed. 'No, he was just here because Beatrice was booked up until yesterday. He's a nature photographer from our sister agency, Great Heart Adventures, but he doesn't do weddings. He only agreed to yesterday's job because it involved an ice cave.'

'A shame,' Tonya said with a pout, pouring Mattia a glass of wine. 'Is this sort of the hen party?' she asked with a giggle. 'While the boys are up there drinking – I mean skiing?'

A shiver made its way down Mattia's spine. Through the window, he saw the fat flakes of snow still falling and wondered what it was like up on the mountain right now. Sidling towards the electric radiator in one corner, he turned the thermostat up as high as it went.

'Tonya, maybe you could take over from me here?' Ginny asked so brightly, another person might not have detected the tightness in her tone. 'We need to hang the gauze just like this along all the pews. And now I'm really sorry, Alessandra, but I have to go get the mistletoe. Will you be okay here for an hour or so?'

'Hmm?' She looked up from the spray of flowers she was carefully binding onto the end of the pew. Her distraction sent Mattia's alarm up another few notches.

He approached Ginny. 'Go. I'll make sure everything's okay here.'

The relief in her expression was easy to read. 'Great. Can you make sure she eats something?'

'Of course.' Trailing Ginny to the door, he tapped her on the shoulder before she could leave. 'Do you think everything is okay, or should I talk to her?'

'It's pretty normal so far,' Ginny replied. 'Brides always forget to eat.'

'And grooms go drinking on ski slopes?'

Ginny peered at him, her smile dimming. 'Kira will have that in hand.'

He nodded. 'I suppose you're right. If anyone can have that group in hand, it's Kira.'

'I'm sure they're all scared of her.'

His gaze snapped to hers. 'Kira told you about yesterday—?'

Ginny nodded, giving him a conspiratorial smile. 'Don't worry. Your secret is safe with me.'

His chest expanded, imagining Kira seeking advice from Ginny because her feelings were as mixed up as his. 'Good, because she was worried and I don't want to get her into any trouble.'

'No,' Ginny said with a chuckle. 'I'm sure she couldn't help it that she got an eyeful.'

He drew back in confusion, but Ginny was already sweeping the door open and stepping into the Snowmageddon outside.

* * *

Nothing cleared Kira's head as thoroughly as biting, high mountain air. At over three thousand metres of altitude, each breath was a reminder of the tenacity and value of life. Digging her skis into the fresh powder on top of the glacier, her heart pounded with something that wasn't joy, but it was a celebration of some kind – of the strength in her body, of the great landscape she had the privilege to be part of for this moment.

If someone had asked her teenage self if she'd ever ski down a mountain, she'd have scoffed. She wasn't a preppy city banker. She had no interest in expensive hotels and après-ski. But then she'd met Willard as an angry nineteen-year-old with some poor decisions and one enormous disappointment behind her and he'd shown her the magic of working with the slope to conquer it – the elation of playing with gravity.

He'd taken her to Chamonix her first winter on the crew, taught her the basics of skiing and left her there for the season. After five months, she'd pulled thousands of pints in the Irish pub, skied the Vallée Blanche and narrowly passed her first ski instructor's certificate. And she'd slowly rebuilt her shattered pride – the pride that still felt fragile every time she thought about seeing Christian tomorrow.

Roaring down a steep, snowy slope was almost as good as reaching the top of a challenging crag and she certainly needed to feel the icy wind in her face the day before the wedding – feel herself again. And hopefully banish the disturbing suspicion that, down in the valley, Alessandra was manoeuvring Mattia and Carla beneath a bunch of mistletoe. At least she had to try not to care, if that was the case.

She couldn't focus only on the euphoria of being alive that day. She had three clients who, although good skiers, were increasingly erratic as the morning wore on. Joe vacillated between daring descents with whoops of excitement and almost desperate dips in his temper. Rav and Hugh seemed to be ignoring his mood, but Kira couldn't. The clouds had moved in as well, shrouding the ski fields in fog.

Around lunchtime, as Kira sat in the chairlift with her charges, preparing to raise the bar and disembark, she was alarmed to see Joe pitch forward, mumbling something unintelligible. Something dropped into the snow far below them and a sizzle of panic shot up her spine.

The lift approached the station rapidly. 'Hold him up!' she snapped at Rav as she yanked Joe back in his seat so she could shove at the safety bar. 'Help me get him out! What on earth is going on?'

The second question turned out to be unnecessary. As she hauled him out of the chair, thankful that he stayed on his feet for long enough to slide out of the way, it quickly became clear that the groom was stinking drunk.

'How much has he had?' she demanded of Hugh and Rav.

'I dunno,' Rav answered, wringing his hands. 'But he mixed it with a few energy drinks too and I don't know what he's eaten today.'

Joe collapsed onto his bottom in the snow at her feet, swaying gently in the wind and singing snatches of Frank Sinatra.

'How are we going to get him down?' Hugh asked. He had the nerve to tug out his own hip flask and take a swig. Kira hoped he'd accidentally mixed *his* with arsenic.

'Under no circumstances are we getting him down ourselves. You and Rav can go and I'll see you in the car park, but Joe is about to meet the ski patrol.' She pulled out her phone to dial the resort number, berating herself for not noticing what he'd been sipping all morning.

'We'll wait with you,' Rav offered, but she only spared him a glance as she spoke to the office.

She wished she'd firmly *ordered* them to meet her in the car park fifteen minutes later when she loaded Joe onto the back of the snowmobile while Hugh filmed everything. The thought of Alessandra seeing that video made her stomach turn.

'I'm very sorry,' she said to the laid-back patroller as she climbed on behind Joe, holding him steady with one arm while she clutched their skis with her other.

'Bachelor party?' he asked.

'How did you guess?' she responded drily.

'Didn't have a real bachelor party!' Joe piped up. His dark mood had returned.

Kira ignored him and turned to the groomsmen. 'You two, go straight back down to the Sommerbergalm and get the gondola to the car park from there.

Straight down! I don't want to have to come back up here and dig either of you out of the snow.'

'Yes, ma'am,' Rav said with a smile that did not cheer her.

She lost sight of them amongst the throng of skiers as the engine of the snowmobile sprang to life. She hoped Joe might sober up with the wind in his face, but the snow pelted them, visibility so poor, she would have been uneasy continuing even if Joe had been sober. The powerful headlights of the snowmobile created eerie figures out of the skiers, hurtling down the slope in star-shaped silhouettes.

In the queue for the gondola, Joe propped up next to her, but mercifully steady on his feet, she glanced at him and asked, 'Why didn't you have a bachelor party? It would have been safer – and more fun – than getting drunk on skis.' *And ruining my chance to clear my head.*

'You say that now, but drinking sounded good this morning,' he slurred. 'I didn't think I wanted the usual sort of bachelor party,' he continued. 'Strippers would only make me think of Alessandra. Her body is a fucking dream. And none of my friends are married yet, so they'd all be mocking me.'

'That's... insightful,' Kira replied, 'apart from the bit in the middle.' She ushered him through the turnstile and wrapped an arm around his waist to help him step into the moving gondola. Thankfully, there was space on the padded bench.

Joe leaned his head back on the glass, eyes closed, face drawn and ashen. He looked ten years older than he had two days ago.

'But maybe I should have done it, had a huge bender – licked a stripper, got high.'

Kira studied him for a moment and then laughed, heartily enough that the couple across from them glanced up. 'That would have saved me some trouble, but do you think that would have made you feel better? That's a real question,' she qualified. 'I don't have any answers for you and I'm the last person to guide you in any direction except safely down.'

'I appreciate that, Kira,' he said softly and she wished she'd separated him from his friends sooner to discover the person underneath his false bravado. 'I don't know if I would have felt better, but at least I wouldn't be wondering. It's like trying out a different life so you can see you have the right one.'

Kira's heart thumped in her chest as his words brought Christian to mind – again. But there was a difference this time. She hadn't had the chance to try out a different life, but what if the one she had was the right one? What did that mean for what Christian had put her through?

She still couldn't bear the thought of the same happening to Alessandra.

'Joe, do you think you're going to remember this tomorrow?'

'God, I hope not,' he said with a grimace, clutching his stomach.

'Well, I'll tell you again when you've sobered up. Whatever this was today, whatever is going on in your mind, if you don't show up tomorrow and sign on the dotted line, I'm going to throw you off a cliff.'

A smile twitched on his lips. 'I didn't think adventure guides were supposed to do that.'

'Adventure guides who are also wedding planners can, and I most definitely *will* do it. Don't even think of abandoning Alessandra there, after everything she's put into the arrangements. Divorce later if you have to, but do not leave her standing there.'

He cracked an eye open and she bit her lip, afraid she'd said too much, too strongly. '"Go through with it now, divorce later" is your pep talk? You're not a very good wedding planner, you know.'

Joe was joking, she suspected, but his words still hit right on target. 'No, I'm not,' she agreed tightly.

21

Conditions were just as poor down in the valley as at the top of the mountain and Kira grimaced as she shepherded the groaning, bleary-eyed groom through the car park at the ski area to the minivan, through ice and slush and a layer of fresh snow as thick as whipped cream on an apple strudel.

What a week for a wedding. If Alessandra believed in bad omens, there had been a ton of them. Kira was without a doubt the most awful wedding planner in the history of the profession. Instead of Ginny's perky helpfulness, she was brooding just as darkly as the groom.

Leaving Hugh and Rav to get him settled into a seat, she took out her phone and called her colleague.

'I am never a winter wedding ever again,' Ginny said instead of a greeting. 'It took me *an hour* to get here. Google told me twenty-six minutes. Google obviously thinks I am a competent driver in snow. I thought Google was supposed to know more about us than we do about ourselves. It should have fucking known.'

Kira would have laughed, if she weren't so strung out herself. 'You're on your mistletoe mission? Where are the others?'

'Yes, I'm in Mayrhofen collecting the damn greenery. And that's another thing. The florist is so busy, she's still binding up the bunches, so it'll be at least another hour before I'm back. Alessandra and the others are decorating the chapel. I left Mattia in charge.'

'You—' Kira choked.

'What else could I do? Alessandra has bride fog.'

'Bride fog, jitters, existential crises – I think weddings must be a kind of mental illness,' Kira muttered.

'We're just in the "mental illness" phase of the preparations. It happens every time.'

Kira cursed under her breath. 'I'll head to the chapel to check on the others.'

'Wait, you're done skiing already?'

'Yep,' she said in a clipped tone. 'We're done. I can't

see a thing up there and Joe... needs to get back to Alessandra.' He could be the bride's responsibility and not Kira's.

'Aw, that's sweet. It's probably a good idea, since Alessandra was spacing out a bit. It's claustrophobic having the whole wedding party around all the time and they should probably talk before tomorrow.'

Kira's stomach churned, remembering Joe's words, Ginny's strange ideas about nurturing doubts and the precarious state of this entire event. 'What if they talk things through and call the whole thing off?'

'That doesn't happen in real life,' Ginny insisted. 'If they got this far, it's the real thing.'

Kira gritted her teeth, desperate to contradict her, but she knew she'd wish the words unsaid again, if she uttered them. 'All right. But don't you worry anyway. You get the mistletoe; I can handle a few guests and a lot of snow.'

'I am soooo glad to have you here,' Ginny gushed, making Kira swallow a sigh.

'Even if it takes you three hours, drive safe, okay? Your hire car will have winter tyres, but there might be chains in the boot, if you feel really insecure.'

'That's assuming I can work out how to put the chains on.'

Ginny ended the call with a grumble and Kira

checked to see that her charges had fastened their seat belts before she pulled out of the car park, the tyres spinning out once or twice as she manoeuvred. Even with, the glass was pelted with snow and traffic inched along the narrow road through the valley.

When she'd parked safely in the usual spot by the stream, she released a huff of relief, peering grimly up at the mountainside. How different it looked from two nights ago when she'd arrived with Mattia. If he'd stepped out into this snow and twirled, his tailored trousers would have been soaked up to his knees and his fancy leather shoes would have resembled snow cones.

But she was struck by how vividly she remembered him standing under the lamp, his long, fine coat whirling around him as he held his arms out. If Christian hadn't left her so publicly that day, if they'd gone through with everything as planned... Her skin prickled and she shook off the feeling.

'Stay there,' she ordered the three men as she shoved open the car door. 'I'm going to check on the others at the chapel.'

'Alessandra will kill me,' Joe moaned, his tone pained.

'If you didn't want her to see you like this, maybe you shouldn't have got yourself into this state.'

'She's seen him in worse,' Rav commented with a laugh.

Kira glanced doubtfully at him. 'And she still wants to get married?'

Rav's smile died and Kira cursed herself for nudging the can of worms open a little more. She did *not* want to talk to Rav about this, not when Joe's words had made her think of her own past from a different perspective.

'I'll be back soon.'

Battling her way to the chapel, the first thing she noticed was a satin banner with gold lettering that she assumed was supposed to be fixed above the entrance, but was currently flapping in the wind. Catching the loose end, she tilted her head to read *Joseph and Alessandra, Always and Forever 31.12*. There were numerous discoloured patches where snow had soaked the material. She hoped it would dry pristine.

With a frown, she untied the other end to save the splotched ribbon from further damage before tomorrow. If the weather didn't improve, not only the decorations would suffer. She hoped Alessandra had chosen a pair of white snow boots to match her dress.

After the comments about bride fog, her increasing reservations about the bridal couple and the knowledge that Mattia had been left in charge, Kira grasped the door-handle hesitantly, wary of what she'd find inside.

But when she spilled into the tiny wooden chapel, tracking clumps of snow with her, her mouth swung open in surprise. Outdoors, there might be a storm raging strongly enough to herald the apocalypse, but inside...

The air was warm and scented with pine and orange and a hint of spices. The overhead lamp was off and only wall sconces complemented the muted daylight struggling through the windows. The soft ambience seemed to show up the gold and silver touches everywhere Kira looked. The simple, wooden pews were artfully draped in white; tiny bouquets of flowers with a single twig of pine decorated the ends. And at the front of the church, an effusion of flowers and leaves where she could already imagine Joe and Alessandra standing to face each other, a matching dusky rose in Joe's buttonhole and a floral coronet with a long veil for Alessandra.

She gulped. It was almost enough to convince her that Ginny was right and this wedding would go ahead come rain or shine – or catastrophic snowfall, in this case.

'Kira! What are you doing here? Did something happen? Where's Joe?'

She nodded quickly. 'He's fine.' At least he would be, once the substances were out of his system. 'Nothing happened. It's not very pleasant up there in this weather.'

To Kira's surprise, Alessandra laughed. 'My mother tells me rain on a wedding day is auspicious. I believe it must be doubly true for snow. Come and take a look at... everything!' Alessandra's smile was bright with excitement and Kira was not looking forward to bursting her bubble.

'Alessandra this is... a wonderland!' She wasn't even being sarcastic.

Tonya turned from where she'd been looking out of the window, wine glass in hand. 'A winter wedding wonderland!'

Kira glanced warily at her glass, wondering if two members of the wedding party would need to sleep off their morning drinking.

The door behind Kira flew open on a flurry of snow. She jumped out of the way as the tall form of Mattia shuffled into the church backwards, Carla trailing behind him with a giggle. He turned with a flourish, a wide smile on his face – which dimmed as soon as he saw Kira. *Ouch.* Just when she'd thought she might belong in this picture, even if only as the adventure guide and wedding dogsbody.

'Everything okay?' he asked.

'We found pizza!' Carla announced, taking the enormous box from Mattia's hands.

Alessandra lifted her nose and her eyes widened, rushing to the door. 'Santo cielo, I am suddenly *starving*! What time is it?'

Carla laughed. 'Matty said you'd be hungrier than you thought.'

As if on cue, Kira's stomach creaked in complaint. She willed away the blush of embarrassment at the inappropriate rush of jealousy she was experiencing. How utterly ridiculous.

'Kira?'

She obviously still wasn't used to the sound of her name in his voice – the rich, low syllables and the lilt of the 'r' in his accent. The tone that sent her thoughts instantly to kissing in cupboards and secret, meaningful looks.

'Yeah, everything's fine – or it will be.'

She was distracted by Alessandra tearing out a piece of pizza and shoving a third of it into her mouth, collapsing into the rearmost pew with a dramatic sigh. Carla and Mattia shared a conspiratorial smile that punched Kira in the gut.

'I can't vouch for the quality of the pizza, but it was the only place open and we had to pass the

South Pole on our way,' Mattia said with a satisfied huff.

'You're my hero, Matty,' Alessandra cooed.

'Carla too,' he said affably. Glancing at Kira, he added, 'I didn't dare go alone in case someone had to call for a rescue.'

Confused about a message he seemed to be trying to send her with his eyes, she asked, 'Who would you have called?'

'You?' he said hopefully. 'Are *you* hungry? Do you want some pizza? I got party size.'

'*Look!*' Alessandra cried all of a sudden. Pointing one manicured nail at the door of the church, she finished chewing and continued, 'You're under the mistletoe. You know what that means. Let me get my phone. I want to capture the first mistletoe kiss at my wedding!'

Kira's stomach sank to her toes. It was unfortunately true: Carla and Mattia stood in the doorway of the church, just beneath the little bunch of bright green leaves with white berries.

They seemed to have bonded over the pizza. Despite what had gone wrong with their relationship, Carla seemed to be a nice person – friendly and a little shy, but that would be perfect for Mattia. They knew each other well, wanted the same things. They made sense together. Surely he would be starting to realise that.

'Eh...' His throat bobbed with a swallow. 'I don't think—'

'If you don't kiss, then neither of you will get married for the next year. I'm sure I read that somewhere.'

Kira stifled a snort at the weak threat, but Carla looked stricken. She bit her lip and glanced up at Mattia.

Kira gritted her teeth. 'Oh, just kiss her. As soon as you've finished eating, I think we should call Norbert and head back up to the chalet.' She turned away, fiddling with one of the bows at the end of the pew, hoping they interpreted her behaviour as contemptuous and not ragingly jealous. When she accidentally unravelled the bow, she snatched her hand back.

Behind her, Mattia cleared his throat and there was a muffled 'hmph' followed by a deep sigh.

'That was a poor excuse for a kiss,' Alessandra grumbled, Kira's cue to turn back around – to find Mattia's unnerving gaze on her. 'But I suppose you have an audience. Are the boys already up at the chalet? I suppose we're finished here until Ginny brings the mistletoe.'

'Um, Alessandra...' Kira trailed off, hesitating over the explanation. Leaning closer to where the bride was looking up expectantly, her second piece of pizza heading towards her mouth, she whispered, 'Joe's drunk.'

'What?' Mattia bellowed behind her.

Shit, she'd forgotten about his superhuman hearing. Alessandra held up a quelling hand in his direction.

'Perdio!' she exclaimed. 'The day before our wedding! He's lucky he didn't break his leg! Or maybe I'll break it for him!'

'I don't know that he—' Kira sighed heavily. She wasn't even sure why she was defending him. 'He might have sobered up by now anyway. They're in the van in the car park waiting for us.'

Alessandra threw the crust of her pizza slice into the box and meticulously cleaned her fingers, before rising with a long breath through her nose. Stuffing her arms into her enormous, puffy jacket, she lifted her chin and stalked towards the door.

'I'm going to talk to him,' Alessandra declared, her voice wavering.

'If you just wait—' Kira began, that *I'm going to ruin this wedding* feeling solidifying inside her again.

'I've had *enough* of him not taking this seriously. Nobody is forcing him to marry me and if he doesn't want to, all he has to do is say it!' She swung open the door, flinching at the howling wind and swirling snowflakes, but she sailed through it and even managed to slam the door as an extra exclamation point.

When Mattia didn't move, Kira gestured frantically at him. 'Go after her! It's a freaking snowstorm out there!'

'What about you?'

'I don't need you to hold my hand while I cross the road,' she snapped. 'I'll help Carla bring this shit back to the van.'

She expected him to hurl back a gritty *Fine!* and stomp angrily to the door, as people usually did when she pushed them away. But he simply studied her, for long enough that she started to worry he could *hear* emotions.

'Go,' she repeated, but her voice had lost its belligerence and sounded alarmingly like pleading. 'I'll call Norbert to pick you all up. He can come back for the rest of us.'

He considered her request once more, brows raised, his earring winking in the soft light. Then he nodded, his jaw tight. 'I'll make sure she gets back to the car safely.'

Winding his colourful scarf once more around his neck, he braced himself and headed back out into the snow.

22

Just when he'd thought he'd done something right.

Hurrying to catch up with Alessandra, he thought absently that at least he didn't have to worry about drenching his trousers, as they were already soaked. He needn't have hurried either. Alessandra hadn't got far through the snowdrifts.

Mattia walked more easily now in the brand-new snow boots he'd hastily bought while waiting for the pizza – boots that had pleased him mainly when he imagined showing them to Kira. She hadn't even seen them; she'd been so busy being grumpy at him.

Being grumpy about the wedding, he was beginning to understand, but she'd told him to kiss Carla too and he was less willing to forgive that.

Alessandra clutched at his arm, muttering in relief when he reached her, and he realised Kira had been right again: Alessandra needed help. Wrapping an arm around her shoulders, he concentrated on taking solid steps and let her lean on him.

'Are you okay?' he asked over the wind. 'I mean about Joe?'

'Non lo so, Matty,' she said, her voice barely strong enough to carry. 'I don't know. I feel like he's insulting me.'

'I'm sure he doesn't realise—'

'Are you defending him? *You*?'

'I don't know him well,' he responded, peeved, 'but I can't imagine anyone purposefully insulting their fiancée the day before their wedding.'

Alessandra stopped, blinking at him. 'What's happened to you?'

'You can stop worrying about me for a minute while you get married, Ale. I'm not the emotional wreck I used to be.'

She studied him closely enough that he came up in goosebumps – or perhaps that was the cold. He considered asking her to stop pushing him with Carla, but the wind picked up her hair and now certainly didn't feel like the right time.

He urged her on. 'Dai, it's freezing, carissima. Joe's waiting for you.'

'He's probably passed out by now,' she muttered.

Battling across the slippery street together, they found the van – ice caked around the wheels – and Rav opened the door for them to get inside.

'Where's Kira?' he asked.

''sKira?' Joe repeated, his eyelids heavy.

'She's finishing up in the chapel, but Joe, here's Alessandra.'

The man had the good grace to look sheepish as he hoisted his brow high enough that he could squint at her. ''m s-s-sorry, baby. I'll be better tomorrow. Promise. I love you s'much.'

Mattia could almost see Alessandra's resentment crack – that quickly. A smile touched his lips. His old friend was no stranger to resentment; she'd been known to hold a grudge – for months, on occasion. But with Joe, she barely lasted a minute.

He had no doubt Joe had some grovelling to do to get back in her good books, but he could already see she'd forgive him. Mattia only hoped Joe understood what a gift that was.

A distant buzz alerted him to Norbert's approach and he peered through the gloom to see the head-lights of the snowmobile tracking slowly down the mountain. When the concierge pulled up, he was wearing ski goggles and heavy-duty gloves, and his moustache was caked in snow.

The sled that had brought them down this morning was attached to the snowmobile and Mattia shuddered, imagining another loud, juddering trip in heavy snow.

'Where's the wedding planner?' he asked gruffly after he cut the engine. 'This is record snowfall and I'd like to get home to check on my cows.'

'Ah,' was all Mattia could say at first, not quite understanding the comment about the cows. 'She'll be here soon. But maybe you could take this group up first? By the time you're back, the others will be finished.'

He offered Alessandra his arm for balance as she settled into the passenger sled while Rav and Hugh kept Joe steady. She clutched at him when he would have tugged his arm back.

'Aren't you coming?'

He shook his head. 'The van's not locked.' That was his excuse anyway. She looked ready to protest, so he continued, 'Go get warm and then talk to him. You can work it out, the two of you. It's not your wedding day yet. He's allowed to see you.'

She nodded, placated, but what she said next

made him grit his teeth. 'And you can wait here for Carla – and the mistletoe. I'm sure Ginny will need help hanging it.'

He waved off Alessandra and the groomsmen as the sled leapt forward. After they'd disappeared into the gloom on the other side of the stream, he shivered, stomping his feet to keep warm. Even inside his new boots, his toes were turning numb. He considered retreating into the van and closing the door, but it was cold in there as well, so he kept moving instead. He hoped Kira would notice what he'd put himself through because he wanted to talk to her, if he could still speak through his chattering teeth.

'What are you still doing here?'

With the wind whipping in his ears, he hadn't heard Kira approaching. She trudged over to the van, shoving the box of decorations inside and locking up. He didn't answer her question, preoccupied by her belligerent tone.

The buzz of the snowmobile reached his ears again and he glanced warily at Carla and Tonya before leaning close and saying, 'I was waiting for you.'

He let that sink in, watching surprise and pleasure give way to dismay on her face. She'd kissed him – *kissed* him, in a way no one else in his life had ever kissed him. But she seemed keen to forget it had ever happened, pretend she'd never felt anything.

'Did Alessandra tell you to wait for Carla?'

He suspected her flat tone might hide jealousy, but he wanted that too much to trust his judgement. 'Yes, but—'

Norbert roared back into the car park, the layer of ice in his moustache even thicker than before. He shook Kira's hand.

'I'm glad you made it. There's some food for Yolanda to warm for you later, but Katy had to go and collect her children and I don't want to make any more trips up after this.'

Mattia frowned, glancing between Kira and the concierge in alarm.

'Thanks. What about tomorrow?' she asked. 'The forecast is clear, but what state will the road be in? Are we going to be able to get down?'

Norbert grimaced. 'I'll organise you a snow groomer, just to be safe.'

Mattia's mind wandered, picturing a snow groomer as a dapper older man with slicked-back hair and a wide selection of razors for shaving snowmen, before he remembered it was the hulking vehicle that had taken them down the slopes to the restaurant yesterday.

'Okay, thanks,' Kira responded.

'Where's the other one?' Norbert asked gruffly, gesturing just below his lip to indicate Ginny's piercing. Mattia's gaze shot to Kira's in alarm.

She muttered a curse and rummaged for her phone. 'Give me a second to find out where she is.'

* * *

'This cannot be happening!' Ginny whined over the line. Kira heard a thud that was probably her colleague banging a hand on the steering wheel. 'I'm not going to make it. The traffic isn't moving and I'm only just out of Mayrhofen.'

Kira pulled the phone from her ear to check the time. There were barely two hours of daylight left. 'Okay, Ginny, listen up. Turn around and go back to Mayrhofen.'

'What? There's a wedding tomorrow!'

'I haven't forgotten,' she said drily. 'But I'm a guide, remember, and this is a snow emergency, not a wedding emergency.' The kind of emergency she could actually deal with.

Ginny took a deep breath. 'Right. You're right.'

'I don't want to risk you getting stuck on the road in the middle of nowhere this afternoon. Find a hotel in Mayrhofen and keep warm. Overnight, the snow-ploughs will clear the roads and you'll get here in plenty of time. Norbert has said he'll arrange a snow groomer, so you'll be able to catch a lift back up.' At least she hoped so. If she ended up in charge of this wedding, she didn't want to know what might go wrong. But ensuring Ginny stayed safe was a bigger priority even than the vows.

'A snow groomer?' Ginny said. 'But I booked rein-deer. Alessandra wanted to arrive at her wedding in a sleigh with reindeer. They're coming all the way from—'

'I'm sorry, Ginny, but I doubt Alessandra is getting her reindeer,' Kira said tightly.

'This is such a dis—'

'It'll make a great story once it's all over,' she as-sured Ginny – another mountaineering dictum that she didn't exactly trust in this context.

'I could tell my grandchildren,' she said with a chuckle, 'if I ever meet someone to have the children with,' she added with a groan. 'Isn't this just my rotten luck? I haven't kissed anyone in a year and now I'm up to my neck in mistletoe – *all alone!*'

Kira couldn't stop her gaze sliding to where Mattia was gazing up at the mountain, which was partially obscured by the thick fog of snow. She hadn't kissed anyone in longer than a year – until yesterday. And this morning. But then he'd kissed Carla under the mistletoe and reminded her of how stupid she'd been.

With tingles up to her hairline, she wrenched her eyes off him and focused on her conversation with Ginny.

'But you'll be back in the morning to help me get them to the church, because right now, I can't guarantee that this wedding will go ahead. They need therapy, the lot of them.'

'All normal. Love is for the brave. If they start yelling at each other, distraction works well – on wedding parties as well as toddlers. I'll see you tomorrow.'

Kira ended the call with a grimace. *Love is for the brave.* That would have looked better on the banner over the church door.

'Everything okay?' Mattia asked. The wind picked up his curls and his intent look made her feel as though all of her worries were shared, which was strange, because he was one of them.

Nothing is okay. I don't know how you feel – I don't know how I feel and I'm thinking about my fucking feelings instead of fretting about Alessandra's reindeer!

'Everything's fine,' she said with a sigh and dropped her gaze – which fell on his feet. 'You bought shoes?'

'I heard there's no such thing as bad weather, only bad shoes.' His expression was so inviting – inviting her to come far too close and do too many things she really shouldn't.

'Is that true?' she asked drily.

'Unfortunately not,' he said with mock earnestness. 'I bought these shoes and the weather is still atrocious! Plus they don't match my outfit.'

'Maybe you need a new outfit.'

'I will if you will.'

Were they still talking about clothes?

He leaned closer. 'I kissed her on the cheek,' he said in a low voice. 'And even that... I didn't want her to be the one there under the mistletoe with me.'

Kira's breath was suddenly too tight. 'It doesn't matter. We agreed it shouldn't be us under the mistletoe anyway.'

'I know, but...' His sigh held a thousand unspoken words.

'Uh, guys?' Tonya's voice was a bucket of freezing water over the silly flirtation that Kira shouldn't have indulged in anyway.

Kira forced her eyes from Mattia's face only to meet Carla's wary gaze, and heat flushed up her neck. At least her cheeks were already red from the cold.

The wedding was a mess. Kira suspected even *she*

needed therapy – or she would when this was all over. On top of everything, she had to put on her dress tomorrow, an outfit that made her feel ten kinds of exposed. And she had to wear it in front of Christian.

Sharing her worries was a complete illusion. She was all alone and she always would be, because although it was sad sometimes, it was safe.

'We'd better head up,' she said flatly, stomping over to where Norbert was waiting with the snowmobile and the passenger trailer.

'Is everything okay? Are we going to get snowed in up there?' Tonya asked.

Carla cut straight to the point. 'Is the wedding going to happen?'

Kira was already the worst wedding planner in the history of the profession, so she rubbed the deep groove between her brows and muttered, 'Who the hell knows?'

23

Mattia awoke sometime in the middle of the night with a sense of something gone very wrong. It could have been any number of things, since Alessandra's course of true love was not running smoothly. The sense was confirmed as soon as he came fully awake, by the fact that his feet were *ice*. When he rolled over on the bed, the sheet beside him felt like a slice of provolone straight from the fridge.

He lay frozen in the bed – in both senses of the word – paralysed in fear of what awaited him when he threw off the covers. Perhaps if he went back to sleep, he'd be warm in the morning. They were in the Alps, for the love of God. He shouldn't be surprised to be a bit cold. Maybe he was even dreaming.

Squeezing his eyes shut, he only succeeded in curling his muscles in tighter knots until he was scared he'd strain something.

He heard only thick silence, as though he were insulated with cotton wool. There was no creak of wooden floorboards, no whistle of wind through the pines and most importantly, no gurgle from the radiator. The silence might have scared him if he hadn't been so panicked about the cold.

'Porca miseria!' he cursed through his chattering teeth. There was no way he could get back to sleep. He hoped his was the only room that was so icy.

Folding back the blanket, he shook violently, more from the fear of the cold than the cold itself. The polished timber floor tortured his feet with every step as he hurtled for the jute rug. Shuddering violently, he pulled on his thickest merino pullover and rummaged for a pair of socks, and then another pair of socks when the first was clearly insufficient.

Touching the back of his hand to the radiator, he found it completely cold, even though he'd turned up the thermostat as soon as he'd been shown to his room on arrival.

Tugging the duvet from the bed and wrapping it around himself, he slipped into the felt slippers with embroidered antlers on them provided by the chalet and braced himself to open the door. The hallway would be toasty warm. His radiator was probably broken – that was all. With the concierge down in the valley, maybe Kira could fix it or he could just sleep in her room.

That was what he called serendipity.

Pulling open the door, he stepped tentatively into the hall. Damn, he could see his own breath in here. The window at the end was obscured with condensation, but glowed bright with the light of the moon reflected on snow.

Crossing the hall, he approached Kira's door and knocked. He was too cold to pause and reflect on the last time he'd stood here and had his world turned upside down by a vulnerable kiss.

'What?' he heard, her voice groggy.

'Kira, there's something wrong with the heating,' he said, standing close to the door and speaking as quietly as possible. When the door swung open abruptly, he nearly teetered inside, especially as he only managed to extract one arm from his duvet to grab the doorframe for balance.

Kira blinked up at him, her hair a tousled bluebird's nest and her lips puffy. She was wearing a ribbed tank top and leggings, her skin radiating heat, making him think of wrapping his body around hers.

She crossed her arms instinctively against the cold she mustn't have registered yet, in her bleary state, and that also made him want to wrap his body around hers.

When she noticed him with the duvet all the way up to his neck, she cocked her head and frowned. 'What the matter?'

'T-the h-heating. It's not working.'

Her frown was eloquent. Mattia rather liked sleepy, sluggish Kira. He wanted to scoop her up and take them both back to bed. Sharing body heat sounded like a dream right now.

She groped for the light as she turned back with a shiver, but when she flicked the switch, nothing happened. *Click, click.* Still nothing. His stomach clenched with the first spasms of panic.

She muttered a curse and stalked away, swiping a fleece off the floor and tugging it over her head. This room was dim, with the window facing the steep slope behind the chalet, but the light of the moon penetrated enough for him to see more piles of clothes and even a tablet lying on the floor of the room.

'You have something against tables?'

'I'm messy. Get over it.'

With thick socks on her feet, she nabbed a quilted

jacket from a hook and beckoned for him to follow her.

Downstairs, the light from the panoramic windows in the den shot vivid shadows across the floorboards. He caught a glimpse of an enormous,
pearlescent moon in a black sky.

'At least it's stopped snowing,' he commented, his
voice hushed.

Kira knocked on the door marked 'Privat' and they
waited for the manager to appear.

Mattia hovered next to her in his duvet, feeling
faintly ridiculous. 'I'm sorry I woke you,' he belatedly
apologised. 'I probably could have managed this
myself.'

'It's okay,' she said mildly. 'I needed to know what's
going on.' And there was no answer from behind the
door. Kira knocked again, more firmly this time.
'Katy?' she called through the door. Straightening, she
glanced over her shoulder at Mattia. 'Did Norbert say
something about Katy leaving to collect her children?'

'She didn't... She can't have left us alone here, can
she?' A scraping sound reached his ears and he
jumped. 'There's something outside.' A distant crack.
'Did you hear that? Was it thunder?'

She shook her head. 'Unlikely in this weather.
Large amounts of snow can be pretty powerful though

– and noisy.' Unease rippled across her features, alarming Mattia further. 'But we're safe here, okay? You only need to worry when there's something to worry about. We're safe.'

Her rough, matter-of-fact tone took him back to the first night in Salzburg, when she'd vanquished the fridge for him. He nodded. 'Safe,' he agreed. 'Just cold.'

The moonlight illuminated the smile curving her lips. 'The cold won't hurt you in here.'

'Ahem. It *is* hurting my toes.'

She knocked again, this time with force, and finally, he made out a rustling sound behind the door.

'There's someone there,' he said with a sigh of relief.

But when the door opened a crack, it wasn't Katy standing there, but Yolanda, the waitress. 'It's very cold. What time is it?'

Mattia's relief caught in his throat.

'The electricity's gone off. Do you know where the fuse box is?'

It took a little more explaining, but eventually, Yolanda showed them to a storage cellar off the kitchen, where the big boiler and various other devices usually would have whirred and hummed and ticked. That was the most disturbing silence of all.

Kira located the fuse cupboard and flung it open, but quickly shook her head. 'The fuses aren't tripped.'

As the first glow of dawn touched the sky over the valley on New Year's Eve, Alessandra and Joe's wedding day, Kira confirmed his worst fears.

'The power is out.'

* * *

'Here, have some breakfast. Nothing hot or cooked yet, sorry, but the orange juice is nice and cold this morning! The good news is, we'll be able to make coffee as soon as Kira's off the phone. Yes, it is necessary for survival, which is lucky. Sit over here by the fire and I'll join you in a minute.'

Kira leaned heavily on the kitchen bench and listened to Mattia calming the wedding party on the other side of the door, trying to force herself to go out there. She heard him speaking in lilting Italian and imagined him performing the same spiel, this time for Alessandra's parents rather than Joe's mother.

It was official. The wedding was ruined.

She couldn't blame herself for the ultimate nail in the coffin; she was well aware the weather was a greater force than she could hope to tame. But they were stuck here with no contingency plan. These people had not expected a cold night in a mountain cabin and Kira had no idea how to fix things.

Worse, she was dreading facing Alessandra. What a time to understand that she should have taken Ginny's advice. She was emotionally involved and it was hell – and not only because of her coincidental connection to the groomsman.

No, she hadn't had a chance of keeping her distance from the moment she'd heard Mattia sing.

Avoiding the issue a moment longer, she rummaged for something to light the stove and found a pack of matches. Filling a saucepan with water, she managed to get the stove lit manually, which was a blessing. She hadn't been looking forward to going outside with the little gas burner she'd seen in the storage cupboard where Mattia had kissed her.

Yolanda bustled into the kitchen and out again with more bread and cheese. She'd spoken to Katy, the manager, but it was clear she was out of her depth with backup equipment and safety, so it was best if she focused on food. That left Kira to work out the next course of action.

The kitchen door swung open again and Mattia appeared, studying her. 'Okay?'

She eyed him. It was usually her asking him that, but he seemed to be holding up well. He'd swapped the duvet for his long coat and scarf, but he was still wearing loose sweats and looking far too approach-able, his hair curling wildly and a little silver hoop in his ear this morning. She wondered if he'd ever played a baritone pirate.

'I've got water on for coffee. I'll have to run it man-ually through the filter, but the stovetop works.'

He hesitated, as though he had something else to say, but changed his mind, heading for the pantry. He emerged with eggs and a bedraggled plant and rum-maged for a bowl. Before she'd registered what he was doing, he'd whipped up the makings of an omelette and drizzled olive oil in a pan.

'Light it for me? I'm not good with fire. Ever since my costume caught alight during a performance of *Il Trovatore*, I don't like to get too close.'

More vulnerability. She lit an element under the frying pan and he tossed a few leaves from the plant into the oil.

'You make your opera performances sound like life-or-death situations.'

His response was a shrug. 'It took some therapy to convince me that wasn't the case. Maybe it was all pre-paring me for this moment, I suppose. Are we snowed in? We'll be stuck here until Easter?'

She didn't think he was serious, but she couldn't

be certain. 'When Ginny joked about the wedding party having to eat someone to survive, I didn't think it would actually come to that.'

He gagged theatrically. 'I suspect I know who would be eaten.'

She patted him on the arm as he grated cheese into the egg. 'There's not enough meat on your bones.'

When he caught her gaze with one of his warm, prompting looks, she belatedly recognised his ploy: he was softening her up to receive tenderness. Her stomach swooped as she saw it coming.

'Want to talk through the options? Whatever you think, I trust you. We can tell Alessandra the damage together.'

It was too much. The strain of fitting into the wedding planner box over the past few days, feeling inadequate and out of place and now the responsibility for a wedding that wasn't going to happen – at least not as planned – sapped her remaining strength. Her shoulders fell and the urge to cry rose up and she hated how Mattia made her feel all this stuff too vividly.

But as soon as her misery began, it stopped again, replaced by the touch of fine wool on her cheek, a warm, vital body pressed to hers, enveloping hers. She needed to repeat this when the heating was on, without coats to interfere with the sublime closeness.

She wanted to repeat it without any clothing at all – exposed, sincere. *Dangerous.* She could so clearly see why Mattia didn't understand casual intimacy. Perhaps he wasn't capable of it.

His hold loosened, but she wasn't prepared to let him go yet. A chuckle echoed in his chest, under her ear, and he steered them towards the pantry. Rummaging one-handed in a box, he produced a small morsel she couldn't properly see, then tugged at her bottom lip with one finger.

'Open.'

Her heartbeat stalled at the sensation of his fingertip on her mouth, but she did as he instructed without thought. A moment later, the flavour of dark chocolate burst on her tongue and she savoured it with a sigh.

Realising she'd closed her eyes, she wrenched them open to see Mattia watching her from close range, a small, pained smile on his expressive lips. His thumb brushed her mouth once more.

'I love how your bottom lip is so firm and strong and practical.' His voice wasn't quite steady. Pressing up with his thumb, he continued, 'But your top lip is soft and giving.'

Kira froze, recognising the panicked reflex that was demanding she push him away, mock him for his sentimental words and re-establish her comfortable equilibrium where she could plausibly deny feeling *anything* that would push her too far. But she remembered too well the sensation of his mouth on hers, full of wanting, demanding she believe him. All of a sudden, the best solution to all of her problems appeared to be more kissing.

Until he was the one to move away.

24

The hiss and crackle of the eggs reverberating in Mattia's ears, he whirled and stumbled in his rush to save the food – and therefore the wooden building – from burning.

Che cavolo, he suspected he might have just missed out on another kiss. But he was trying to be practical – helpful – not dreamy Matty with his head in the clouds.

He hadn't ruined the eggs, thankfully. Just the moment. Stealing another glance at her, he wondered when – if – he'd get another chance. Even the way she frowned lightly at the coffee grounds made him want to pull her close. He was so sick of staying away from her.

He wanted to know how she was feeling about seeing her ex, convince her she was doing a great job in difficult circumstances. He wanted to hug her again – kiss her until she gave him that giddy smile she saved for special occasions.

Anything between them would be the definition of casual, but... he could try that out. He could turn this wedding delay into a blessing in disguise, like their first night together in Salzburg.

'Has Alessandra come down yet?' she mumbled before he had a chance to cheer her up. 'I haven't seen her since I built the fire in her room.'

He shook his head. 'She won't take a chance on Joe seeing her in case the wedding is still going ahead.'

He wasn't surprised when Kira grimaced and said flatly, 'It's not.' She poured the coffee into an insulated pot and closed the lid. 'I suppose I'd better go see her.'

'I'll come with you. Here, have some eggs first.'

'Mattia, I—'

Before she could protest further, he slipped a forkful into her mouth, expecting and rather enjoying her put-out expression.

'This is ridicul—' Her tone already lacked conviction and when she licked her lips and gave a satisfying 'Mmm', he knew he'd done the right thing. The next time he prepared a bite for her, she opened her mouth eagerly. 'Delicious. This is delicious.'

'You're hungry,' he said mildly.

She snatched the plate from him and wolfed down two more mouthfuls. She finished the omelette before he'd even gathered his thoughts, brushing past him with a sigh.

In the dining room, she greeted the wedding party with a tight smile and the assurance that she'd be right back with an update on the weather and they should sit tight.

'I can imagine you as an expedition leader,' he said when he caught up with her in the hallway, shoving his hands in his pockets against the sudden cold so far from the fireplace.

'Better than as a wedding planner,' she said. Stopping suddenly at the top of the stairs, she whirled to face him. 'You seem *happy* that the wedding isn't going ahead.'

He hesitated, his mind racing. 'I'm not happy,' he insisted. 'I know she'll be upset and I'm not looking forward to that, but I did see certain other possibilities now this has happened.'

'What *possibilities*?' she asked with a snort.

He gave half a shrug. 'Like... what nearly happened in the kitchen.'

'What nearly happened in the—' She sucked in a swift breath. 'I don't know what you were trying to do in the kitchen.'

'Look after you.'

'I don't need—' Her chest rose and fell with heavy breaths. Perhaps she realised she was lying and stopped talking. Pressing the heel of her hand to her forehead, she groaned, 'I'm supposed to be throwing you together with Carla.'

'Carissima,' he began, taking a step closer, but he forgot he was on the steps and scuffed his foot. With a cry of alarm, he groped for something to hold onto and ended up suspended in the stairwell, one hand clutching the banister and the other around her waist, his face pressed into her chest. He froze, expecting her to grab him and steady him – then push him away. But instead, there was a hitch in her breathing and a swallow and he stayed where he was, breathing in the strength of her.

'What is going on here?'

He cursed Alessandra's impeccable – or terrible – timing. He opened his eyes and reluctantly extracted his face from Kira's fleece. Her nostrils flared and he considered for a moment leaving Alessandra to wonder for a few more minutes and talking all of this out. Poor Kira. She was afraid – probably of her own feelings. How she must hate that.

But Alessandra was watching, wide-eyed and expectant, from the door of her room. All Mattia could do was lift his eyebrows at Kira, give her arm a squeeze in the hope she understood that to mean *We'll talk later. Hang in there.*

'Eh, I slipped. We were coming to see you.'

Shut inside the bridal suite for warmth, Kira invited Alessandra to sit down, while his old friend still looked between them as though they were about to announce their own marriage – and she'd be horrified.

'We can't have the wedding today,' he blurted out.

'What?'

Kira's gaze flew to the ceiling. 'Bloody hell, Mattia, even *I* could have done that with more tact.'

He was distracted by how good his name sounded in her voice.

'I'm so sorry,' she said to Alessandra. 'There's an avalanche warning for this area and we've been strongly advised to stay put.'

'An avalanche?' Alessandra cried, echoing Mattia's thoughts.

'A warning,' Kira reassured them. 'This position is

protected or they wouldn't have built the chalet here. It's the road in and out that's the concern. Norbert won't risk it, which is fair. But I've spoken to Ginny and she's already checked that the priest is available tomorrow or the next day and he's been very accommodating.'

'The next day! Our wedding day was supposed to be *today*! I'm supposed to be married before the new year! I even had a commemorative plaque engraved with this year on it! I can't get married *next year*!'

'It isn't safe for the reindeer anyway,' Kira pointed out.

What reindeer?

'But at least it gives us lots of time for Ginny to get back from Mayrhofen with the mistletoe.'

'The mistletoe!' Alessandra exclaimed and then she burst into tears. 'All the flowers! Everything will be wilted!'

His friend had her own dramatic streak, but he'd never seen her worked up like this. His gaze flickered to Kira in horror. She glared back.

Patting Alessandra's shoulder awkwardly, she said, 'There, there. The low temperature might slow the process.' She shot him another look, clearly expecting him to do something.

He sat down next to Alessandra, wrapping an arm around her shoulders, and tried to reason with her.

'Given the fact that we're safe and warm... enough, anyway, during a catastrophic snowfall event, aren't your flowers and the commemorative plaque a side issue, Ale? We're all together, like you wanted.'

His words only seemed to get her more worked up. 'This was supposed to be the happiest day of my life and instead I'm *freezing* in fifteen layers of clothing, and what I *wanted* was for you to fall in love with Carla again so at least you'd have each other when I'm gone, but you've decided you want to let your horse run, chasing every woman in this chalet *except* the one who's interested in you!'

Kira stepped back so suddenly, *she* nearly tripped. 'I'm not... I don't want to be involved in this.'

Mattia's throat closed, terrified she didn't want anything to do with *him*, but not certain that was what she meant.

'Look, I'm going to go—'

'No!' Mattia stopped her. 'We haven't finished—'

When Kira wrenched open the door, Carla stood behind it, her hand raised to knock. Mattia's groan came from deep in his chest as he watched them exchange a wide-eyed look across the threshold.

He'd been wrong. It would have been better if they'd got Alessandra married and out of the way so he could talk to Kira in peace – except after the wedding, they'd have no reason to ever see each other again.

'I have to—' Kira made a jerky hand gesture. Moving stiffly past Carla, she fled into the corridor and was gone in a blur of blue.

'What happened to her?' Carla asked.

'Nothing,' Mattia insisted. 'We were just telling Alessandra the bad news about the weather.'

'*We?*' Alessandra repeated, her brow low.

'Yes?' He gave an elaborate shrug, hoping that made him more convincing. 'It's a pronoun. First person plural, I believe.'

'Matty,' she continued – but thankfully, her shrill tone had abated – 'you're a terrible liar.' She studied Carla as she came into the room. 'There's... no hope of the two of you getting back together, is there?'

Afraid of another outburst – or getting Kira into trouble – Mattia hesitated.

'No chance at all.'

That pronouncement was the last thing he'd expected to hear. His gaze snapped up to see Carla giving him a sad smile.

'I hope we'll always be friends, though.'

'Of course.'

'Ale,' Carla said, taking the bride's hand and patting it, 'we don't need each other to make up for your absence from Naples and you don't need to feel guilty for leaving. Matty's not your little brother and I think he'd like the chance to choose his own partner.'

She raised her brow at him, as though challenging him to disagree, but he couldn't.

'I would like to have been better friends with Joe, but you know the most important thing to me is your happiness,' he added emphatically. 'It doesn't matter what's going on with Carla or me.' At least, he hoped she'd stop giving him suspicious looks and heavily implied pronouns. 'Once the snow is cleared, it's your day. Your marriage.'

To his horror, her tears returned.

'Shhhh, Ale. I'm sorry. I didn't mean to make you cry.' He grimaced at the door. It might be a while before he could go after Kira.

'For more than a year, my whole life has been about this wedding: these wild ideas for the destination, the decorations. Joe never once told me "no".'

'And that's a problem because...?' Carla prompted.

'After all this, I'm not sure he cares. I just wanted him to *care*.'

'Oh, Ale,' Mattia said with a shake of his head. The first thing that entered his mind was how much he wanted to discuss this with Kira. 'Have you talked to him about this?'

'I tried yesterday, but he was drunk; he would have told me anything if he thought I'd forgive him.'

'Surely that's true love?' Mattia suggested with a wince.

'I thought you had *ideals* about love, Matty,' she said softly.

With an awkward glance at Carla, he considered his response. 'Maybe my ideals are finally being tempered with realism.'

Alessandra's sigh was deep. 'That's a shame, but I suppose it really means you don't need me to look after you any more.'

He thought of the difficult years at school and university, as he'd come to terms with his sensitive ears and even more sensitive brain. A lot had changed since then; something had changed over the past seventy-two hours.

'No, Ale. I don't.'

* * *

Upstairs in the loft, Kira grabbed a squeegee from the storage cupboard and continued into the bouldering room, heading straight to the slanting window. She hadn't come up here to reminisce, but memories assailed her anyway: Mattia appearing, mostly naked and out of breath, all because he was worried about her and he liked her and he cared about her pathetic past – even though she hadn't told him the full extent of Christian's betrayal.

She'd had her fingers in his hair and he'd called her *carissima*.

Gritting her teeth, she ignored the urge to haul herself up on the grips to prove her resilience and clear her head and opened the window instead. As Norbert had said on the phone, the roof was dotted with solar panels, currently buried under a layer of snow.

Grasping the squeegee, she nudged aside as much snow as she could, clearing the two nearest panels. The rest would come online as the snow softened and slid off and hopefully, they'd have enough power to run the boiler for a few hours.

Returning downstairs, she refused to glance at the closed door of Alessandra's room or wonder what they might be talking about.

Kira's phone rang as she made her way through the dining room, giving her the perfect excuse for slipping past the guests apologetically without pausing. When she tugged her phone out of the pocket of her ski jacket, she was surprised to see Willard's name.

With a tug in her chest, she connected the call to

talk to her boss. 'Will? Everything okay?' Great Heart Adventures, Will's pride and joy, had caused him more than its share of grey hairs over the past five years of financial trouble. Since the merger, Kira still hadn't quite processed the end of the money worries or got used to Will's new enthusiasm for life – and, remarkably, weddings.

'I'm calling to ask *you* that, Watling.' Just hearing his gruff voice set her emotions bubbling.

'I've been snowed in before,' she answered.

A pause. 'Kira?' Damn it, when someone had climbed a mountain with you, they were too good at picking up on what you didn't want to say. 'I can't get up there to help you, so talk to me.'

Nobody could get up there to help her. She was used to shouldering everything alone, so it shouldn't have made any difference, but she felt exposed and it had everything to do with Mattia and his fine feelings. 'Everything's all right,' she insisted. 'The heating will spring on for a few hours when the snow melts off the solar panels and we have wood and plenty of food. It's fine.'

'I have every confidence in you,' Will said.

'Yes, well, I'll keep everyone alive. Survival is more along the lines of my qualifications.'

'But?' he prompted.

She'd arrived in the kitchen to see the frying pan on the stove and a plate on the bench. Her stomach flipped, thinking of Mattia feeding her egg. He'd touched her, talked to her – *looked* at her. But she'd always known there could be nothing between them except 'it's complicated'.

The man was afraid of fire and fridges, for goodness' sake.

'Weddings aren't for me,' she grumbled, hoping her old friend would accept the flippant explanation.

'No one's asking *you* to get married,' Will joked. 'What's the problem?'

She laughed, leaning her forehead against the door to the technical room. She was tired – physically, but also running low on emotional resources, which were usually in scarce enough supply anyway. 'What *isn't* the problem? I'm ruining this wedding. I implied the decorations were frivolous the first time I met the bride and I accidentally insulted the groom's mother. I'm going to see my ex-boyfriend at the ceremony for the first time in twelve years and it's going to cause a scene. The groom got drunk on my watch and the opera singer I'm supposed to be keeping safe has a head injury and makes me cry when he performs.' She took a breath. 'Worst of all, I kissed him. I kissed the bridesman.'

Silence. She'd expected some reaction from Will, even just a laugh. Perhaps she'd been lucky and the connection had cut out before he'd heard the end of her tirade. She shouldn't have said anything, even if she could count on Will not to pass on her faux pas to anyone at I Do.

'Are you still there?'

'Um.'

'Um? Will, what's going on?'

'I, er, probably should have told you that Reshma's here.'

'Reshma's where?'

'Right beside me,' he said gently. 'Listening to every word.'

There was only one word she could say in reaction, even if it was another that probably wasn't appropriate for the ears of the head of I Do Destinations. 'Fuck.'

She heard a muffled, 'Give me the phone,' and then Reshma's voice in her ear. 'Have you told Ginny any of this?' Reshma didn't sound as though she'd kill Kira, but perhaps she'd just wait until she could do it in person.

'She was there when I screwed up on the first night.'

'But the... other things?'

Her throat closed as she wondered which one was considered worse: ruining the ceremony with her own dramas or kissing a member of the wedding party. 'Ginny doesn't know,' she managed to explain. 'I'd hoped *no one* would have to know.'

She heard a deep sigh over the line and recognised Willard – and his disappointment in her. It hurt more than she wanted to admit, even to herself.

'Kira,' he began, his voice so smooth, she knew something bad must be coming. 'I know this is your personal history, but perhaps it's better if the team at I Do understand *why* you struggle with weddings?'

Tears pricked in her eyes and all the heightened emotions collapsed on her at once in an avalanche she could no longer hold off. With a flash, she saw the decorated church, Alessandra and Joe toasting the gathered family and friends, Mattia's rich, haunting voice travelling through the violent landscape – and her thoughts raced back to a day she'd hoped she'd left behind, but was evidently still as fresh in her memory as though it had been yesterday.

'I wish it made no difference,' she began grimly, 'and I don't want sympathy, or for you to think any differently about me, but maybe you should know.' Taking a deep breath, she forced herself to continue. 'I was engaged once, when I was very young – too young. I nearly got married. But on the day of the wedding, he... he left me at the altar.'

A noise made her turn, slowing in horror as she began to suspect who was behind her. Gathered in the doorway of the kitchen, ears pricked and eyes round with shock, stood Joe, Rav and Hugh, the parents of the couple, Tonya and even Yolanda the waitress – all witnesses to her mortifying confession.

25

'Do I look like I've been crying?'

'Not at all,' Mattia assured Alessandra, the lie falling smoothly for once from his lips. 'You look absolutely beautiful, as always.'

She smacked him on the arm. 'I have got the message,' she said with a sniff.

He trailed her and Carla out of her room, feeling five years older than the moment he'd gone in, but rather brightly thinking that would make him a year older than Kira.

Bracing himself as they reached the door to the dining room, he was expecting an uproar as the group came to terms with avalanche risk and frozen bodies and *no wedding*, but what he saw instead made him stop short.

Kira sat at a table with a coffee cup in front of her, a pained grimace on her face, while Tonya clasped an arm around her shoulder and Alessandra's mother held her hand, stroking it periodically.

'What's happened now?' Alessandra asked.

Kira stiffened, glancing from him to Alessandra. 'I have to, um, get more wood.' Her face was flaming as she scooted out of the door to make her escape. He found Rav giving him a pained look and with a lurch in his stomach, he guessed what she was upset about.

He squeezed Alessandra's arm. 'Are you okay, now? I just have to—' He gestured wildly after Kira, his feet already moving in the direction she'd gone.

She gave him a perplexed smile. 'You have another fire to put out?'

'I'm a real firefighter today,' he called over his shoulder as he took off after Kira.

He lost time lacing his complicated boots and once he'd swung open the door, he had his breath knocked out of him. The valley sparkled and glowed in bright sunlight. The sky was such a vivid blue, it hurt his eyes. The air was so still, he heard the muted mumble of running water under ice and the cry of a bird of prey in the distance – and the loud crunch of Kira's boots in the snow.

There was two feet of it, in lopsided piles with vivid shadows and blinding, untouched white. Studying the surface uneasily, he tried not to think of what might be underneath, which didn't work very well, and he eventually had to make himself move anyway.

Limbs flailing as though he were a giraffe walking in quicksand, he stumbled in the direction Kira had gone, to a lean-to built against the rock face behind the chalet. Hunks of wood were stacked against the back wall, under a snow-covered tarpaulin, and Kira stood in front of an old, pockmarked stump, wielding an axe.

Mattia jerked a step back as she hauled the axe over her head and brought it down with a precise thwack, neatly splitting the piece of wood in front of her. The sound rang in his ears, the violence of the blade meeting rough wood digging into his chest. Picking up one side and setting it back on the stump, she repeated the action – *thwack* – sending the two smaller pieces flying. He flinched, but he was more fascinated than concerned by the outward manifestation of Kira's prickly defences.

'Wow.'

She didn't even turn around. 'Go back inside,' she snapped. 'It's too cold out here for you.'

'It's rather nice in the sunshine,' he responded mildly. 'But I think after the conversation I just had with Alessandra, I'm the one who should decide what's too cold for me or not.'

That earned him a wary glance. 'What conversation? I thought you were going to talk to Carla.'

'Oh, that too. She's not as stubborn as Alessandra. But we're all friends again. *Just* friends. I've got to make my own way through the confusing world of relationships.'

Her only response was another juddering thwack of the axe. Her strength struck him under his skin, like beauty – with awe. But today, it was clearer than ever that she was trying to protect herself – and not quite succeeding.

'Will you tell me what's upset you? Did Rav say something?'

She gave a snort and turned to face him. 'You can ask anyone inside. They all know now.'

Even someone without sensitive hearing would have made out the hurt in her voice. 'Can I hear it from you instead?'

'Why?' She swung the axe again, the sound ringing out through the still valley.

'I'm not asking because I'm curious – well, not only because I'm curious. I'm asking because, whatever it is, I want to understand.' *I want to protect you.*

'I'm not sure I want you to understand.' The breathy quality of her voice, the tentative words sent a shiver through Mattia. Not *I don't want*, but *I'm not sure I want*. For Kira, that was like running into his arms.

'It's all right, Kira.' He kept his voice steady. 'It's just me.'

Her quick glance from underneath a lopsided brow gave him a spark of hope for – quite a lot. 'Just you,' she repeated with a huff. 'Mattia, you don't know me very well.'

'I politely beg to differ.'

Turning, she looked him square in the face and the flash of longing that shot down his spine took him by surprise. 'You know all that stuff I said in the van on the way here? About how I don't do commitment?'

'You don't get attached to people who could hurt you.'

Her eyes narrowed and he was glad he had a vivid memory of that conversation – of every conversation he'd shared with this prickly, colourful woman who possibly didn't realise she held everyone else at a safe distance because she felt *too deeply*.

'This is about Christian, yes? Why everything changed for you after you broke up with him?'

Another snort. 'I did not break up with him.'

'That's a yes,' he said on a sigh. 'What happened? Why don't you want me to know?'

Crossing her arms in a gesture she'd probably meant as combative, but only made her look vulnerable, she said, 'Because it makes me a liar and a hypocrite.'

He shook his head. 'I'm sure—'

'I was about to marry him! I was wearing a long, white dress covered in lace, my hair done up, in *heels* and a lace garter, for fuck's sake. They were playing Pachelbel's fucking Canon.'

Oh. Mattia's eyes swung shut, blinking open again as he tried to make sense of what she said. *Oh.* He sucked in a deep, shaky breath, blowing it out again on a cloud of moisture particles in the cold air.

'He didn't show up,' she said with a caustic smile. 'Lucky near miss for my marital status.'

But a lasting blow to her pride. 'How old were you?' He grimaced even before she answered him, knowing the answer could only be: *too young.*

'Nineteen. I thought I was in love. I was an idiot.' Her jaw set, she turned back to the stump and swung the axe again. She didn't quite find the middle that time and a smaller piece splintered off the wood. She cursed under her breath.

Her words echoed in his mind. She thought the story made her a hypocrite, but he could picture it so clearly. Kira head over heels in love – bravely, faithfully, loyally.

'Christian was the idiot.'

She dropped the axe. 'Don't say that. You can't possibly mean it.'

'Why not? Because we've only known each other for four days or because you're trying so hard not to let me see who you really are?'

The breath left her mouth on a sharp exhale and then she shoved him half-heartedly on one shoulder. 'You play all innocent and weak, but you have superpowers,' she said accusingly. 'You can make people *feel* things, even when they don't want to.'

He shook his head. 'I'm only telling you what I see, what everyone would see, if they looked more closely.'

'If you look closely, you'll find crooked teeth and brown hair growing back under the bleached bit.'

He stared at her, marvelling at the vibrant image of her imprinting on his mind – his heart – in real time. 'I am curious about the natural colour of your hair, but I like the blue. I love how you rebuilt your pride even bigger and stronger than before. I wish more people saw what I see when I look at you, but I can also understand why you protect your soft heart, why you make people *earn* the real you. I hate how the memory of this one mistake colours your world still, but I love how you hold onto things so tightly.'

Her smile died. 'I don't have a soft heart. I *can't*. Maybe I did once, when I was reckless and too trusting, but now... It won't do you any good to believe I'm like you.'

She wasn't like him. She'd been brave and loved as she found, while he floated with the dreams and ideals of a child. She'd been more grown up at nineteen than he was at twenty-seven.

He gave a single nod. She'd been right, the way he thought about her had changed with the knowledge that she'd nearly married someone once, but not the way she'd feared. From a disjointed bundle of instincts and impressions, she'd come into focus. No matter what happened – or didn't happen – over the next few days, forming that image had been important to him, proof that the mess of real life could be just as gripping as art and ideals.

He gestured to the axe, its crude blade lying harmless on the snowy ground. 'Will you show me how to do that?'

'What?'

Her doubtful expression pinched, but he wouldn't give up yet. 'I'm not asking you to just hand me the axe so I can try to swing it. You'd have to actually teach me. But I'm asking you to.'

He waited, imagining Alessandra laughing off a similar request with a joke about the wisdom of handing him an axe. Kira didn't laugh.

'All right,' she said hesitantly. 'Come here.'

* * *

Hot blood tingled under Kira's skin and every cell in her body felt warm and alive and the sensation was so different from what she'd been feeling twenty minutes ago that she kept asking herself if it was real.

After the mortification of everyone discovering her wretched history and the reason for her infantile resentment of weddings, after the relentless confusion of her feelings about Mattia, now she was smiling, her chest floating and expanding – like the shock of sunlight after yesterday's blizzard.

'Allora, okay, I line it up.'

Mattia – a light sheen of sweat on his forehead and his coat discarded to reveal those wide, bony shoulders – placed the axe blade carefully onto the piece of wood on the chopping block, matching a crack in the grain. Standing back, a firm nod was all the encouragement she gave him.

His words were on repeat in her mind: *It's just me.* He accepted her, trusted her, *liked* her. But that statement was more dangerous to her state of mind than anything any other man had ever said to her. Mattia Bentivoglio wasn't *just* anything.

Taking a deep breath, he raised the axe over his head and let it fall back down as she'd shown him, the weight lodging the blade into the wood. He tried to haul it out again, but it was stuck.

'Oh,' he said with a disappointed flick of his eyebrows.

'That's fine. Just lift the whole piece and drop it down again.'

With a grunt of effort, he hauled up the axe – and the wood with it – and slammed it back down, rending the wood with a creak and a clang. He jumped in surprise and dropped the axe, the handle landing on his foot.

'Cazzo!'

'There, you did it,' Kira said placidly.

Lifting his gaze to hers, his eyes bright with disbelief, he said, 'But that was—' Taking in the wood, neatly split into two pieces along the crack, he cleared his throat and tried again. 'I did it.'

Picking up one of the pieces and setting it onto the block, she fetched the axe for him and pressed it into his soft hands. 'It needs one more split.'

The way he stared at her as he nodded seemed to open up a world she'd refused to acknowledge.

She nudged his waist. 'Stand a little farther back and keep your arms straight.' Her hand seemed involuntarily drawn down his arm to his wrist and she was glad he was the one holding the axe, because her knees were unsteady.

It's just you. When he nodded again, his hair fell over his forehead, tempting her fingers, but she forced herself to step back. He wanted to learn to chop wood. He certainly didn't need her to teach him anything about kissing. He was very good at that already.

Concentrating with his bottom lip between his teeth, he regarded the wood earnestly as Kira studied him, quietly falling apart. Setting the blade onto the wood, he set up another swing and brought the blade down. He flinched again, powerfully, but the wood split obediently into two. The sound must have been ringing in his ears.

He looked up with a grin, the sun winking off the hoop in his ear and highlighting his angular features, and Kira tumbled, sprawling through her mess of feelings.

It's you. While part of her wallowed in the burn of recognition, the sensible part panicked, warned her not to get caught up in this whirlwind. She was stressed, that's all. Not in love. That would be ridiculous.

He seemed thankfully oblivious to the tectonics inside her. Lifting a fist, he tensed the muscles in his arm with a pout. 'There! I can keep everyone warm! My first survival skill.'

She chuckled. 'You can keep everyone warm for about an hour. Well done.' Taking his hand, she rubbed her thumb over his palm, enjoying the way his smile dimmed and that brightness lit his gaze again at the touch. 'But don't give yourself blisters.'

Before she could take her hand away, he slipped his fingers between hers and her stomach swooped.

'Are you suggesting I have soft hands?'

Very soft. She untangled her fingers while she still could. 'I don't think I'm supposed to be letting the wedding guests do this,' she said over her shoulder as she went to fetch another chunk of wood.

But before she could get there, a gentle blow to her shoulder stopped her in her tracks and a shock of cold seeped down her neck. She whirled around, her mouth falling open in surprise.

'Did you just—?'

His studied, innocent look wasn't convincing in the slightest.

She inclined her head. 'Seriously? How *old* are you?'

Up went his shoulders, hands out in a picture of blamelessness. 'I never got to throw snowballs as a child. You're my first target.'

'Oh, I'm so sorry for your deprived childhood,' Kira said, feigning thoughtfulness while she snaked a hand behind her to scrape some snow off the tarpaulin protecting the wood. 'In that case, allow me to—'

She hurled the snowball at him, catching him square in the chest. He jumped in shock, swiping at the patch of snow left stuck in his pullover.

'—be the first one to ever hit *you* with a snowball,' Kira finished with a grin.

'You have an unfair advantage!' he called out as he crouched, scooping up more snow. He flung it at her before he'd packed it down properly and it showered over her rather than hitting.

'You'll have to learn under pressure,' she quipped, her snowball glancing off his shoulder as he moved.

He did learn – quickly. After several minutes of flinging snow at each other and squealing – although Mattia's baritone squeal was much more appealing than her own choked, laughing one – she had snow in her hair and down her back and her collar was damp and cold. Mattia had fared worse, without his coat on.

'You know if you caught a cold and damaged your precious vocal chords because of this, I'd probably lose my job.'

He rolled his eyes and took a step closer. 'That's not how viruses work and besides, I started it.' His pointed look made her wonder if they were still talking about the snowball fight.

'I'm glad we didn't harm your expensive coat, though. I know it's much warmer than yesterday, but don't you think we should go ins—'

'You're surrendering?'

How had he suddenly got so close?

'A-a truce. Snowball fights don't end in surrender.'

'Are you sure?'

Her heart thumped against her ribs. 'I am the more experienced one here.'

Leaning close, his lips were a breath from her ear when he whispered, 'But I'm the one holding a snowball.'

She only had a moment to brace herself before he brought it down right on top of her head. With a shriek, she prioritised shoving him over clearing the freezing snow from her hair, but he caught her, laughing, and then helped her, his fingers gentle on her head and then the organ failure seemed to be spreading to her lungs, because her breath would only come fitfully.

Staring at his mouth, she knew exactly what could cure this illness. His small smile when he caught her looking suggested he wouldn't mind administering the treatment. Being snowed in at the chalet was so much better than being at the wedding. She hoped it would be another few days before they could go back down again.

She'd just snaked a hand around the back of his neck when the door swung open with a creak and Mattia jumped.

'Are you both all right? We heard a shout!' Alessandra's voice sounded, along with the rustling and shuffling off footsteps. Kira just had time to wrench away from him before the bride and seemingly every other member of the wedding party arrived around the back of the building. 'What *are* you two doing?'

26

Mattia could think of several inconveniences of being snowed in with Alessandra's wedding party, but the worst was definitely the interrupted kisses. He tramped forlornly back inside the chalet.

'Come and get warm. I can't believe you were out there with no coat on! You're lucky the heating has come back on, by some miracle. I will *never* take heating for granted again. But come and sit by the fire and warm up.' Alessandra obviously hadn't quite given up fussing, but she had the grace to give him a sheepish look when she realised what she was doing.

'It wasn't a miracle,' Kira explained. 'The solar panels have come online. Unfortunately, it will all go off again when the sun goes down, but at least we're prepared this time.'

Mattia straightened his shoulders. 'With all the wood I cut!'

She eyed him. 'Yes, all that wood. If the electricity's on, I should go and charge my phone and check in with Ginny.'

'And I guess the rest of us will sit around and... do nothing?'

Kira gave him a shrug, clearly communicating that his entertainment was not her responsibility, and disappeared up the stairs.

'What did she mean, the heating is going to go off again?' Alessandra asked in a small voice.

'Exactly what she said,' he replied as he followed her into the den. 'But it certainly feels warm in here now I've been outside. It's a beautiful day,' he insisted, waving at the panoramic windows that showed— He grimaced. Clouds had rolled in again and a flurry of snowflakes gusted against the glass as he watched.

Alessandra sighed and threw herself into an armchair with all of the disappointment of a postponed wedding and he looked up to find eight concerned gazes meeting his. Joe looked especially helpless, especially since Mattia had switched to Italian without thinking and Joe wouldn't have understood.

'Tonight was supposed to be my wedding reception. Joe was going to feed me pomegranate and I would give him lentils and I was going to kiss him at midnight – my *husband*. I had red underwear to go under my dress,' she lamented, listing New Year's traditions that he had to admit seemed fitting for a wedding celebration.

'You could throw Joe out of the window instead, now,' Mattia couldn't resist teasing, referencing the one Italian tradition that *didn't* fit.

'I could throw *you*. It's supposed to be old things we throw out of the window at midnight, *old friend*.'

His first thought was that Kira would save him, which put a crooked smile on his face.

'What are you smiling for? It's going to be at least a year before I can laugh about this.'

He squeezed her arm, glad she realised that one day, she might be able to. 'Have you talked to Joe since...?'

'Since he got drunk? No, he fell asleep and then I thought it was the night before my wedding, so I made him sleep in a different room. He didn't protest,' she said bitterly.

Mattia glanced up to find the groom watching them with increasing concern. 'I think you'd better, Ale. Do you want that midnight kiss or not?'

'But it might be the day before my—'

'Alessandra,' he stopped her firmly. 'There might not be a wedding unless you talk this through. All your preparations might have been for nothing.'

Her lips wobbled. 'I think that's what I'm afraid of: that I've already pushed him too far. He's just too polite to say it.'

Mattia snorted. 'I'm sure he's not that polite, even if he is British.'

He stood, shooting Joe a meaningful glance and looking around for an excuse to leave and something helpful to occupy him while the wedding party navigated this crisis. Alessandra's mother provided it unexpectedly, standing as well and grasping his arm as he brushed past.

'It is still New Year's Eve, you know,' she said. 'We might be stuck halfway up a mountain and there will be no wedding, but there are still traditions to be observed.'

He paused, his mind racing. 'You're right, Zia Francesca. Would you care to join me in the kitchen?'

* * *

By the late afternoon, each bedroom had wood stacked by the stove, both Kira's phone and battery pack were fully charged in case of an emergency and she'd cleared the snow from around the front and back doors.

The solar panels had run the boiler for five hours, but only with all other appliances switched off. While the guests had grumbled about not being able to charge their own phones, when they realised the choice was between heating and entertainment, heating won out easily.

Despite the claustrophobic setting, stuck up here with the wedding party, Kira still considered herself lucky. If she'd been the one down in the valley explaining to the other guests that the wedding had been postponed, she might have wanted to shoot herself – to say nothing of the mother-lode of mistletoe slowly wilting in Ginny's hire car.

But she'd been avoiding the rest of the party and was worried about the inevitable mood swing as the evening grew cold. Happy New Year indeed.

She trudged through to the kitchen, hoping there were tins of beans or something similar to feed the many mouths. Poor Alessandra with her fine taste and rich parents would have to make do, since they'd been stuck with Kira and not a gourmet chef, but when she swung open the door, she was surprised to see

Francesca Martinelli herself at the stove, Yolanda busy chopping at the kitchen bench.

'What's—' She inhaled on a deep breath through her nose. 'That smells amazing.'

Signora Martinelli nodded austerely, wiping her hands on the apron embroidered with edelweiss that she'd apparently adopted. Reaching up to a high shelf, she poured a drink into a small, tulip-shaped glass and held it out to Kira.

'Go. Sit. Drink.' She continued with something further in Italian.

'She says you need it.' Kira turned to find Mattia entering the room behind her, a smile lighting his face.

Throwing up her hands, Signora Martinelli puttered back to the cupboard and poured another, handing it to Mattia.

'You need it too?' Kira guessed as Alessandra's mother shooed them out of the kitchen.

Following him into the dining room, Kira slowed in shock to see the table set with festive finery. The runner was embroidered with pine trees and little crochet flakes of snow. The plates were painted with stars or deer, edged in red. Gold coins – euro ten and twenty-cent pieces – were scattered through the middle, along with several pink pigs.

Rav hopped hurriedly down from a chair as Kira caught sight of him, along with Alessandra's father, where they were standing by the door into the den. Looking warily up, Kira noted the bunch of mistletoe that they must have moved from the main entrance.

Mattia's sheepish look, when she glanced back to him, warmed her from the inside.

'You've been busy,' she commented.

'The other option was playing cards,' he said with a shrug. 'I hate cards.'

'I hope you'll stay and celebrate the new year with us tonight?' Rav asked. The invitation seemed sincere. Although she'd had to endure more pity – from him and all the others – than she was comfortable with, she had to acknowledge that nothing else had changed now everyone knew about Christian. She was still herself. She hadn't regressed to the impulsive and naive nineteen-year-old she'd been. There were other things on her mind right now – another person.

She didn't want to keep herself apart from everyone else tonight.

'I'm looking forward to it.'

When Rav and Signor Martinelli left the room, the urge to hug Mattia was nearly overpowering. 'Thank you,' she muttered. 'This is a great idea.'

'It wasn't my idea. It's New Year's Eve. Wedding or no wedding, we have to celebrate.'

'I suppose we do.' She could think of a few ways she'd like to do that, if Mattia would just come a little closer.

'There are all those evil spirits to scare away.'

'I thought your necklace took care of that?' she teased.

'On the last day of the year, you also need fire and red underwear to do the job.'

She dropped her gaze pointedly and his cheeks turned a nice colour to scare away more evil spirits. 'The evil spirits are scared of your red underwear?'

He grinned. 'Something like that. We also throw stuff out of the window in Naples – plates and small items of furniture. We have to make room for the new things.'

Before Kira could tease him, the door behind them banged open and Signora Martinelli bustled in with a salad, followed by Joe's mother. 'I have no idea what this is, but it smells divine!' Nadine declared.

Mattia leaned close to whisper, 'Zia Francesca probably doesn't know either, as the tins were all in German. She just doused everything in garlic and herbs and olive oil.'

As the doors opened and closed, guests bustling

through to build the potluck celebration of the year about to start in a manner none of them had expected, Kira groped for Mattia's hand, linking her fingers with his and leaning back against him, close enough to catch his indrawn breath.

Staring at the table but seeing nothing, time seemed to slow around her. She knew exactly who she wanted to kiss at midnight – and what memories she wanted to throw out of the window. It was what happened tomorrow that she was less certain of.

27

'It is so quiet here; we *must* make more noise!' Signor Martinelli declared, tapping his spoon against his glass.

Kira thought this Neapolitan New Year, snowed in at the Kitzingalm Hütte, had certainly been a noisy affair so far, despite the lack of electricity. Conversation never stopped, between Alessandra – perhaps a little desperately gregarious tonight – and her lively parents, who drew everyone into the conversation in a mix of Italian and halting English.

There were rousing serenades with a percussion accompaniment of knocking on the table. Mattia had allowed himself to be imposed upon for an occasional tune which at least gave Kira a breather from the whirlwind of conversation, even though it brought on the familiar ache in her chest when his voice wrapped around her heart.

He'd taken the seat next to her and her evening had been pleasantly punctuated by nudges from his elbow and the occasional brush of his fingers on her arm. Kira was less worried about the eyes on them, because everyone was carefully tiptoeing around Alessandra and Joe, sitting together at the other end of the table.

Ever since the disaster on the ski slopes, Joe had been subdued. He joined in with the conversation, but he only perked up on the occasions when Alessandra leaned close and said something softly just for him.

Francesca had found a single tin of mountain lentils and warmed it on the stove once more as the hour ticked towards midnight, setting the dish in the middle of the table with a flourish and the tangy scent of bay leaves.

'For good luck,' she explained to Nadine. 'I only wish we had more.' With a glance at the bride and groom, her meaning was clear.

'We have some grapes,' Yolanda added, moving the bowl nearer to the bridal couple. 'There is a big clock in the hallway that will chime. You should feed each other one grape for each chime of the clock. That's what we do in Spain.'

'Some people at home do that too,' Carla added.

'I don't think there's enough luck for everyone this year,' Mattia muttered with a wry smile.

'Maybe I could find some raisins?' Yolanda suggested apologetically.

Mattia's melodramatic gag earned him a poke from her elbow, but Kira chuckled at him. 'I wouldn't eat raisins, even for luck.'

'You know what's strange,' Hugh piped up. 'Without that clock, we wouldn't even know when it's midnight, since all our phones are dead.'

'And we won't have any photos!' Tonya lamented.

'I could turn my phone on for a photo, I suppose,' Kira suggested. 'One photo won't take too much of the battery.'

By the time she'd got the old device switched on, the numbers on the screen read 23:59 and Yolanda dashed back into the dining room from the hallway, clapping her hands excitedly.

All eyes turned to Alessandra and Joe, the not-wedded couple, and Kira was dismayed to see tears in Alessandra's eyes. She'd never been so relieved to see a man step up, when Joe took her chin and turned her face to his, speaking urgently in a low voice.

A chime sounded from the hallway and Signor Martinelli raised his glass with a cheer. After four strikes to signal the hour, the moment stretched as they held their breath for a cue from the beleaguered bride and groom.

With a sniff, Alessandra fumbled for the bowl of grapes and at the first gong, she slipped one into Joe's mouth. The collective sigh of relief became rather manic amusement as the clock gonged much too quickly for the couple to eat their grapes. Alessandra laughed and a grape tumbled out of Joe's mouth as he joined her.

Kira groped for her phone and snapped a few hurried photos. The torchlight was dim, making the photos grainy and eerie. Candid wedding shots were hopefully on-trend.

'¡Dios mío!' Yolanda groaned, throwing up her hands.

'Don't worry, cara,' Francesca declared, coming at the couple with the bowl of lentils and dropping a spoonful into each mouth.

'Mamma!' Alessandra mumbled while chewing, but her mother ignored her, shovelling in another spoonful before handing the bowl to the others to share. Kira took more photos, capturing the guests passing around the bowl of humble lentils.

When it reached Mattia, he held it out to her first and she sneaked a photo of him, eyebrows up, chiselled features dramatic in the harsh light, peering at her from under those astonishing lashes. She wondered if she'd regret that photo later when she found herself mooning over it, long after they'd all gone home.

Setting down her phone, she picked up her fork and took some lentils as he said softly, 'Buon anno nuovo, Kira.'

'Happy New Year,' she whispered back.

A raucous cheer drew her attention back to the rest of the group and she saw Joe pulling Alessandra gently to her feet. Taking a deep breath, he picked up her hand and drew her into a slow waltz. He stumbled a few times without music, but Francesca clapped a gentle beat and her husband hummed a well-known tune.

After giving her a twirl, he pressed his forehead to hers and whispered something that made her smile through the tears tumbling down her cheeks.

'I promise we'll have an amazing wedding, with every detail perfect, because that's what you deserve, Alessandra.'

Carla snorted a sob and Nadine was dabbing at her eyes.

'Oh look, mistletoe!' Joe said in mock surprise. He pressed a soft, lingering kiss onto Alessandra's lips to a chorus of cheering and raised glasses.

It appeared they would have a wedding after all, as soon as the snow cleared. Alessandra wouldn't be jilted at the altar. Kira would have to stand there awkwardly in her dress and face Christian while trying to keep it together.

Then the next day, they'd all go home, as though nothing had changed. Nothing *had* changed. She had her crags and her adventures, friends who couldn't hurt her. She'd only held hands with him – that was all.

She stood with a huff, trying to clear her self-pity, and mumbled something about checking on the wood-burning stoves. She could feel Mattia behind her, narrowly evaded the touch of his hand on her arm. What was she even doing, leaning on him?

Trying to squeeze past Alessandra and Joe surreptitiously, she was appalled to hear Carla's voice.

'Kira, wait!'

'Hmm?' was all she managed in reply.

The bridesmaid's tentative smile only confused Kira. 'You're standing under the mistletoe.'

Her throat clogged. Her shoulder brushed something – or rather someone – standing equally still just behind her and she heard his gulp.

Alessandra laughed. 'Yes, go on, Matty. The two of you have been wonderful today, making all of this happen.'

Kira's cheeks were unbearably hot, her chest tight. What would Reshma say about this, given that the bride had now dictated a kiss? Glancing warily up at Mattia, she found his head already ducked towards her.

'Okay?' he whispered.

She nodded curtly and squeezed her eyes shut. They'd done this before. He only had to give her a quick peck—

Her eyes flew open, wondering if she should have offered her cheek, whether he was embarrassed to kiss her in front of his friends. He was very close, his eyelids heavy, the sharp lines of his face as familiar as the citrus-and-honey scent of him. Catching the alarm in her expression, he paused, then lifted a hand to her cheek.

It was that touch she couldn't resist. Her eyes falling closed again, she lifted her chin and met him in the middle.

* * *

Mattia felt as though he could power the house, his nerves were crackling so rigorously through his body. He'd been thinking about kissing Kira all day, nearly done it on several occasions. Alessandra's family was watching, expecting, but he was mainly thinking about Kira, about the emotions that she didn't realise flickered on her face and in her voice, her layers of strength and softness – and the dismay on her face when she started questioning herself.

So he soothed her with his thumb on her cheek and honoured her with a slow kiss. He'd worked it out now, the way he could steal her breath with a hint of pressure, the perfect angle to seal his open mouth to hers so she melted with him.

Her fingers fisted in his sleeves. The softest noise of frustrated restraint reached his ears and his thoughts blurred. Kissing her brought something to life, something he hadn't known he needed.

His hand slipped from her cheek to her neck, his thumb finding a pulse point that made his own heart leap. Following blind instinct, he opened his mouth further against hers and sparks ignited under his skin as he flicked his tongue along her lip.

She jerked back with a breathy, 'Whoa,' steadying

him – or herself – with her hands on his waist. Risking a glance at the wedding party, he glimpsed Alessandra's frozen, slack-jawed incredulity and wished he hadn't.

Kira turned, tripping over her own feet. 'I was— Fireplace lighting. Stoves. Night – not cold.' Lifting her chin, she took off out the door.

Alessandra snapped out of her shocked stupor more quickly than Mattia was prepared for. 'What was—?'

He pointed firmly at the door Kira had disappeared through. 'I'm going to—' He pointed again when no words came, then dashed out after her, refusing to imagine what the others would say when he was gone.

'Kira!' he called after her.

She didn't stop, so he followed her onto the stairs. 'Unless you want them to think we're jumping into bed together, you should go back down,' she said gruffly.

At the top of the stairs, he reached for her hand and tugged her to a stop. She didn't turn. 'I don't want to go back down. But I will if that's what you want – I mean if you *don't* want...'

'Mattia,' she began with a huff, her voice thick, 'are you suggesting we *actually*...' She shook herself and tugged him along the hallway to his room, barging inside, since he hadn't bothered locking the door.

As she leaned on the wall studying him warily, he was reminded of the night in Salzburg, when her uneven features had intrigued him, woken something in him, but he'd had no idea he would be here with her like this, just four days later.

'You don't do casual,' she reminded him steadily.

'With you, I could.' There was a lot more he could say, but he didn't want to spook her.

Her indrawn breath echoed in his ears. 'I don't—' She bit her lip against a wobble in her voice. 'I won't be your soulmate.'

'I know.' She had her feet too firmly on the ground to believe in that.

'Are you sure I won't... hurt your feelings?' She grimaced at her own word choice.

He took a step closer, enjoying the way she couldn't hide her reaction when they were near each other. He shook his head. 'I can take responsibility for my own feelings.'

Her faint smile made him stand a little straighter. His blood coursed through his veins as though pressurised, as though he were on stage – except he was playing *himself*, a version of himself, anyway. One he liked.

Holding her gaze while a giddy smile contorted his features and adrenaline surged, he marvelled at the absence of worries or embarrassment or insecurity.

And then she said the sweetest word he'd heard all day. 'Okay.'

28

This wasn't remotely a good idea. In no universe did she belong in this room, with this man – who was currently inhaling deeply at her neck, turning her spine to custard. But when she slipped one hand up his back, and another into his hair, her palms recognised him.

With you, I could...

Under the circumstances, she figured Reshma's rule book no longer applied.

It wasn't in her nature, but she knew she had to let him dictate the pace, manage his own comfort zone, so she held on and bore it as the gust of his breath, the warmth of his body drew her own feelings to the surface. He touched her as though memorising her, lingering at her jaw, pausing every now and again to meet her wide-eyed gaze and kiss her as though she were the one needing reassurance.

She had to pull away to stoke the fire in the stove and add more wood and he used the time to fetch a condom from the bathroom, but instead of the interruption awkwardly halting their progress, she turned to find him peeling off his pullover and reaching for the buttons of his shirt – no hesitation.

The fact that she'd seen him almost naked before only made her less patient. Her fingers skimmed his skin before he'd even freed his arms from the sleeves. His chest heaved at the touch. Tucking herself close, she soaked up the warmth, the familiarity of his body and pressed a kiss to his sternum without thought, then another when he swayed on his feet and groped for her to steady himself.

'Ahi,' he whispered, pressing a kiss to the top of her head and spearing his fingers though her hair. 'I think I need to sit down.'

He tugged her with him to the bed, sitting on the edge and pulling her between his knees with a casual intimacy that rang alarm bells somewhere deep and distant in Kira's mind. His easy touch wasn't practised, informed by previous experiences with other women.

It was *genuine*, a response to the fragile feelings he spilled everywhere.

She might regret it later, but that insight spurred her on, rather than giving her the wisdom to withdraw, keep things light. Peeling off her fleece, the thermal base layer followed quickly. When she would have rushed ahead to her bra – the same simple design as the one she'd been wearing when they'd arrived – his hands stopped her and a groan made its way up from deep in his chest.

'I was not prepared that time in the van,' he murmured. 'I shouldn't have peeked – I tried not to.' Trailing a hand up her arm and along her shoulder blade, his eyes avidly following its progress, he licked his lips and continued. 'But look at you.' His voice was high and breathy. 'So soft and strong and beautiful.'

The urge to laugh rose in her chest – or was it the urge to cry? Men had admired her breasts before, but usually with cruder language. Running her fingers through his hair, she brought him close, until his chin lined up with the seam of her bra.

God, *he* was beautiful, with his intent gaze and expressive mouth. After studying her for a dangerous moment where she began to wonder what he saw, he dropped his gaze and pressed kisses to her skin, along the edge of her bra.

The kisses were almost chaste, except for the occasional swipe with the tip of his tongue, but the pull of desire flared through her, hot and sharp. By the time he helped her shed her bra, her breath was ragged and she was desperate for more.

He didn't make her wait, closing his mouth over her nipple with a grunt of relief that matched her sigh.

None of this felt like an awkward first time. She didn't have to tell him what she liked, because he heard every involuntary sigh, every hitched inhale – every gasp. She told him everything with her breath, with noises from the back of her throat that might have embarrassed her with anyone else, but she could tell by his choked response that he liked them.

It was easy to let go and allow him the intimacy of hearing because she couldn't hold in everything she was feeling at the glorious press of his body against her, then over her and, after a fumble with the condom, inside her.

He buried his face in her neck, his body strung taut, and she wrapped her arms and legs around him as though holding him together. Locked tight to each other, her hurtful past and lonely future seemed distant and abstract.

Only the moment existed: the tickle of his hair on her face; clumsy kisses to her throat; an urgent touch pulling her knee up and the unthinking perfection of her own body's response. She could see from his rigid jaw and heavy eyelids that he was holding on by a thread.

As he pressed one last, desperate kiss to her lips, she encouraged them both over, soaking up every shudder and gasp.

He remained close, panting heavily, long enough for Kira to notice the gaping crack in her defences. He might have been sweeter and more earnest than anyone she'd ever been intimate with, but the next part was always painful and this time, it could be doubly awkward.

She only hoped he didn't open his mouth. Whatever he said right now was sure to make everything worse – one way or another.

* * *

The temptation to hold on – to her, to the connection – was strong, but Mattia knew he had to let her withdraw. He'd agreed to casual, even though he wasn't quite sure he'd achieved it in the end.

He flopped onto his back, lacking the energy to even pull the duvet over his naked body, while Kira sat up, her beautiful, bare back to him, and rummaged for her underwear.

'Every time I hear the crackle of a fire, I'm going to think of you and get turned on.'

She stilled and he made out the soft sound of her blinking. '*That's* what you have to say right now?'

'I didn't think anything else would be... appropriate.'

'Well, I'm glad you have a different association with fire now.' She shoved her thermal shirt over her head without bothering with her bra.

'I think... I have a different association with sex.'

She was in the middle of tugging her underwear up her legs and she stumbled, scowling at him.

'A positive association – a *casual* one,' he insisted, rolling onto his side to give her a reassuring look. 'That was... I've never been so good in bed before.'

She snorted a laugh. '*You've* never been so good in bed before?'

'That's what I meant. Because of *you*, I was—' He gave up when she only laughed harder. He rolled onto his back in defeat. 'Will you at least come back to bed and pretend I'm not the only one completely wrecked?'

Her laughter puttered out and he inwardly winced. 'Mattia,' she began, warning in her tone.

He flung out an arm and snagged the waistband of her underwear, just lightly. Tugging too hard – holding too tight – would only send her running. 'To keep warm,' he pointed out, although the roaring fire in the stove – crackling pleasantly – had heated the room a little past comfortable. 'Casual body heat.'

'I'm not a snuggler,' she insisted, although the way she practically purred when he rubbed a hand up her back suggested she was only fooling herself with those words.

'You're not a snuggler; you're not a wedding plan-ner,' he teased lightly. 'What *are* you, Kira Watling?'

'A loner,' she insisted, slipping out of his reach.

Mattia sobered at her words. He had to take her at face value, even though he felt more than a glimmer of doubt. For a loner, she'd allowed him very close.

She pulled up her technical trousers and perched on the bed to adjust her socks, sitting up to run a hand over her tousled blue hair. It was still in a ponytail, but was barely recognisable as such, most of it now in loose, wild strands around her head.

'Do you dye it blue so people don't have a chance to judge the real you?'

She stiffened and he snapped his mouth shut a few seconds too late. The thought had just tumbled out. He hadn't considered whether she wanted to talk about this right now.

'If that's true, it's not working. You... all the others – you've found out more about me than my oldest friends know.'

His stomach dropped as he realised she was thinking about her ex, about the unwelcome reunion – whenever they made it down the mountain.

'How are you feeling? About seeing him?'

She glanced over her shoulder at him. 'Maybe a little better now,' she answered with a dark chuckle.

'Well, I'm glad of... that.'

The mattress dipped as she shifted closer and he propped himself up on one arm to meet her wary gaze. Lifting a hand haltingly, she brushed her finger-tips over his cheek and he wasn't sure whether to beg for more or berate her for touching him in such a pa-tronising manner after everything they'd just shared.

'I hope you find your soulmate. You're capable of it.'

He frowned. 'You think you're not?' She'd loved Christian enough to hurt for twelve years.

'It's a bit too late for me to believe.'

She stood before he could formulate a rebuttal. He hauled himself upright, reaching for her hand – when a distant roar made him pause and listen.

'Do you hear that?' he asked, alarm zipping up his spine as the rumble grew louder, punctuated by a crack that made him jump.

'I heard *that*!' Kira groped for him, hauling him up. 'Away from the window!' Pulling him into the corner away from the fire, she threw herself over him just as a resounding crash broke the silence of the early hour and he thought he felt the walls shake.

A moment later, the eerie mountain quiet descended again – muted and immense. Kira exhaled on a long breath, her expression tight. Glancing around as though to check that everything was still standing around them, she moved off him.

'That was a few minutes too late to feel the earth move,' he blurted out. 'What just happened?'

The grim light in her eyes told him Alessandra's wedding had just gone from hell to hell frozen over. 'An avalanche. Come on, we have to check on the others!'

29

Kira burst out of Mattia's room, racing for the stairs, but she stopped short when her gaze snagged on the door to her own room – off its hinges and teetering on a pile of snow, *in* the hallway.

'Che cazzo!' she heard behind her.

Stepping slowly towards the rubble of snow and rocks, she caught sight of her own suitcase, bent and knocked open, stuck halfway out of the doorway. Shards of glass and wood from the window frame were scattered at the sides. The beds must have been under there somewhere, but they were buried to the last inch.

A squeeze of her hand brought her racing thoughts back to the present. 'I'm even more glad you were with me.' The thought of what might have happened if she'd gone to bed alone instead of making the reckless choice to share the last hour with Mattia made her legs wobbly. 'It was only this side of the building.'

'You should stay back,' was all she said in reply. 'There's glass. Get some shoes on! No wait, go downstairs. I don't know if the floor is stable.' An alarming creak sounded from somewhere in the guts of the building.

'What about you?'

A door flew open at the end of the hall and a white-faced Carla emerged. 'What's happ—' She shrank back when she saw the rubble pouring from Kira and Ginny's room.

On a hiss and a crash, a secondary snowslip threw powdered ice into the air around them and Carla ran for the stairs with a squeal. The wedding guests had all been given rooms on the other side of the hotel with a view, meaning they were probably safe—

A terrifying thought occurred to Kira and she raced for the stairs after Carla, hoping Mattia was following her down to safety. Rushing through the hallway on the ground floor, she skidded to a stop in front of the door marked 'Privat' and pushed it open.

'Yolanda!'

The staff area was a mess, the back wall of the chalet caved in. The door to the bedroom hung open and Kira hurtled inside to see a mass of snow. She'd never had to do this outside of training, but the dread didn't allow her to hesitate. She scanned the room, guessing where a bed might have been, and with no tool available, she used her hands to shift the snow as quickly as she could, her lungs stinging with the exertion.

She registered voices behind her, but she knew every second counted when there might be a person trapped under the snow.

'Is Yolanda out there?' she called out, panic rising in her throat because she hadn't moved nearly enough snow yet. 'Someone come and help me!'

'She's not in the kitchen!' she heard Joe calling and then another pair of hands joined hers – fine, small hands with a giant diamond on the left ring finger.

'Make sure everyone else is accounted for!' Kira yelled back to Joe, just as her hand struck something harder and smoother than the snow. 'Here!'

She and Alessandra worked frantically, uncovering part of the bedframe. Kira punched at the ice to dislodge it and as she dug down, her hand found fabric. *Please let it just be bedclothes. Let her be somewhere else – safe!*

With a grunt of effort, she hauled away a drift of snow and choked to see Yolanda's uniform shirt. 'Her head! We have to clear her head! Someone call the emergency services!'

'I'm already on the call,' came a calm response.

Another pair of hands joined them and a moment later, Yolanda's face emerged from under the snow – pale and still.

'Keep clearing the snow off her and get blankets! Does anyone else know CPR?' As soon as Yolanda's chest was clear of snow, Kira was already climbing into position, checking for breathing and trying not to panic when there was none – and no pulse. Her focus narrowed and she locked her fingers to begin chest compressions, shutting out everything except the numbers counting up on her lips, refusing to wonder how long it had been since Yolanda had last taken a breath.

Kira reached thirty and leaned down to deliver a rescue breath. With a sudden jerk, Yolanda's mouth dropped open and a strangled cough emerged from her throat. Kira's blood rushed with relief, so hot and sharp that her vision blurred with tears.

'Get her on her side. More blankets! We have to keep her warm. Is there someone coming to help?'

Yolanda continued to breathe in choking gasps,

but Alessandra soothed a hand over her hair as blankets were piled on top of her and the remaining snow cleared.

'There's a paramedic coming with a helicopter. They'll be about ten minutes.' The same calm voice from earlier reached through Kira's adrenaline fog and she looked up in confusion to see Mattia standing in the doorway, his pullover on backwards and her own phone in his hand.

Kira would never have expected Mattia to keep his head in a crisis, but it seemed everyone had been underestimating him for a long time – including himself.

Her coat fell around her shoulders and he was suddenly closer, urging her in the direction of the hallway.

'We'd better get outside in case there's damage to the building,' he said to the rest of the group. 'Joe, can you and Rav move Yolanda?'

The front door was impassable, but the side door was free, although the sauna had disappeared under a pile of snow. The beleaguered wedding party stumbled out into the clear night to await rescue, dragging out a chair for the weak and shivering Yolanda.

When the shock of the cold entered Kira's lungs, the enormity of what had happened over the past half hour flooded her synapses and she shivered uncontrollably. 'I-I've never had to d-do that before in r-real life,' she stammered. 'Only in training.' None of her expeditions or tours as a guide had ended as disastrously as this wedding.

The whump-whump of a helicopter sounded overhead, lights flashing as the aircraft banked in search of the nearby helipad. It was over. Everyone was safe.

She hadn't noticed Mattia's arms settle around her, but then her forehead was pressed to his chest and his fingers were at the back of her neck. He was muttering something, low and smooth and rhythmic and it didn't matter that she didn't understand the language.

'Shhhh, Kira,' he said on a sigh, the concern in his voice tipping her off to the hot tears streaming down her cheeks.

'Alessandra was amazing,' she choked out. 'She was supposed to be thinking about bows and favours and that shit and instead she s-saved a life. H-how awesome is that?'

The bride was now enveloped in the groom's arms, her hair damp and bedraggled, her expression pained. Rav and Carla were crouched by Yolanda, supporting her and keeping her wrapped up tight while they waited.

'*You* were supposed to be here to help with bows and favours and shit, but lucky for us, you're an adventure guide and not a wedding planner.' Mattia's arms tightened around Kira. 'The right place at the right time. Exactly the right person – just as you are.'

Closing her eyes and letting the strain of the evening wash through her, trusting that Mattia would hold her up when her legs grew wobbly, she marvelled that he was the right person at the right time as well. Only this, the strangest set of circumstances, could have brought together a grumpy adventure guide and a sensitive, clumsy opera singer to grow an intimacy she would never have thought possible – one she would never forget.

Wavering lights in the distance announced the arrival of their rescuers, but Kira clutched Mattia's arm, refusing to move for a moment longer. He might be the right person, but how long did they have this 'right time' magic? Would he still hold her when they arrived down in the valley?

What if he wanted to stay in touch? Could she risk all the uncertainty of that?

'Kira!'

She snapped her head up, startled by the voice she knew well, the familiar figure jogging in her direction. He paused, taking in Mattia, his expression contorting with alarm.

'Are you all right?'

Reluctantly stepping out of Mattia's arms, she approached her friend and threw her arms around him. The tight – almost too tight – hold made her heart squeeze, but not the way her loopy heart bumped in her chest when Mattia looked at her.

'I'm all right. What are you doing here?' she asked as two paramedics rushed past to take charge of Yolanda, preparing a stretcher to load her into the helicopter to be evacuated first.

'We drove up yesterday as soon as I heard you were stuck here. I discussed the situation with the mountain rescue team. I was coming up to get you today, as soon as it was safe.'

She hugged him tight again, remembering all the reasons why Great Heart was her family. 'I didn't need rescuing, but it's nice to know you had my back.'

'I'm not surprised *you* were the one doing the rescuing,' he said with a gruff laugh. His smile dimmed when he looked over at Mattia. 'But who is he?'

She extricated herself and gestured awkwardly in Mattia's direction. 'This is... the opera singer.' How inadequate that introduction was.

'The opera singer?'

'Mattia, this is my friend Andreas.'

30

Mattia was reeling from the range of experiences the night had shot at him: suspense at dinner, wondering whether Kira would talk to him; the beautiful moments when they'd done much more than talk; the sudden emergency; and now, the harsh lighting of a hospital waiting room, seated next to a stranger of few words and many, many muscles.

Kira's bed friend. Both of them had been her bed friends.

She'd shrugged off all offers of help and waited until first Yolanda and then Alessandra, Joe and their parents had been airlifted from the chalet to Innsbruck to be checked at the hospital. Only then had she reluctantly showed the rescue officers her scratched and bleeding hands and allowed them to escort her to the helicopter.

Mattia still wasn't sure how he'd managed to remain standing under the hot, disapproving look from Kira's 'friend' in the helicopter. Possibly, he should have handed her over to Andreas to look after her, but he was the one who'd held her while she shuddered in the aftermath of giving life-saving first aid. He didn't imagine she would run back into his arms, but he would stay until she told him she didn't want him there – at the very least until she came out of the treatment room.

'You made the emergency call?'

The question from Andreas broke the silence in the waiting room out of nowhere, making Mattia jump. 'Yes,' he managed to answer. 'She was... busy. It was lucky her phone wasn't in her room, as it was the only one charged.' The way the man looked at him, Mattia felt as though he stood in the witness box.

'What do you mean?' Andreas asked.

'We didn't have electricity. She only charged hers—'

'I mean about her phone not being in her room?'

Mattia's throat closed and he bit his lip, his mind racing for an appropriate response. 'Her room was on the wrong side of the building. It's basically full of snow now.'

He didn't miss Andreas's indrawn breath. He might have been a frightening figure, but his obvious concern for Kira settled Mattia's nerves. But the next question brought a fresh blush of heat to his cheeks. 'She got out in time?'

Opening his mouth, he grimaced before answering, 'She wasn't in her room.'

Andreas's only response was a tic in his jaw. Mattia looked away, tapping his foot compulsively, imagining various disapproving – or threatening – things that might be running through her friend's mind.

What he eventually said was nothing like any of the scenarios Mattia had prepared himself for. 'I didn't know. About this guy – her ex. I thought she was just scared of commitment like the rest of us. I didn't realise she'd been hurt.'

'I'm sure she didn't want you to know.'

Andreas looked at him askance. 'Are you giving me sympathy?'

'You obviously... care a lot...' Mattia cleared his throat. 'As a friend.'

'Of course as a friend. My fiancée is currently on her way here.'

Mattia wasn't sure if Andreas realised how his

chest puffed up when he said that word. He was obviously one of these cavemen who were too scared to admit they wanted love and then grabbed it by the neck when it finally found them.

He probably should have kept silent, but he was tired and high on Kira's attention to him, so he continued. 'But she told me about you.'

That earned him a dark look. 'What are you trying to say?'

He came right out with it. 'I like her. If things were different...'

Andreas's expression turned reflective. 'Are you going to make things different?'

The words gave Mattia a start. He *couldn't* change the things that would keep them apart once they left Tyrol. That was up to Kira. And yet...

In a flurry of a woollen coat, scarf and subtle perfume, a woman rushed to where they were sitting, making Andreas leap out of his chair to catch her. The fiancée. She was blonde and pretty, but with a chin that suggested she could keep him in line.

Grasping his lapels, she asked, 'How is she? Can we see her? I picked Ginny up because she was beside herself with worry. Apparently, their room was completely destroyed, all of their belongings buried under the snow!'

Ginny approached at a more sedate pace, smiling a weak greeting at Mattia. 'You're still here, you poor thing. Alessandra texted that she and her parents are settled into a hotel here in Innsbruck. I don't know how I'll be able to make it up to her!'

'She won't expect you to,' Mattia attempted, but Ginny was obviously too worked up to take anything in.

Turning to Andreas, she said, 'I hate to think what might have happened if we'd been in the room, especially after poor Yolanda—' She cut herself off with a choke.

Andreas's fiancée drew back with a frown. 'It's lucky that Kira wasn't in the room.'

Mattia's face heated afresh and he looked anxiously to the double doors Kira had disappeared through too long ago.

'Very lucky,' Andreas responded drily, with a look in Mattia's direction that he felt in his skin.

He was saved by those doors opening, Kira finally appearing with her jacket over her arm and both hands wrapped in bandages. He rushed at her, but unfortunately, he wasn't the only one with that idea.

The two women wrapped her in a hug before he could reach her.

'Thank *God*!'

'You are everyone's hero!'

'We officially need a guide on board for *every* wedding from now on!'

She met his gaze with a small smile and he felt immediately lighter. The faint rumble of her stomach reached his ears, reminding him of the evening they'd met – grumpy, hungry Kira who'd still saved him from a fridge worse than death.

So, he took a risk. Lifting his brow in invitation, he held out a hand. 'Come on,' was all he said, softly. 'Food.'

While her friends looked on, mouths ajar, Kira's smile blossomed fully and she came to him, letting him help her with her jacket.

Glancing back at her colleagues, she said, 'We'll talk later today, hmm? Thanks for coming.'

'Always.'

'Any time.'

Andreas added in a low grumble, 'Even when we're not needed, it seems,' that he probably hadn't intended anyone to hear.

Ushering her towards the exit, he heard Andreas's fiancée marvel, 'Did she just leave with the opera singer?'

'Reshma said she'd kissed him, the dark horse. I had no idea!' Ginny added.

'Pretty sure they did more than kiss,' Andreas said, 'since she was in his room when the avalanche hit.'

'That's official: mistletoe doesn't work,' Ginny declared. 'They got together even without it and absolutely *nothing* happened for me while I was stuck in Mayrhofen with a car full of it.'

'I like your friends,' Mattia commented as the conversation behind them faded into the background noise. 'Even if Andreas is a little scary.'

'He's really not,' she said with a snort.

'You didn't see him when he worked out why you weren't in your room when the avalanche hit.'

'Yikes,' she said with an apologetic glance. 'But it's none of his business.' She glanced at her feet. 'I can't believe they came all this way to check on me.'

'It's not every day you narrowly avoid an avalanche by having amazing sex.'

She nudged him with her shoulder. 'You don't have to look after me.'

'I know,' he assured her, 'but I like it.' *I like you.* 'You don't have to hang out with me if you don't want to, of course.'

'I know,' she repeated. After a pause and a tentative glance up at him, she continued, 'But I like it.'

* * *

Kira stirred from the sleep of the dead, slapping a hand over her ear to shut out the pounding in her head. Her pillow was soft and the bed incredibly comfortable and warm. Her subconscious was telling her that she hadn't a care in the world and sleep was such a beautiful, delicious experience, especially with her body pressed against another, all smooth skin and heady tenderness.

But the other body shifted, first the legs and then a hand nudged her to the side, making her protest the loss of her comfort human, although she was too tired to give more than a forlorn grumble when he got out of bed.

The pounding stopped, but she heard voices and realised it hadn't been in her head. Someone was at the door. She still wasn't sure if she cared.

Amidst a rush of Italian that sounded as though it were in double time, she heard her own name and finally roused.

'She's here?' That was a deeper voice, in English: Joe.

'Why is *Kira* in your bed?' If Alessandra thought she was speaking in a hushed tone, she was mistaken.

'I think the answer to that should be obvious,' Joe muttered.

'Are you *together*?'

She didn't need superhuman hearing to catch the strangled sound Mattia made in response.

'Mattia!'

'We've been through this, Ale,' he said, his tone pained. 'Don't worry about me. I'm all grown up. If I want to have a casual relationship with someone, it's not going to break my heart.'

Kira stilled, all thoughts of rolling over and announcing that she was awake flying from her mind. His words didn't change anything. She'd been at pains to remind him that she didn't want a serious relationship. She *didn't* want a serious relationship. But... hearing him say it wrenched at some new, vulnerable growth in the vicinity of her heart.

It appeared he'd learned how to do casual just when Kira was wondering if she could try something a little more intimate. Who was she kidding? All of their time together had been more intimate than any casual relationship she'd ever had. Their very first conversation had had more depth than most of the things she discussed with her closest friends.

All the more reason to keep her distance now. If his words could hurt after only five days – words that weren't unexpected – how much more could he hurt her in the future? It was lucky they'd say goodbye in a matter of days – perhaps even hours.

'I suppose it's lucky she's here, anyway. I wanted to let you know we're meeting Ginny in the lobby in twenty minutes.'

'What for?'

Alessandra's sigh was pained and full of feeling. 'If there's one thing I see clearly after all of this, it's that I want to marry Joe – as soon as possible. I don't care if it can't be exactly as I envisioned it. I just want us to finally be a family. Everything else is only a detail.'

Kira heard a light smack that was probably a kiss from Joe and she gagged, thankful they thought she was asleep. The wedding nonsense wasn't over yet. She hadn't escaped all the romantic rubbish – perhaps it had even got worse, now they were so desperate to marry.

She'd have to put back on her ill-fitting wedding planner hat and pretend it didn't all make her uneasy, especially now she'd walked too close to the fire, by starting to feel something for Mattia.

'Okay,' she heard Mattia saying. 'We'll meet you downstairs then.' And with a click, the door closed on the bridal couple, leaving her alone with her *casual sexual partner.*

She heard rustling from the vicinity of the doorway, then a creak that made her imagine him leaning on the door.

'I know you're awake, Kira.'

She groaned, rolling over to face him. He was shirtless, his jeans hanging off his hips with the top button undone, barefoot – and utterly delicious, her fallen angel with his dark curls, hunched shoulders and tall figure.

'How much did you hear?'

'Enough,' she said, her voice rough. She hoped he thought she meant about Alessandra's wishes and not his bald summary of their relationship. 'I'd better get dressed.'

'I'm sorry, you'll have to see Christian after all – unless perhaps he had to go home rather than wait for the rescheduled wedding.'

Oh, Christ, she'd forgotten. But at least the horror at the prospect had paled in comparison to the rest of the wedding disasters and she was so sick of feeling embarrassed and out of place.

'No such luck. Ginny told me the photographer got stuck at the airport with all flights grounded. I'm pretty sure he'll still be here.'

'But we'll all stand behind you, now we know what happened.'

Oh fuck, everyone knew what had happened.

'Ehi, carissima,' he said with a chuckle. She heard footsteps and then a thud and when she opened her eyes, he'd dropped down beside the bed. 'Your pride is a wonderful, powerful thing, but it's okay that we know. You're human like the rest of us.'

'Sometimes, I think you're not,' she mumbled, 'with your sensitive soul and other-worldly voice. You're more angel than human.'

'In that case, you're lucky angel physiology is compatible with humans, because—'

She swiped the pillow from his side and walloped him with it before he could finish the sentence. Laughing, he climbed back onto the bed, pinning her beneath him as he leaned down for a slow kiss.

Kira hesitated, wondering if she should let him kiss her now she had an inkling of how bruised her heart would be when they said goodbye, but no part of her truly wanted to stop him. One soft kiss became several longer ones, her thoughts blurring and her body warming just from the lazy, teasing, coaxing press and tug of his lips. She darted her tongue out to find his bottom lip and he groaned, allowing the kiss to heat only for a heartbeat before pulling away, resting his forehead on her sternum.

'Why couldn't she have said an hour instead of twenty minutes?'

She struggled to sit up, urging him off her. 'I don't even know what time it is.'

'I don't care,' he pouted. 'I was enjoying being human with you.'

He'd made her a little too human, since she could already feel herself cracking. He peered at her, his dangerous, sensitive hearing tipping him off to her strange mood.

'It'll be okay,' he said, obviously not quite understanding her turmoil. 'You saved someone's life today. Don't let that turd Christian make you feel any less than you are.'

She studied him, tracing her bandaged thumb over his cheek. No matter what happened after Alessandra's wedding, she'd discovered she wasn't as broken as she'd always thought. There was still life in the old organ taking up space in her chest.

'I'll have to try. I've spent twelve years allowing him to have an impact on my life. Maybe it's time I stopped.'

31

If Kira had learned anything about weddings in her fledgling career working alongside Ginny and Sophie, it was that there was always chaos. Perhaps the two weddings she'd worked on so far had been particularly disastrous, one featuring a surprise Lake Garda thunderstorm and the next interrupted by an avalanche. She'd rarely had such bad luck on her adventure trips.

But in both of those cases, she also couldn't deny that love had proved resilient in the end. Or lovers were particularly proud and stubborn.

Getting Alessandra and Joe's nuptials off the ground had taken the entire team of I Do and Great

Heart working together. Willard and Reshma had pulled strings over the phone while Kira had slept off her rocky night and even Tita and Toni back in the office had been glued to their emails, helping with last-minute arrangements.

Andreas, it turned out, was well connected with the municipality of the ski area, since he lived only three hours away and the mountaineering community was a small fraternity. He'd helped Sophie secure the folk museum as an alternative location for the wedding reception and Ginny and Kira had cobbled together catering from various local restaurants.

The biggest challenge had been the photographer, who'd had to fly out again to her next gig, now the runway was clear. With Tita muttering over the phone about her constant battle with photographers, I Do had finally prevailed upon Rhys to return for the ceremony and reception. He hadn't even left Tyrol after accompanying them to the glacier, so it had made sense, even though Kira wished they'd been able to respect his genuine reservations about photographing wedding guests.

To everyone's relief, arrangements fell into place – perhaps missing some of the smaller details – for the second of January, only two days late.

Other guests had given up their rooms for the bride and her parents so she didn't have to travel on the big day. The rest of them had taken whatever they could find in Mayrhofen and hoped the little road winding through the valley would stay open, which looked likely, since the area hadn't seen a single flake since New Year's Eve.

The list of tasks was endless for the day of the wedding, but Kira enjoyed the busyness and the camaraderie, especially now the ambience was 'make do' rather than 'absolute perfection'.

She would never have expected to wake up on the morning of the wedding and join in with a quiet sunrise yoga session. The two of them didn't quite fit on Mattia's mat, which had been salvaged from the chalet by Andreas and the mountain rescue volunteers, along with the rest of his things, but the hotel carpet was soft enough to manage and they only occasionally poked each other with an outstretched hand or foot – and only even more occasionally on purpose, usually after Mattia had patronised her with uplifting yoga-speak that only made her more determined *not* to connect with her centre.

'And lift,' he said smoothly as they transitioned from a warrior pose to a side angle, 'the corners of your mouth.'

'Fuck you,' Kira replied lightly, her balance wavering. She wasn't great at holding still without a goal.

'You can take that energy,' he continued in his infuriating yoga teacher voice, 'and wrap it up in a lovely, big bow.'

She eyed him, trying not to be impressed by how his lean muscles tensed and relaxed.

'In a few hours, you can give that present to that fucking bastard Christian.'

Kira collapsed onto the mat, laughter causing her stomach muscles to give in. 'What kind of karma is that?'

'I'm pretty sure my baptism protects me from karma – and the curniciello.' The horn-shaped charm around his neck hung down towards the ground as he held a forward bend position.

She gave him a shove, but he remained infuriatingly stable. 'It doesn't protect *me*.'

'You're not Catholic?' he asked in mock horror.

'Of course I'm not Catholic!' She chuckled, but there was a little sting in the banter, realising it didn't matter if she was Catholic or not, because their relationship was casual.

'I could get you a curniciello, but I'm not sure you'd appreciate the other meaning: my mother's secret wish for grandchildren.'

'Whaaat?' She tumbled onto her bottom, imagining him one day with a bunch of kids. He'd be a great father, which was the strangest thought she'd ever had about *anyone*.

'It's a fertility charm, as well as warding off the evil eye,' he explained sheepishly. 'Luckily, we foiled it.'

'I think you should probably shut up now,' Kira said, not quite stifling her chuckle. 'But thanks for making me laugh about seeing Christian. You know when I brought Joe down in the cable car the day before New Year's Eve?'

'I was ordering pizza.'

'Yeah, I was thinking about what I told him. He had reservations about the marriage. Ginny tells me this is normal, as strange as it sounds. But I told him he could do anything he wanted after the wedding, as long as he actually turned up at the altar and didn't embarrass her.'

She crossed her legs on the carpet as she stared out the window at the slanted roofs of Mayrhofen, under a layer of marshmallow snow.

'What's wrong with that?' Mattia prompted gently.

'It was bad advice,' she insisted. 'Surely it's better for everyone involved if they *don't* get married, when there's a serious problem, something that might lead to divorce. That's heartbreak packaged up in bureaucracy.'

'That does sound bad.'

'Exactly. I realised I was thankful Christian hadn't gone through with it. He tried to explain it to me afterwards, but all I remember was something about me being a friend with boobs, so I definitely had a lucky escape.'

'I told you, he's a turd!'

'He is a turd,' she said softly, smiling at Mattia. 'I assume that's more poetic in Italian.'

'Poetic? No. Emphatic – yes. He's a stronzo, that's for certain.'

She nodded slowly. 'He's a stronzo, who destroyed my pride at a delicate age.' Her next words caught on her tongue and she couldn't bring herself to say them aloud. *But maybe he didn't kill my heart the way I thought he did?* 'He's *not* going to ruin Alessandra's wedding, though. And neither am I.'

'Did you really think you could?'

'I thought I could ruin certain aspects of the preparations, yes. But those aren't the things that matter, even for a bride like Alessandra. I'm starting to understand that.'

He sat next to her, his arms propped on his knees,

as a sprinkling of snow tumbled down past the window. 'This reminds me of the hotel in Salzburg,' he said softly. 'But no fridge.'

Turning from the window to regard him, she asked, 'What about your future? You'll be back in Salzburg in the summer, and then what?'

But he flashed her a tight smile. 'I'm sure I'll... land on my feet somewhere. Maybe I was holding onto Alessandra and her circle in Naples. I really was a hopeless teenager, trapped in my own fears and insecurities, but—' He shrugged. 'Things change. I have the chance to make more of my music career and I'll see where it takes me.'

She nearly regretted asking, when the answer was so clearly, *It won't take me to you.*

'Thanks for teaching me to chop wood and reminding me that sometimes, the solution is as simple as switching off the fridge.' He stared at his knees for a moment, spots of colour on his cheeks. 'And, you know, the sex.'

She gave him a shove. '*Do not* thank me for sex!'

He held up his hands in surrender. 'It was kind of life-changing. I had to say something.'

Kira's chest hurt. The pressure on her lungs was similar to being at altitude, but there should have been plenty of air in this room. It was Mattia and his wild ability to bring feelings up to her pores.

She patted his shoulder. 'Maybe you just needed an older woman,' she said as lightly as she could, hoping his hearing wouldn't betray the churning in her stomach.

Hauling herself to her feet and ignoring his doubtful snort in reply, she fetched her water bottle and took a long sip, glancing at her watch. Eight fifteen.

'I should get ready,' she said, shaking off the lingering effects of Mattia on her system. 'The wedding's in just over six hours. Hopefully, not enough time for anything else to go wrong.'

* * *

'You look great!' Ginny said as she squeezed Kira in a hug. The chirpy wedding planner wore a two-tone dress in baby blue and turquoise with a belt and heels and a diamond stud winking in her piercing. She was in her element, directing museum staff to rearrange furniture and checking – and double-checking – every last detail. *She* looked great. *She* was the real wedding planner. And yet...

Kira was some kind of wedding planner too – her

own kind. And she did look good. She wore a pair of neat trousers and a patterned, silky blouse that Mattia had helped her pick out – that did not require decorative knots to finish the look. Ginny must have also bought her outfit in Mayrhofen, since their luggage was ruined.

Kira wasn't wearing make-up. Mattia had silently dissuaded her with a hand gesture, his fingers at his neck. Although she'd scowled at him, the memory of the last time he'd seen her with make-up – seen her applying it poorly – and the knowledge that he thought she was fine without had lightened her mood.

It was difficult *not* to feel optimistic, now the wedding was on track after so many obstacles. There was only a light sprinkle of snow coming down – just enough for Alessandra's superstitions. The reception could take place in this historic farmhouse, under the low, wooden ceilings strung with pine boughs and holly, a roaring fire in the old, whitewashed stove.

It was perhaps more rustic than Alessandra had imagined, but Kira rather liked the charming building, its wooden balconies discoloured with age and many, many marriages in its history.

Ginny counted off on her fingers. 'I've checked on the caterers, Andreas is sorting out transport and Sophie's at the church performing CPR on the decorations— Oh fuck, that was a poor choice of words!'

'It's fine,' Kira assured her.

Ginny clutched her arm. 'And I'm under strict instructions not to let you lift anything with those hands!'

Although the scrapes had scabbed over, Kira's fingertips were still tender. 'I know my limits,' Kira insisted drily. 'You can tell Andreas to back off.'

Ginny's eyes widened. 'I could *never*! Anyway, I do have a job I need you to do.'

Of course she did, which was how Kira found herself spending the morning asking Carla and Joe and anyone else she could find what music to put into the wedding playlist, now they had to do without both the string quartet and the DJ.

Andreas had found a trumpet player and a clarinettist among the mountain rescue volunteers and, from Mattia's reports, the music for the ceremony was all arranged, but it was a big job ensuring hours of music for the reception – and making sure the sound system at the museum worked when required.

At lunchtime, Andreas appeared with an enormous tray of bread and cheeses, pickles, grilled vegetables and cured meat.

Ginny shoved bites into her mouth and chewed

while she worked ceaselessly on her tablet, stylus in hand. 'Where *is* Rhys?' she asked, her mouth full.

'Right here,' Kira's old friend mumbled from the opposite side of the room, where he was topping a piece of bread with grilled courgette.

'Oh, Christ, I didn't see you there!' Ginny exclaimed, her hand on her chest. 'You're always so *quiet!*' Kira saw her lips moving and suspected she was adding under her breath, *For someone so tall.*

His eyes lingered on Ginny, his expression grim, while Kira made her way over to him. With a nudge to his shoulder, she said, 'It's good of you to step in.'

'Don't tell me *you've* come to terms with this wedding stuff too, now? I'm only here today because of everything that's gone wrong.'

'The photos will be fine,' she said, cutting through to what she knew must be his concern. 'They understand you don't know anyone. The bride is the one in the white dress. The groom is the one with a fancy steel watch with a blue face. It will all be clear at the ceremony.'

His expression suggested he didn't share her confidence. 'I'll take the photos, but then I'm just sending them over. I don't want any commentary. And I'm never doing this again. Someone will have to explain that to the tenacious woman in the office at I Do.'

'Fair enough,' Kira replied, thinking of Tita, the whirlwind of an older woman who kept the administration running at I Do. 'You're an amazing photographer.' If his subject had been mountain peaks or caves, birds of prey or chubby little marmots, Rhys wouldn't have needed the encouragement, but Kira knew taking photos of people was far out of his comfort zone. Ginny probably thought he was simply a miserable person.

He was rather miserable, but he had his reasons.

Ginny approached and Rhys backed away rather conspicuously. Shooting him a puzzled look, Kira didn't have time to wonder why as Ginny grabbed her attention. 'It's just about time to head over to the chapel.'

Kira realised too late that Ginny had cornered her.

'Are you doing okay? I heard this story about your ex. It's a shitty coincidence.'

'I'm not going to ruin the wedding with my own drama, don't worry.'

'That's not what I'm worried about,' she said gently. 'I'd probably be throwing up in the corner if I had to see an ex while trying to run a wedding.'

'I have a strong stomach,' Kira replied curtly.

'I bet you do,' Ginny replied with something like

admiration in her tone – that Kira didn't want to accept at first. 'But we're all here to help if you need it.'

Kira sighed. 'To be honest, I just want to get it over with.'

Especially now she understood the greater hurt was still to come, when she woke up in her own bed at home with the knowledge that she was not going to see Mattia ever again.

32

T minus twenty minutes.

Half of the pews were full already and other guests were milling around, kissing friends and acquaintances on the cheek and probably doing exactly what they would have done at this wedding, if it had been at a bog-standard church wherever Joe had grown up.

Kira had to admit, though, that a bog-standard church was not Alessandra's style, and this way, the wedding took place on neutral ground.

The placid priest was speaking to Rav, Hugh and a very twitchy Joe in the corner by the gold icon. Thankfully, the holy father had dispensed with all of the possible funny hats he could have pulled out of his vestry, although he was wearing a robe with festive red panels and gold detailing. After having so much trouble deciding on her own outfit, Kira had to admit the priest was rocking his with very little apparent self-consciousness.

Recorded orchestral music subtly bolstered the mood from the four tiny Bluetooth speakers placed around the church. It wasn't a string quartet, but Sophie had known the perfect volume to set to enable comfortable conversation. More wedding magic Kira had yet to learn.

Everything was calm and organised, as serene as the spray of dusky-pink roses in the bower. Kira was shitting herself.

There had to be something she'd forgotten. There was still time to tactlessly ask Grandma how her dead husband was doing. Her phone might ring in the middle of the ceremony, even though she never had it set on anything other than vibrate because she couldn't stand all the pinging and beeps. She might accidentally stand in Rhys's line of sight while he tried to capture the big moment – or worse, sneeze right when they said 'I do.'

Her nose *was* itchy.

The only redeeming feature of her stress levels was that they were drowning out any residual concern she had about seeing Christian. She'd built the encounter up in her mind to apocalyptic proportions, but in comparison to what Joe and Alessandra had been through over the past few days, what was a twinge of hurt pride?

In comparison to what Kira had experienced over the past few days...

Deciding to ask Sophie if there were more last-minute jobs, she stomped to the back of the chapel, clenching and unclenching her fists. Sophie looked up, her expression carefully neutral and kind, looking poised and perfect from her chignon to her brand-name tablet and stylus.

If she hadn't seen Sophie soaked and bedraggled and officiating the world's most moving wedding ceremony with mud in her hair back in September, Kira wouldn't have liked her so much. But Sophie – and especially Ginny – had welcomed her on board with nothing but friendly and frank acceptance, even when she'd been resistant to the change and wary of... everything about this situation.

It didn't mean they'd be happy if Kira screwed up.

'Is there anything—?' Her gaze snagged on the altar and she thought of something to do. 'The candles. We haven't lit the candles.'

'Thanks,' Sophie said. 'And Kira?'

Kira skidded to a stop and turned.

'No matter how things go, it's too late to worry now. And remember, we're all here to share the load.'

'I don't know how you guys do this over and over again,' Kira grumbled. Snatching the lighter she'd seen under the lectern, she started with the pillar candles, releasing the subtle fragrances of rose and honey.

The scent of honey brought a smile to her lips. A hint of spice and fresh citrus and she'd imagine Mattia behind her. He'd be here soon, with Alessandra. Perhaps she should have been bracing herself for the emotional onslaught of hearing him sing, especially given the strange mood she was already in, but she let her mind wander pleasantly instead.

Which was why she wasn't prepared when a voice from her distant past sounded behind her.

'Kira.'

She froze, which was a little awkward, given she was leaning over the altar to light a candle right up the back.

Twelve years. It was more than a third of her life. She was most definitely an adult now, with a rational perspective on life. She was a rock climbing instructor, she'd summited two 6,000ers in Nepal and led countless adventure tours.

But hearing that voice made her nineteen again –

the tomboy misfit who soaked up every drop of affection her inadequate friend-turned-lover gave her. A friend she never should have believed she was in love with.

'Kira, the candle!' Sophie's choked cry broke through her foggy thoughts and she looked down – and yelped.

Flailing for the nearest piece of cloth, she grabbed the linen under the big old Bible and slapped frantically at her stomach, registering the bite of pain.

The unassuming priest must have had super-human speed, because he appeared in a heartbeat with a fire extinguisher. A puff of white powder exploded over her torso, raining down on the altar and filling the front of the church with chemical fog. After one more blast for good measure, the priest stepped back to assess his handiwork.

'That could have been very bad,' he said emphatically.

Spluttering, Kira swiped at her chin, noticing the fine, white powder residue all over herself. This *was* very bad.

'Kira! Can I—?'

She whirled around, hearing Christian's voice much closer. He drew back when he saw her face – or perhaps it was in reaction to her current state.

'Wow, it's been a long time.'

Kira gritted her teeth. Did he mean good 'wow' or bad 'wow'? What kind of reaction was 'wow' anyway? The wedding was due to start and she'd just set herself on fire. This was no time for 'wow'.

'It really has,' she said woodenly.

'It's good to see you.'

A few days ago, she might have given a snarky retort, something like *It obviously wasn't good to see me in a fucking wedding dress!* But all she wanted was for Alessandra's nuptials to get underway – and to fix her latest mishap.

'Maybe at the reception we could... catch up?'

She gave him a withering look. 'Let's not,' she said with a laugh. 'I need to go get cleaned up.'

That was that. She'd seen him again. And she'd felt more standing in the Christmas market while Mattia shared the tiniest glimpse of his soul.

Sophie bustled up to them, nudging the trigger-happy priest with the fire extinguisher and Kira's gawping ex-fiancé out of the way. 'Are you okay? Let me see.'

Kira turned to allow Sophie to assess the damage. 'I'm so sorry, Sophie. I did warn you I'm not cut out for weddings, although I didn't expect I'd nearly burn down the church.'

Her eyes flickered to where Christian was retreating to the back of the chapel to stand with a tall woman in a pencil-straight dress. At least with the perspective of the continual disasters, she was barely even curious about his girlfriend.

'My shirt is ruined. And maybe the wedding.'

Sophie snorted a laugh, obviously assuming she was joking. 'We'll get this cleaned up. It's not the first fire I've had to put out before a wedding. I promise we've had our share of mishaps over the years,' she said ruefully. 'I'll call this one "Fire and Ice" in the file.'

'More like crash and burn?' Kira muttered. 'That's just my pride. Oh, and my wardrobe, apparently. I literally have nothing else to wear.'

'That's easily solved. Here's the key to the van. There are wet wipes in the centre console and you can grab something out of my suitcase to wear. It might be a little loose on you, but better that than the other way around.'

Kira took in Sophie's fine, wrap-around dress with a doubtful look. 'It's more the style that concerns me.'

'You can pull it off. Just wait until you see Andreas in a tie.'

Kira's eyes widened. 'You didn't? He's going to wear a tie?'

'I told him it was a gesture of respect for the couple. It'll probably last about ten minutes and then he'll say he made the gesture and they should be happy now.'

'Sounds like Andreas.' Holding up the key, she said, 'Thanks for this. I'll be as quick as I can.'

Thoughts crowding in, she was distracted as she picked her way to the car park in her presentable patent leather court shoes – highly inappropriate for the weather. The minivan was there, the snow cleared from the windscreen and the tyres, since Andreas had been using it to ferry guests around the valley. The vehicle reminded her of the drive from Salzburg – and the way Mattia's eyes had gone round at the sight of her rather tatty old T-shirt bra. The weirdo.

Knowing she'd see him in a few minutes loosened the tightness in her chest. No matter what regrets she had about this week, she refused to count her time with Mattia among them, even though she was certain a lecture from Reshma was on its way when they got back to the UK.

After scrubbing her face and hands with enough wet wipes to give her the scent of a freshly changed baby bum, she found a single top amongst Sophie's extensive collection of dresses – why she'd brought so many dresses for a short wedding emergency, Kira couldn't tell. She'd just whipped her ruined blouse over her head when she heard a shout from outside the van.

'Kira!'

What a day for her pride.

Shoving Sophie's top on, she peered out to see Andreas waving at her from where he sat at the front of a sleigh decorated with pine garlands and bells and pulled by two real reindeer.

Alessandra's reindeer. She couldn't contain a gleeful laugh – and a shared eye-roll with Rhys, who stood to one side capturing the moment with the livestock.

'Kira!' Andreas called out again. 'Why didn't you tell me about Christian? We've known each other for *twelve* years!'

Jumping down from the van and slamming the door closed, she yelled back, 'I wanted your respect! And I didn't want you to think I was a pathetic woman who'd put on a white dress and wait in a church for a guy who wasn't coming!' She glanced at Alessandra, where she was wrapped up in the back of the sleigh with Carla. 'Not that you're pathetic, or that Joe will leave you at the altar. Someone just tell me to shut up!'

Andreas obliged. 'Shut up! You aren't that pathetic woman. You've never been, since I've known you.'

She wanted to protest that she must have been pathetic back at the beginning, when the hurt was still fresh, but it didn't seem to matter. He was right. She wasn't that woman.

Coming to stand by the sleigh, she lifted her chin. 'Are you saying you won't tease me rotten about the fact that I nearly got married?'

He shot her a smile. 'No, but we all did stupid things when we were young. Now I know you're human too. And sometimes...' He gave an eloquent shrug. 'Sometimes, humans need another human.'

She groaned. 'Sometimes, I think marriage is some kind of pyramid scheme. When you get engaged, you have to match everybody else up to prove you're doing the right thing.' With another wince in Alessandra's direction, Kira added, 'No offence.'

The bride leaned forward graciously. 'I'm only sorry I expended my energy matchmaking the wrong people.'

Kira's face heated. 'Don't you all have a wedding to get to? Those reindeer must be getting cold.'

One of the animals obligingly stamped a hoof.

'We'll talk later,' Andreas said. It was a threat.

'I'm not joining your pyramid scheme,' she insisted, shooing them in the direction of the church. The reindeer snorted as their handler urged them off again, turning to cross the road into the field where the church sat under a cushion of snow.

'He likes you!' Andreas called over his shoulder. 'He told me.'

'That boy blabs!' she shot back, ignoring the buzz of heat through her middle. He wasn't for her and she had to remember that for another eighteen hours to make it out unscathed. 'It's just a crush. He'll get over it.'

'What if it's not?'

Kira didn't want to wonder about what she and Mattia could mean to each other if they weren't walking away tomorrow. They *would* walk away. There was no other sensible course of action.

By the time she trudged back to the church, Alessandra's parents were fussing over her. But Kira was lost in her own thoughts about mistakes and commitment and desire. Shaking herself, she hurried up the steps, shoved open the door of the church – and came to an abrupt stop.

Every eye was on her. Pachelbel's Canon was playing through the speakers. And Mattia stood near the altar, giving her a lopsided smile.

33

She couldn't tear her eyes off Mattia, tall and distinguished in a well-cut suit with a white bow tie. A hint of dark eyeliner enhanced his dramatic features and a graze decorated his forehead, giving him a rakish look. His jacket was open and as Kira's eyes sneaked down his body, she noticed he was wearing a burgundy cummerbund, and she could barely contain her snort of laughter at the memory of that first evening in Salzburg.

He gave her a wink and a flash of his eyebrows in greeting and she was struck by how well she'd got to know him since that night. Perhaps she and Mattia were both chaos muppets who could only perform within their limited comfort zone. Her short time with him had certainly been disastrous – and fun.

Plus, he looked pretty handsome standing at the altar, his gaze locked on her as though he never wanted to look away. Christian had never made it this far – not to the altar and not so far inside her heart.

Someone cleared their throat and loud rustling outside announced the arrival of the bride – and Kira was standing at the back of the church as though *she* were about to take measured steps down the aisle.

'I'm so sorry,' she muttered, her cheeks flaming.

Ginny floated to her, snaking an arm around her waist and ushering her to one side. Kira could tell from the tight hold that Ginny's first instinct had been to rugby tackle her out of the way. It wasn't a moment too soon.

When the door opened once more, Carla emerged through it, beaming over her bouquet of slightly browning roses and baby's breath. Mattia melted off to one side, ready to perform his part when the time came, and Joe straightened his buttonhole, then his shoulders, as he peered eagerly around Carla.

'Oh my fucking God, we did it,' Ginny whispered into Kira's ear.

'They haven't said "I do" yet,' Kira pointed out.

'But if they don't, it won't be our fault.'

Wiping her damp palms on her trousers, Kira asked, 'Do you think priests make the ceremony long to keep us all on the edge of our seats?'

'It's not an action film,' Ginny joked out of the side of her mouth.

Joe's gaze snapped up, his grin widening as he saw past Carla to where Alessandra had paused just inside the door with her father. Slipping out of her faux fur coat, she revealed the intricate wedding gown of hand-made lace and pearl beads in a classic 1940s style.

Sophie appeared from nowhere to take the coat and Kira was even more convinced she had a sixth sense for weddings that defied explanation. After Alessandra's father moved the veil over her face, she took his arm with a serene smile – another skill Kira was fairly certain she'd never master.

Judging the right moment, Ginny faded Pachelbel's Canon and queued the track for the walk down the aisle.

'Alessandra changed this at the last minute. It's a surprise,' Ginny whispered, as the piano melody and string bass from the opening bars of 'Can't Help Falling in Love' filled the chapel.

When the bride and groom's gazes met and softened, the romantic moment had a life of its own among the guests. Kira crossed her arms, annoyed that something as simple as a song could tempt a reaction even from her. But she was happy for Alessandra and she would bear the sentimentality for a few minutes for her sake.

Then, instead of the familiar resonance of Elvis Presley's baritone, Mattia's voice filled the chapel and Kira's knees nearly gave out. There was no other sound but the gentle vibrato and ringing warmth of his singing. His voice wasn't rounded and smooth like Elvis's, but aching and full of colour.

Kira had no defences against his voice. He performed with everything in his heart, even when it cost him his equilibrium. The power wasn't only in his vocal chords and his diaphragm; it was in his ability to mould his audience, communicate through raw emotion. He made her feel human in all its contradictions. Mortal, vulnerable – beautiful.

He sang about fools rushing in and foolish tears pricked her eyes. She wished he meant the words for her, instead of serenading the bridal couple.

She was still that pathetic woman, reaching out for love where it wouldn't be returned. She'd walked too close to the edge and she needed to be very careful she didn't fall.

The rest of the ceremony was a struggle. She was

unexpectedly proud of Alessandra and Joe for what they'd made of the day, for not only showing up physically, but talking through their feelings beforehand as well.

Mattia set the scene with a rousing performance of 'Nessun dorma', his cheeks red and his hair flopping wildly over his forehead as he reached the high notes. He was particularly exposed with only the trumpet and the clarinet in support, but Kira wouldn't have noticed, if she hadn't known the string quartet was missing.

The Catholic wedding vows were surprisingly simple – and very different from the heartfelt original vows Kira had heard at the last wedding, in the summer. But the words rang with the weight of generations, a marriage built on the tradition of all the marriages that had come before it.

It was when Mattia sang 'One Hand, One Heart' from *West Side Story* as the witnesses signed the register that Kira seriously worried about bursting into tears. She wouldn't have been the only one. Tissue packets were making the rounds of the pews and even Sophie was dabbing at her eyes.

But with great effort, Kira swiped at her nose and straightened. Mattia might touch her heart with everything he did, but she wouldn't be foolish enough to give it to him.

* * *

After readings and homilies, prayers and communion – as well as the actually rather short marriage vows – the priest finally invited Alessandra and Joe to rise from their kneeling position and raised his hand.

'Go in peace to glorify the Lord with your life.'

Rather than the sedate response Mattia was fairly sure was supposed to follow, the guests cheered, snapping photos of the radiant bride and the rather dazed groom. Mattia hoped the moment had lived up to every one of Alessandra's dreams – and been worth Joe converting to Catholicism.

His chest was light, partly with happiness and re-lief and partly the physical aftermath of singing the liturgy and two arias.

As soon as the bridal party retreated back up the aisle, he headed straight for Kira, where she was standing awkwardly in the corner, clutching her hands together. He'd seen her dabbing at her eyes – once while he'd been singing – and he needed to know...

He wasn't quite sure what was driving him, especially since nothing had changed. A few tears at a wedding didn't mean she'd apply for the job as his soulmate. Even if she'd started to realise she'd been shutting out romance after being hurt, he was in all likelihood not the person she'd risk making an exception to her 'just casual' rule for.

As much as he fancied the idea of that.

'How do you think it went?' he asked her.

She looked at him warily, but that was nothing new. 'Surprisingly smoothly. She was lucky to have you to sing.'

He gave a shrug, even as his smile stretched to silly proportions. 'I had to sing "Nessun dorma" in a tenor key. These instrumentalists couldn't transpose it in time and unfortunately, I'm not Pavarotti. But I think it was okay.'

'It was more than okay,' she said, her tone oddly fragile. 'You don't need to be Pavarotti.'

'I suppose I am slimmer, although his charisma was—'

She whacked him with the backs of her fingers. 'You know that's not what I meant.'

'You don't think I'm slimmer?'

She rolled her eyes, but a smile turned up the corners of her mouth and that had been his goal.

'That top is nice, but what happened to the one we

bought yesterday?' He'd enjoyed going shopping with her, even though she'd complained at every boutique he'd dragged her into and shown an almost complete lack of taste.

Tugging at the blouse that was definitely too big in the chest, she grimaced. 'It caught on fire. I knew I was bad luck at weddings.'

Mattia felt a jab in those words, as though she'd meant them as a reminder that this thing between them was casual – as though she didn't know the word 'casual' had been stamped all over him as he tried to remind himself while also sliding helplessly into something very much like admiration for prickly, practical Kira Watling.

'If you caught on fire, but the wedding was still as beautiful as that, I think there's more good luck involved than you think. You didn't burn yourself?'

She shook her head.

'I'm glad of that, but it's a shame. I liked that shirt.'

'So did I,' she admitted, 'but I don't have much call for blouses. I probably wouldn't have worn it again.'

She stared at the altar as she spoke, as though fascinated by the crochet cloths and the gold chalice, but discomfort skittered over Mattia's skin. She wasn't interested in the altar. She was forcing out flat words to

cool any feelings that might flare – specifically between them, he guessed.

He had the answer to the question he'd been too
skittish to ask. She would let him down gently and
tomorrow, they'd say goodbye. He'd said he'd take responsibility for his own feelings. Now he had to do it.

He just didn't want to.

34

'I *must* add this place to our files,' Sophie was muttering after dinner, tablet and stylus in hand. 'This rustic style is right on trend and the municipality was so helpful organising this. Do you think the manager has a second to—'

'No,' Andreas grunted from the other side of their table. 'You're not supposed to be working right now. If we're missing out on the ski tour I had planned for us over New Year's, the least you can do is dance with me.'

'Aw, so romantic,' Ginny gushed as Andreas snatched the tablet out of Sophie's hands and hauled her to her feet.

Kira rolled her eyes.

'Excuse me,' Sophie said indignantly. 'If you left me for six weeks to climb some mountain after we'd only just got engaged, you can wait five minutes for me to finish what I was doing.'

'Aw,' Kira repeated with a pointed look at Ginny. 'That's romance.'

The wedding planner shrugged. 'What do I know about romance?' Her eyes drifted to the dance floor, where Alessandra and Joe were swaying to 'At Last' – the Beyoncé version. Kira caught sight of Rhys hunched in the corner, his camera to his eye – pointed right at Kira.

She flipped him the middle finger and he lowered the camera to return the gesture with a smile.

Alessandra's mother Francesca chose that moment to appear at their table and Kira flushed to the roots of her hair. She didn't expect that particular hand gesture was approved by Italians. But if Francesca had seen it, she didn't mention it.

'I think it's time for tarantella!' she declared with a clap. 'And you all *must* join in.'

Andreas's stifled groan wasn't quite stifled enough.

'Come, you are Italian!' Francesca said with enough enthusiasm for all of them.

'Technically,' Andreas mumbled. 'But I'm not tarantella Italian,' he continued as Francesca ignored him, getting the rest of the team from Great Heart and I Do up on their feet.

'What is it?' Kira asked warily as she followed the others into the back room that had been cleared to make a dance floor.

'You'll see,' Ginny said brightly.

As the entire wedding party, as well as all the guests and the planners, formed a circle around Alessandra and Joe, holding hands, Kira was glad of the excuse of queuing the music and escaped into the corner with Rhys. Sophie's strong grip on Andreas dragged him into the circle as the jaunty accordion music started.

But he obviously knew how to do the dance, kicking his feet out and moving in time to the music. The tipsy, happy group made a wonky circle and Kira smiled, unable to resist the sheer goodwill in the room.

There was something about weddings.

As the team from I Do came around again, Ginny broke ranks, holding out her hand to Kira and shaking it. There was no time to hesitate. Kira took the outstretched hand and allowed herself to be pulled in. As though she belonged. As though they all wanted her there, despite her blue hair and her scepticism, her bluntness and rude gestures.

When she looked up, Mattia was smiling brightly at her from across the circle. Christian was somewhere there too, but she'd finally dropped the memories – and her embarrassment – off the back of a proverbial truck.

She was reminded of her unconsidered words a moment later when Joe kneeled to tug off Alessandra's garter to a soundtrack of raucous laughter as he fumbled under her skirt. But when Ginny winked at her, she couldn't feel embarrassed about that incident either.

As the accordion music finished, Kira was pleasantly out of breath and high on the experience shared with her new – and old – friends. When Mattia approached with tentative footsteps, she didn't quite pull up her defences in time.

'Dance with me,' he said softly, drawing her close.

She was too weak to resist, even though the song that came on next was 'Make You Feel My Love' and they weren't so much dancing as holding each other awkwardly in a slow sway.

They moved in silence through the first bars of piano. Kira kept her eyes averted, her hand gripped in his white, formal shirt, unwilling to give herself over to the intimacy, but also unwilling to let go of him.

He held her loosely, the embrace ridiculously

formal in comparison to the way their bodies had moved together in the bedroom. But as though he knew she couldn't handle anything more, he simply held her solicitously, not too close, but near enough to keep the beat. When she risked a glance at him, he was gazing into the distance.

Only as the song was coming to an end did he take a deep breath, pausing, despite the obvious words on his lips.

'Do you... Would you rather be alone tonight?'

Her stomach clenched as though a tower of beautiful bricks were crashing down inside her. She'd forgotten they'd shared a hotel room the past two nights. Her new toothbrush sat next to his. The yoga mat where they'd bantered this morning was still rolled out by the window.

'It's all right if you do,' he continued. 'I don't expect anything.'

He expected a soulmate – just not her. It made sense. 'What do you want?' she managed to ask.

He hesitated for so long that she had to peer up at him. His expression was so twisted, she was alarmed. Lifting a hand out of instinct, she smoothed her fingers over his brow.

'What is it?'

He caught her hand in his, lowering it from his face. 'I want you to stay – one last night.'

His words shivered down her spine. 'Okay,' she replied with a measure of relief she didn't want to analyse.

A smile tipped up his lips, but it wasn't his usual bright one. 'That's what you said that first time. I don't think I'll ever forget.'

Her eyes stung and she wasn't happy to discover it wasn't only his singing voice that could make her cry.

'How soon do you think we can wrap up this party?'

* * *

Mattia slept fitfully and awoke often, usually to find his hand patting the bed frantically to reassure him that Kira was still there. His thoughts spiralled between the certainty that she'd started pushing him away last night and the realisation of exactly how close she'd let him come over the previous days.

She was a heavy sleeper, so he wrapped his body around hers like an octopus, soaking up the subtle scent of her and wallowing in the sensation of her skin pressed to his. He studied her blue hair, pale in the dim moonlight penetrating the curtains, the crescent-moon scar on her cheek. The line of her shoulder was unbearably beautiful, the musculature an outward sign of her strength of character.

Stirring, she moved instinctively closer and he pressed a light kiss to the side of her neck. Nothing about how he felt was casual, but he knew her layers of armour would not be removed easily and they didn't have any more time.

She felt something – he was certain of that – but it wasn't his place to work out how much.

He must have slept eventually, because he awoke suddenly to find the room brighter and Kira at his neck, using her mouth to bring him out in goosebumps and draw a deep moan from his chest.

His hands threading in her hair, he brought her up for a kiss, long and drowsy and deep. Pausing for a moment, he opened his mouth to say something, but she shook her head and tapped her finger against his lips, kissing him again instead. Then she stole his thoughts completely, moving her body against his and eventually fetching a condom and taking him in.

His agreement not to say anything felt binding, so he showed her instead, with gentle touches to her throat, an urgent clasp on her thighs and finally, tangling his fingers with hers as they tumbled together.

'*Kira.*' He couldn't quite stop the gasp of her name.

She was silent, her chest heaving, where she propped herself up on top of him. She wouldn't meet his gaze, but her mouth wobbled in a frown.

Then she hauled herself off him and left the bed, swiping her clothes up from the floor, flinging them on and disappearing into the bathroom. Five minutes later, she'd gathered up her meagre belongings and, without a backward glance, she left.

35

'Come on! What do you call that? Your head's all over the place today!'

Kira's seventeen-year-old student abseiled down from the top of the climbing wall with a grimace, stumbling over an apology. A twinge of guilt assailed Kira, especially since she knew she'd been a hard-arse and a hypocrite to boot.

She still doubled down. 'It's only three months until Nationals. There's no time for laziness. I expect better on Wednesday.'

The girl ambled away in the direction of the changing rooms, her head hanging. Kira watched her go, consumed by the restlessness that had become a familiar companion over the past three weeks.

The fact that she'd done the right thing – the *only* thing – by leaving before anyone got hurt was no comfort when she seemed to have to readjust to life without him. It made no sense. She'd been fine before – content with her friendships and occasionally scratching the itch in bed with someone. She shouldn't feel starved of touch – a very particular kind of touch.

She'd always been alone, so why did she feel even more alone now?

'I hope you don't go so hard on *me*.'

Turning with relief at the distraction, Kira found Ginny and enfolded her in a hug before she realised what she was doing. God, she'd turned into a sappy mess. It was a good thing Andreas wasn't there to tease her, and Rhys was off photographing pumas in Patagonia.

Actually, Andreas would try to recruit her for his pyramid scheme again and she might choke him before Sophie ever had the chance to drag him to the altar. She was *not* in love, like everyone else seemed to be, all of a sudden.

She just missed Mattia like a part of her own body. Nothing serious.

'Whoa there,' Ginny said with a smile, extricating

herself from the tight hug. 'I need to breathe if I'm going to learn to climb.'

It was Ginny's third session and she was still entirely uncoordinated, but she claimed determination would make up for her lack of natural talent – although she also definitely lacked the self-confidence to test herself against the wall.

It was late January, which could have explained Kira's restlessness. She wanted to get back to the real crags along the Dorset coast, or into the hills – anywhere legitimately outdoors. But the weather was dreary and cold, so she was stuck focusing on her indoor groups and individual training.

But that was just an excuse. She was miserable and it was getting harder to pretend she wasn't.

'Is something bothering you?' Ginny asked.

'I'm always this grumpy,' she joked instead of answering.

Ginny rolled her eyes. 'We are going for a drink afterwards,' she stated, giving Kira no opportunity to protest.

After they'd finished their forty-five-minute session, Ginny was sweating and groaning, but Kira could honestly say, 'You did well today.'

'Yeah, right,' Ginny laughed, still panting from her last ascent.

'A definite improvement on last week.'

Ginny snorted. 'That's because Rhys isn't here. I started to think he haunted this place.'

Kira peered doubtfully at her. 'He's in Patagonia on an expedition.'

'Oh, *Patagonia*,' Ginny said with a dismissive flick of her hand. 'As you do. We've never had a wedding in *Patagonia*. Only the usual places with restaurants and beaches and things.'

'But what does Rhys have to do with it?'

'He *looked* at me last week the whole time,' Ginny grumbled.

'He did not,' Kira defended. 'Rhys doesn't *look* at people.' He truly didn't, but it wasn't Kira's place to explain to Ginny.

'Well, whether he was really looking at me or not, I felt judged and it drained all my confidence. Does he hate *everyone* or just me?'

'Everyone,' Kira confirmed with a smile.

'Oh... that's all right then?'

After showering and changing, they met Toni at The Admiral, the scene of the first, disastrous meeting between the employees of the newly merged 'Great Heart Does Weddings', or whatever Reshma and Willard had decided to call it. Kira would continue to say 'I Do Weddings' just to tease the others, although she was beginning to accept that she truly did weddings too, now.

Toni looked bright that evening and folded Kira in another hug. She'd never hugged so many people in her life and she wasn't sure she was happy with the development, since Great Heart seemed to have gone all mushy.

'How lovely is this? Three girls having dinner at the pub on a school night! With no babysitter required!'

Kira smiled over her pint. 'It's working out well with your parents nearby then?'

'Yes, except I've forgotten how to be presentable. My clothes are all fifteen years old or bought from the supermarket!'

'Oh, Toni, not the supermarket!' Ginny said disapprovingly. Kira couldn't tell if she was being sarcastic.

'At least to come here, I don't need anything special.'

Ginny set down her wine and eyeballed Toni. 'Does that mean you've been thinking about *other* occasions where you might need to wear something special?'

Toni choked on her sip of wine.

'I wouldn't go there, Ginny,' Kira warned her.

'Mmhmm,' Toni managed to agree. 'Dating is my

idea of hell, given the only two topics I can cover are my son and my dead husband. I was thinking about I Do Destinations, now I've had to attend a couple of meetings. There is a certain smart-casual vibe required that I'm too out of touch to master.'

'Don't worry,' Ginny said warmly. 'Kira set her top on fire and had to wear something of Sophie's at our most recent wedding and that was still fine.'

Kira sat back in her chair, sharing the laughter. She was glad the gentle mocking didn't embarrass her – since a miracle had transpired and Ginny was a genuine friend. But remembering that day brought the feelings bubbling back to the surface – all the feelings.

'I did think that's what we'd gathered here today to discuss,' Toni said, lifting her eyebrows at Kira.

'What, my complete lack of grace and poise?'

Toni leaned heavily on the table, shooting Kira a piercing gaze that sent tingles to her hairline. 'Why you've been impossible these past three weeks.'

'I've been just as impossible as I usually am!' Kira insisted. 'You don't have to like it.'

The sympathetic light in Ginny's eyes pricked her. They all knew, now. Seeing Christian had been a strange anticlimax, wrapped up in too many other emotions to truly hurt, but she couldn't hide from her friends any more. Perhaps she couldn't hide from her feelings, which was a terrifying thought, since they got her into trouble.

'To be honest, it makes sense to me now,' Toni said lightly. 'You've been hurt, so you hold yourself away from everyone else – especially someone you could fall in love with.'

'I don't want to fall in love with anyone.' That statement grabbed her by the neck. She meant it, but it sounded desperate and panicky even to her own ears. 'I want to be fine by myself.'

'You are,' Ginny said. 'You're so strong and passionate and I admire that a lot. I wish I were as content as you to be alone.'

'Passionate?' Kira repeated with a snort, taking a sip of her beer in the hope that the conversation would just go away.

But Ginny peered at her with a dubious look. 'I saw how you looked at him.'

Toni gasped. 'Who? What's this? Her ex! Sophie just said it was awkward. What else did I miss?'

'Not her ex,' Ginny said slowly.

Kira took a deep breath through her nose, goose-bumps spreading over her skin. On her own, she could wrestle with the persistent impression of absence, reason with herself that she'd always felt alone and alienated and this was nothing different. But she couldn't fool her friends.

Hell of a time to remember why she didn't have friends.

'Mattia,' Ginny began, enunciating slowly, 'Bentivoglio. Operatic baritone.'

That was all it took. Kira buried her face in her hands, emotions bubbling to the surface even though she didn't want any of them. Her breath was tight and the horrible urge to cry gripped her.

'I hate fucking weddings,' she mumbled.

A hand touched down on her back, rubbing firm circles. 'Poor Kira,' she heard Toni say. 'I'm sorry love hurts.'

The twinge of sadness in her chest wasn't only her own, it was sympathy for Toni, who'd been deeply in love and lost him. Kira had never fully appreciated how devastating it must have been for her.

'It wasn't love,' she insisted. She still had her stubbornness, even if everything hurt. 'Not like you and Miro.'

'Leave me out of it,' Toni said ruefully. 'I'm sick of being the poster girl for grief. What happened?'

'It took me by surprise,' Kira explained. 'Getting on so well with him was unexpected. I never believed anything real could develop between us, so I dropped my guard and then... this happened.'

'They were very cute together,' Ginny commented to Toni.

'What was the problem?' Toni prompted.

'Everything!' Kira insisted, lifting a hand for emphasis. 'Now I *miss* him, like when our favourite takeaway closed down and I couldn't get Chettinad curry.'

'That *is* serious,' Toni said indulgently. 'It was amazing curry,' she added for Ginny's benefit.

'Right, but "I miss you like curry" probably isn't something you should say to him,' Ginny pointed out.

'What do you mean? I'm never going to see him again. He's finally got the courage to build his career. He's so fucking talented, he'll be on a big stage somewhere making everyone cry and—' *not making me cry.* She should have been relieved at that.

'Is *that* the only reason you left without working things out with him?' Ginny asked.

'There was nothing to work out,' Kira insisted. 'We agreed it would be casual. I heard him say it was just casual the day before the wedding. With so many compromises to make to see each other, what would be the point? I just have to get over it. Why do I need an opera singer in my life anyway?'

Ginny tapped a finger against her lip in mock contemplation. 'I can think of a few things.' Dropping her hands to the table, her eyes widened. 'Wait, when we were talking about mistletoe and kissing that night, had you two already— You were getting together with —' Running out of words, she made some vague hand gestures that would have made Kira laugh if she hadn't been so miserable.

'We'd kissed,' she admitted. 'It happened pretty fast. At the very least, I taught the boy some new tricks.'

'Sounds like he taught you something too,' Toni said softly.

Kira crossed her arms. 'I was perfectly happy before I felt all this stuff, thank you very much.'

'You've lasted longer than most people, but I think a time comes when we have to accept that our feelings exist or we just can't cope. We can be hurt. Trusting is scary.' The echo of her life with Miro was in everything Toni said, but Kira wouldn't point it out.

'But what do you do about this disappointment? I can see I held onto the embarrassment of what Christian did for far too long and probably turned it into something it wasn't. I worked out I needed to let that go, but...' She propped her forehead on her hand. 'I've never felt anything like this before. I don't know how to process it.'

Ginny squeezed her arm, the three rings on her hand winking in the dim light of the pub. 'Did you tell him any of that?'

'Of course not!' she said with a dark laugh. 'After insisting the only option was casual, I couldn't turn around and ask him if he wanted to be my video-chat boyfriend!' She shook her head. 'This is stupid. I promise not to be grumpy for twelve years this time and I won't let this stop me making friends.'

Tears pricked again and Toni stretched her arm around Kira's shoulders. She dropped her head to her old friend's shoulder.

'After the curry place closed, I eventually discovered I love jerk chicken as well,' she said with a sigh.

'It's definitely too soon to be thinking about jerk chicken,' Ginny said. 'I'm not ready to give up on you two. He might have said that thing about it being casual, but I bet he didn't mean it. He just didn't want to upstage the wedding.'

'He's had three weeks since the wedding to tell me that without upstaging anything except my Netflix bingeing,' Kira said peevishly.

'Yeah, but what did you tell him when you said goodbye? Knowing you, it was probably something about leaving things as they are.'

Ginny had no right to be so insightful. 'I said nothing,' Kira admitted. 'And I didn't let him say anything either.' She'd just initiated sex and then left – so she didn't have to deal with how much that intimacy had meant to her.

'Oh, Kira!' Toni cried.

'I was scared! He seemed so ready to let me go. He even had to check if we were going to spend the last night together, as though he wasn't bothered!'

Ginny frowned. 'That doesn't sound right. I saw you dancing together at the wedding. He looked at you like he was about to combust if you didn't touch him. Look.'

She fetched her phone out of her bag. Kira was still astonished that she'd managed to become such good friends with someone who decorated her pink phone case with rhinestones and a tassel and had one of those holders for taking selfies.

'I had a feeling you were struggling with this,' she began.

'I'm not—'

Ginny held up her hand. For a small woman who made herself look quite frivolous, she had a skill for commanding people. 'I thought maybe you needed to see this.'

As Ginny turned the device, Kira caught sight of herself on the screen – in the soft lighting of the wood-panelled museum, wearing Sophie's top and no make-up, her blue hair bright. And Mattia. His head was bent, his cheek against her temple. She didn't remember him doing that. She'd been stuck in her own thoughts, obsessed with her own shortcomings.

His eyes were closed, the long lashes visible, and his mouth looked soft, but grim. The photo showed one of his hands, gripped tightly in the loose fabric of her top. He looked pained. He looked exactly as she'd felt.

'Rhys sent a heap of really weird photos, with odd facial expressions and stuff, like he hadn't looked at them at all, but there were enough great ones once we sifted through them – thank God.'

'Aw,' Toni said, snatching the phone for a closer look. 'Wow. That's *something* between the two of you.'

Ginny nodded. 'It was very sweet. The whole time, he stared across the room at her like a stray puppy.'

'He did not!' Kira insisted, her cheeks hot. 'Why would he?'

'Aaaaand we come to our next problem,' Toni said softly.

'I'm starting to think maybe I don't want to fall in love after all,' Ginny said in a small voice.

'It's hell,' Kira muttered.

Ginny stilled, inclining her head to study Kira.

'But did you hear what you just said? You admitted you're in love with Mattia.'

'You know I didn't mean that! I've known him a *week*!'

'A pretty intense week.'

Kira leaned her head back on the wood panelling behind the bench of the booth. 'It was a pretty intense week.'

'You know what I think?' Ginny said.

'I don't want to know.'

'*I* think,' she ploughed on, ignoring Kira, 'you're just the type to fall head over heels straight away. You're tough and loyal and your heart knows what it wants.'

With an unexpected lightness in her chest, Kira admitted to herself that she agreed with Ginny's assessment, but she was no closer to a solution. 'Yeah, well, we can't always have what we want.'

'That's true,' Ginny said thoughtfully. But she pinned Kira with a gaze a moment later and continued, 'Especially if we refuse to go out and get it.'

36

'Matty! Carissimo!'

Alessandra threw her arms around him as though they hadn't seen each other in years. He pressed a kiss to her cheek.

'I'm happy to see you too. How's married life? How was the honeymoon?'

Her smile was soft and wistful and made Mattia reflect on the line she'd crossed without him.

'I can't quite believe it's all over,' she said with a frown. 'I spent months planning everything and I need a new project.' She tucked her arm through his and he was afraid for a moment that he would be her new project. But he'd learned to be firm about that. He was his own project now – which was why he was here.

'But it's wonderful to have you in London with me!'

'I'm only staying a couple of weeks. If things don't work out—'

'They will,' she said with a firm nod. 'You have to believe they will.'

He gave her a smile. 'You're right. I have to believe it. Thanks for offering me your guest room.'

'It's yours for as long as you need it *and* you can get to know Joe properly.'

Arriving at Alessandra's lovely row house in Chiswick, the hum of the boiler and the huge ticking clock in the hall made his eye twitch, but he just took a deep breath and asked her to take the batteries out of the clock before he got too worked up. The sound of the boiler faded as he followed her upstairs to his room, so he would cope. He could chop wood and help out in a snow emergency and hold a strong woman while she cried. He would manage his sound sensitivities.

Especially now he'd made the decision to move away from Naples.

Alessandra had cooked for an army – all her nonna's recipes – so after he'd stuffed himself, he commented, 'You know, that dinner is the best advertisement for London I can think of.'

Joe gave her a quick kiss. 'She certainly brightens up London for me,' he said before disappearing to stack the dishwasher, with only a faint grumble about the kitchen resembling a bomb site.

Allowing Alessandra to settle him on the couch, he waited for her pep talk: the auditions would be fine. He had to get at least one of the jobs because she wanted her friend to live nearby. He'd get used to the strange rules and dreary weather and maybe one day, he'd even like battered fish.

But she only regarded him curiously, for long enough to make him uneasy. 'I doubt my cooking is the best thing about the prospect of moving to London.'

A leap of stubborn excitement rose inside him, but he quashed it quickly. Yes, he was in England, only three hours away from this town called Weymouth that he'd never heard of until he'd looked up Great Heart Adventures, but as often as he imagined travelling down there, catching a glimpse of her, it didn't change the fact that she had left without a word.

There was only one interpretation for her actions that made sense: she'd felt something, but not enough to change her mind about relationships. He needed to accept that.

He had auditions – that was all. His manager had persuaded him that London presented many opportunities and was a good base for extra freelance work if necessary. There was more money in opera in London. That's why he was there – for the horror of auditions.

'Don't hint, Alessandra,' he muttered. 'You're the only friend I have in this country and we both know it.'

After another pause where he could almost hear her protesting, she thankfully let the subject drop.

'And now, I have to show you...' she began dramatically, reaching for a thick, bound tome on the coffee table. 'The photos!'

'I *was* there,' he said indulgently.

'Just look at them!' She dumped the album on his lap a little too heavily.

The photos were printed onto high-quality paper, with subtle, fine design that made Mattia think of the team from I Do Destinations – and the one member who'd never fit in.

The photos from the ice cave gave him goosebumps, remembering the texture of the frozen walls and all of the emotions of that day. Kira had probably already heard about Christian by then, although she'd refused to talk about it. It was a miracle she'd opened up to Mattia at all, although doctoring a minor head wound had definitely brought them closer.

He brushed his fingertip over the scar on his forehead, which only reminded him of the puckered skin on her cheekbone. If he'd bled like a soft drink can and only ended up with this faint line, he hated to think how bad her injury had been to leave a patch of discoloured and misshapen skin, years later.

'It's a bit strange there are no photos from the chalet,' he commented.

'It's probably for the best, given the hot water wasn't working and thermal underwear isn't a good look – even underneath other clothes.'

She turned the pages, skipping over the images of the hotel room where they'd got dressed. Kira wasn't in any of the photos – at least that part of wedding planning she'd mastered – but Mattia painted her back in with his memories. Whenever she'd been in the room, he'd seen everything in brighter colours, felt everything more keenly.

He made the appropriate gushing noises at the posed portraits after the ceremony, in front the old wooden farmhouse with its balconies and slanting roof. Tiny flakes of snow seemed to light up the picture, and the shimmer of rocky mountain peaks in the distance looked too magical to be real.

But the grinning bride and groom were the ones that made the picture into a true fairy tale.

'This one's lovely,' Mattia commented softly, pointing to a photo of Joe tipping Alessandra over his arm, pressing a firm kiss to her cheek while she laughed.

'I asked them to include lots of photos of the guests too,' she said, turning the page again. There was a stunning action shot of the tarantella, taken from a high angle. Mattia hadn't noticed the photographer getting up on a chair, but that's what he must have done. He picked out Kira immediately, with her strong chin and blue hair.

It wasn't the first time he'd seen her face over the past four weeks. She'd unfortunately let him take a photo of her holding her breakfast pretzel at the bakery in Innsbruck. Whenever he looked at her bandaged hands and wry smile, he had a host of contradictory feelings.

He saw none of the other guests in the picture from the tarantella – or even the bridal couple in the middle of the circle. He wondered what Kira was doing and when it would feel normal that he didn't know.

Alessandra surely noticed the focus of his gaze, but he couldn't bring himself to shift it, even though he also didn't want to talk about it. She turned the page slowly, before he was ready, but the photo in the corner of the next page made him freeze, his throat thick.

He was dancing with her. She'd wound her arms around his neck, her body so naturally, so effortlessly close to his. He'd felt her pulling away that night. Had offered to set her free – not that he'd ever tried to hold her back. But she hadn't gone, not until the next day. She'd asked him what he wanted, too scared to be the one to speak first.

Sometime after that, they'd looked like this: intimate and content and easy. He sighed, loudly enough that Alessandra unfortunately saw it as an opening.

'You do still feel something for her.'

He laughed darkly. 'As if that were in doubt!'

'But then why...? Have you kept in touch?'

He shook his head. 'She didn't want to.' As soon as he said the words, he realised they weren't quite true. 'At least, that wasn't the plan.'

'But was it *your* plan?'

'Even I know having feelings for someone who doesn't commit will never work out. I accepted that before we started anything.'

Squeezing his arm affectionately, she scooted closer. 'You changed,' she said lightly. 'I think it's good. I mean, I don't think you should go out and date casually all the time, but you discovered something, right?'

He nodded. He'd discovered how well two people who were wildly different could fit together in the right circumstances.

'But Matty,' she continued, her voice firm, 'I think Kira changed too.'

He stilled, his ears hot. He didn't need much encouragement and he was a little resentful of Alessandra for providing it. 'She didn't say – anything. Except at the beginning, that she only had casual relationships.'

'I don't blame her, after what Christian did. No wonder she was so disparaging of weddings, the poor thing.'

Kira would hate being called a 'poor thing'. She'd learned to be tough, to protect the soft heart under all her layers. He loved that she was tough – he'd needed that. But maybe he had helped her realise that the soft heart wasn't a weakness to hide.

'I understand why she didn't say anything,' Alessandra continued, 'but did you? On that last day, did you say you wanted to see her again? Give her a chance to say no, if that's what it had to be?'

The heat spread to his cheeks. He couldn't exactly tell Alessandra that he hadn't said anything because Kira had pressed a hand to his mouth and moved things on to sex. But the longer he thought about it, the more it made sense that he'd needed to be the one. He'd needed to be brave and promise he wouldn't hurt her, even though she was scared.

Instead, he'd let her go.

'I collected the photo album in person last weekend,' Alessandra said.

'You... Hmm?'

'Joe and I drove out to Bath, to the office of I Do Destinations. It was lovely to see Ginny again, even though she spent ten minutes apologising for the photographer, who I personally think did an amazing job. The pictures in the ice cave in particular are stunning, since he's a nature photographer.'

'That's... nice,' was all Mattia managed to reply. 'How's Ginny? On to the next wedding?'

Alessandra nodded. 'And she's taken up climbing. She said it's been good for her confidence, especially since she might have to do some of these outdoor weddings this summer, now they've merged with the adventure travel company.'

She couldn't have known where Mattia's thoughts would immediately go: Kira hanging from the ceiling of the chalet, her powerful body moving as gracefully as music.

'I asked Ginny about the classes and she gave me all the info,' Alessandra continued, oblivious to Mattia's vivid distraction. 'She drives down to Weymouth to the gym there, partly because she lives in Glastonbury, which isn't as far, but mainly because of her teacher.'

She couldn't quite stifle her smile and Mattia's heart turned somersaults as he caught her meaning.

She leaned close. 'Apparently, Kira's been miserable.'

'Don't sound so glad about that!'

'I bet she's been miserable over you. I *wouldn't* be so happy, except I can see what a mess you are too.'

'I'm not a mess,' he protested, although it was feeble. 'But I could be better,' he admitted, remembering how much better he was with Kira.

'Go and see her,' Alessandra urged.

He studied his hands – his smooth, moisturised hands, so different from her scarred ones. 'She might not talk to me. She might run.' He wasn't sure which was worse: the idea that Kira truly wasn't interested in anything deeper with him or that she felt so much, he could lose her regard anyway if he pushed too hard when she was still scared. One would hurt, but the other would cause the worst regret of his life.

'It can't be any worse than things are now,' Alessandra pointed out with a huff.

His gaze dropped to the album, still open to the photo of the two of them, so unexpected and vulnerable in their tenderness, and he accepted that Alessandra was right. He'd get through his auditions and he'd think of a way to go to her wherever she was comfortable, with no expectations. The obstacles were surely too great and hope could become hurt later on if he indulged it.

But at least he'd get to see her one more time.

37

'I'll be right there! I promise!' Kira knocked on Toni's desk as she hustled in the direction of the changing rooms.

'Class starts in three minutes! Everyone's arrived,' Toni said, her voice raised in alarm.

'Three minutes is plenty,' she called, jogging backwards for a moment to reassure Toni. 'Send any complaints to Reshma. All that wedding business is keeping me from my real work.'

The head of I Do Destinations emerged from the meeting room behind Toni's desk. 'Have a good class, Kira. Thanks for ironing out those details with me. I wish you weren't too busy to help with the Elba wedding.'

'What can I say? Everyone wants me,' she joked. The irony was almost unbearable. She bolted for the changing rooms, whipping on her vest top and lightweight trousers.

If she kept making jokes, they might finally stop treating her as though she'd had her heart broken. And she could mourn those last bits of her heart in private, staring at Mattia's Instagram feed with the duet from *Don Carlo* playing in her earbuds.

God, her pining had got so bad, she'd started appreciating *opera*.

Still hopping as she slipped into her rubber climbing shoes and smoothed the Velcro, she greeted the group of four beginners who were staring up at the wall in awe.

'Right, hi everyone. I'm your instructor, Kira. We just need to start with some safety st—' Her voice gave out.

Even if he weren't in the process of turning around, she would have recognised those shoulders, the soft hands, clenching and unclenching with nerves, the black curls she'd run her fingers through every chance she'd got.

He was wearing grey yoga trousers and a sleeveless workout top that highlighted all the dips and protrusions of bone and muscle in his torso. His shoulders were hunched – as usual. Offstage Mattia.

Mattia. In her gym. In her *class.*

He lifted his gaze to hers and her breath deserted her. That spark in his eyes. The way he seemed to hug her with just a look – the hug she'd spent five weeks longing for.

'What are you doing here?' It wasn't the smoothest greeting, but Kira was all out of politeness *and* rational thought. Her brain had kicked into fight-or-flight and with a job to do, 'flight' was a little difficult.

He inclined his head, the movement reminding her of secret looks across the table. 'I heard that learning to climb is good for confidence.'

That had not been the answer she'd expected, although she didn't know what she'd thought he would say. Certainly not, *I missed you like the sun in winter and I had to see you.*

'I signed up last week,' he continued with a grimace. 'I thought you'd see. I didn't mean for—' He couldn't seem to finish his sentence.

She shot a look back at Toni, who'd paused her banter with Reshma to gape at the scene playing out on the mats. She gave a confused shrug and Kira realised she probably hadn't remembered Mattia's name after one conversation.

No, flight was not an option, at least not yet. She was too curious.

The other three beginners in the class looked at her expectantly; she should have got started five minutes ago. There was only one way forward for now. She had ninety minutes to get through before she could grab a fistful of his soft shirt and demand he explain himself. Or kiss him. Or get the hell out of here. Ninety minutes would be long enough to plan a convincing escape.

Her heart hammering wildly, she swallowed the lump in her throat and tried again. 'We start with safety, with rules and rope handling.'

* * *

Che cazzo, he'd ambushed her. His expectations of this venture had already been low, but now? She wouldn't want to listen to a word he said – right when he was discovering how stupid he'd been to leave this alone for all these weeks.

The instant he'd seen her, the same heat, the potent recognition of a person who meant something – everything – to him had assailed him. He didn't want to be without her, even if it meant pivoting to friendship, which wouldn't be easy, and *learning to climb a terrifying wall.*

While they were fiddling with harnesses, she approached and asked in a low voice, 'Do you really want to learn to climb?', her tone doubtful. 'You don't have anything to prove to me.'

He wanted to dispute the statement, but she was at work and he was starting to realise how awkward the situation was. He'd thought it was a perfect idea when it had occurred to him: the opportunity to spend low-pressure, non-confrontational time together.

'Um, yes,' he began, glancing at the wall with a gulp, 'although it wasn't my only reason for coming here.'

A muscle moved in her jaw, the lines of her face so familiar, it hurt. He wanted to touch her badly, but she looked ready to kill him – figuratively, with those blunt words that showed she cared.

But when she opened her mouth, it wasn't to shoot him down – not quite. 'Next time, book a private lesson!' she hissed.

He blushed to the tips of his ears, which only made her roll her eyes. But even that response was more than he'd expected from her. Did she mean it? Would she be okay to spend time with him and see where things went? Hope surged and he wasn't sure he'd be able to keep it down if she kept saying sweet things like *private lessons.*

'I'm happy to see you,' he tried.

'Don't talk to me until the end of the class,' she snapped in response, 'for *their* sake.' She gestured wildly to the other three. 'They didn't sign up for a...'

'An overture?' he suggested, hoping the word was sufficiently vague not to scare her.

'Just get your butt up the wall or I'll give you an overture.'

I love you.

Oops, those words had popped far too soon into his mind. That wasn't what he had come to say. He didn't want to send her off in a fit of terror. But the sentence lodged rather comfortably in his chest.

Half an hour later, after the safety tutorials and some warm-ups on the mat that reminded him of early-morning yoga, the sensations in his chest were less comfortable as he faced what he was about to do.

Of course they were a long way from attempting the gravity-defying overhangs on the other side of the gym. They stood near the straight vertical wall with plenty of grips. But shit, it was still so high up, he struggled to estimate. Fifteen metres? Twenty? It was death metres high, that much was certain.

In his eagerness, he'd volunteered to go first but

was now realising what a foolish thing he'd agreed to do. The only consolation was that Kira herself would belay him to demonstrate for the others.

'Partner check,' she called out loudly enough for the others to hear. 'Before climbing, always make sure that the belay device is the correct way up with the carabiner locked. Check that your partner's harness is tight above the hips and snug around the thighs.'

She tugged at her own harness, then slipped her fingers through the waistband of his, making him suck in his stomach. She stilled, snatching her hand back.

'You don't need to actually touch it,' she added, her voice wavering. 'Just check with your... you know. Eyes.' She blinked, staring at his harness, although it didn't really look like a partner check she was performing.

The safety device wasn't sexy, with loops around the thighs and an awkward shape at the groin, but Kira looked natural in hers. She was so comfortable in her own body. And her quick hands on the ropes were so capable, he could have swooned.

'Check the tie-in knot,' she continued, giving the rope a yank so he stumbled in her direction. He threw a hand out for balance and it landed on her hip. Wow, that felt good. It took him a little longer than was appropriate to remove it again and he hoped these other clients weren't easily offended, because he was screwing things up badly for Kira in his bumbling attempt to show her she was important to him.

'And up you go,' she said firmly.

He knew that was her version of a pep talk: *get on with it.* It cut through the fog of obsessive thinking and anxiety that would otherwise have crowded his consciousness.

She'd already explained that the yellow grips were the easiest, but they could use any colours at first, so he grasped the plastic lumps at head height, tested his toes against one of the lower holds and pushed up the first two feet.

'Keep your hips close to the wall,' Kira reminded him. 'Use those yoga muscles.'

The thought that she might be appreciating his yoga muscles provided extra motivation. He didn't look up or down, tried to clear his mind of everything except the muted echo of other climbers in the hall and Kira's voice, speaking to the others in the class.

'Focus on the placement of your feet, not your hands. Once you've got more conditioning, hands can do more, but you don't want to injure your fingers at this stage.'

The rope wobbled in front of his face, but he appreciated the reminder that Kira was down there making sure he wouldn't fall. The next grips were within reach, so he stretched and pushed. It wasn't climbing; it was a puzzle for his hands and feet and brain that added a light strain on his muscles as time ticked by.

His knuckles began to ache and his knees were wobbly, but he didn't stop to think. The next grips were in his sights and Kira was watching him. Maybe she didn't care what he thought of climbing, but he was—

A foot away from the ceiling. Christ, he was at the top! His head spun and all the strength in his legs gave out as realisation hit him.

'Porca puttana!' His voice was choked. He lost his grip on the wall and fumbled for the rope, his foot sliding off the grip and leaving him hanging, limbs flailing. The harness dug in and he grunted at the discomfort.

Kira's calm voice reached his ears from a long way below. 'You see what he did there? He lost focus. It's obviously not too difficult to get yourself up the wall with simple grips, right?'

He snorted, but they probably couldn't hear him.

'The difficult part is convincing yourself you're safe and talking down the panicking animal brain that thinks you've put yourself in danger.' Only the tiniest hitch of her breath betrayed that she was taking his whole weight in her harness right now.

The longer he hung suspended, the less it was his animal brain in control and the more his embarrassment cortex took over.

'Can I come down now?'

'Do you remember what you're supposed to do?' she called up, definitely some amusement in her tone.

He took a deep breath. 'Sit in the harness, feet on the wall.' He had to give the wall a bit of a shove to get back into position, but he found some grip with his shoes and when Kira let him down a metre, he managed to plant his feet and walk stiltedly down – all while stubbornly looking up. Down made him too dizzy.

By the time his feet reached the mat, his entire body was the consistency of crema pasticceria and he was shaking violently. Squeezing his eyes shut, he leaned heavily against the wall and waited for the adrenaline to subside.

'Fuck,' he whimpered with a choking laugh.

He sensed her next to him before he felt anything and when he wrenched his eyes open, she was staring up at him with a light in her eyes that gave his spine more substance.

'You did great.'

That melted him into a puddle at her feet – at least his sloppy smile made him feel as though that were the case. 'Thanks.'

'For an absolute beginner,' she added. 'But for the man who hurt himself trying to grab an icicle, you really smashed it.'

He grinned at her. 'I've come a long way.'

Her smile faded and she regarded him thoughtfully – with a hint of wariness, but she wasn't about to bolt. 'You have.'

'Can I... talk to you after this?'

She nodded and said his favourite word to hear from her mouth, so softly, another person might not have heard it. 'Okay, opera boy.'

38

Kira was jittery, as though she'd been one of the beginners making her way up the wall for the first time.

After struggling through the pep talk which closed the class, without remembering anything she said, there was nothing left to protect her from whatever Mattia would throw at her next. Two months ago, if an ex had walked into the climbing gym and said they wanted to talk to her, she would have run the other way screaming, but she'd spent weeks thinking about him, agonising over all the things that had made their time together different from anything she'd previously experienced, even with Christian, before she'd learned to shut people out.

But Mattia, with his angel bone structure and compelling voice, had refused to be shut out.

Her chest was tight, her throat swollen up and whatever he wanted to say, she wasn't ready, but that's what being brave was for. He'd just climbed a wall in her gym, looking rather fine as he did so. She would try to bear her nerves, her embarrassment, her fear – and the giddy excitement that was threatening to choke her.

As the others in the class headed for the changing rooms, sprightly with adrenaline, Mattia swung in her direction with a purposeful stride until the toes of his rubber climbing shoes were half a foot from hers.

She opened her mouth to say something – probably to babble about the class and mock him gently, so he remembered she was prickly and grumpy and not worth his time – but he lifted a hand to her face, brushing her hair back from her forehead, his fingers stretching along her jaw and his thumb pressing gently on her lips.

Her eyes slammed shut and she swayed on her feet. The touch was her kryptonite – no, her drug. She needed it with a physical longing that scared her. How mortifying to be brought low by the human instinct for closeness. She couldn't pretend any more that she didn't need it.

She'd been icy towards others for the past twelve years – for longer, if she were honest – too scared they wouldn't accept her. But Mattia was the spring sunshine and he'd started a thaw she didn't know how to reverse.

'I need to tell you something,' he began, drawing in a few heaving breaths. 'You don't have to say anything in reply. I know this is hard and I know you don't want to hurt me.'

The mushy snow in her chest puddled into liquid. She was hard and blunt and pushed people away, but he was *right*. Hurting him would kill her.

'You didn't want me to say anything in Austria and I respected that, but you don't know what I wanted to say that morning. You can't know, so I have to tell you.'

She'd known she couldn't bear to hear him brush her off. The fact that he'd come all the way to Weymouth suggested this was not a brushing off, but Kira's rational brain seemed to be suffering from hypoxia, given the amount of air she needed just to keep her heart beating.

'I'll start with the little things and you can just say "okay" or "no" if I'm wrong. I'm prepared for any answer – mostly.' His grimace was eloquent as he rubbed his forehead, drawing Kira's attention to the light scar there.

'Okay,' she said, and his eyes snapped to hers in surprise. 'You told me to say "okay".'

'Giusto, I did. Good. Good?'

She nodded, her own nerves settling a little as she noticed his. It was just Mattia – sincere, funny, self-deprecating Mattia. She could do this.

He cleared his throat. 'I don't want to never see you again,' he blurted out, glancing up with a pained look.

'Okay,' she replied immediately.

His face brightened, but he kept his gaze on his feet, concentrating hard. 'I do want to take your class. I don't think I'll ever be good enough to climb with you on a route you'd enjoy too. But I want to know why you love it. I came here today to see you and also to try to understand you.'

'Okay,' she said again, a little wobbly this time as his earnestness touched her.

'Because I know our lives don't overlap much. I only bring you complications.'

She shook her head. 'No.' He'd brought her so much more than that and even the problems had proven to be solutions she hadn't known she'd needed.

When she opened her mouth to say more, he held up his hand again. 'I'll listen to anything you want to say to me soon, but I need you to listen first.' He paused, gathering himself. 'I thought I was learning how to be... intimate with someone without getting my feelings involved. We hadn't known each other long and I'd never been with anyone like you before.'

That was starting to sound like the words she didn't want to hear. He must have noticed her trying not to flinch, because he reached for her hand – her rough, callused hand with bitten nails, held in his smooth, manicured one. But she'd felt that hand all over her body and he'd reached for her now. It might not make sense, but it had all been real.

'But the truth is, my feelings were already involved. What I told you that day in the minivan is still true: I can't do casual. If I'd truly only felt friendship for you...' He flinched at the thought. 'I don't think I *can* get close to someone without those feelings – if it's not right.'

His words struck Kira square in the chest and she couldn't hide any more. Their relationship had never been just physical. She'd stumbled into something she hadn't been prepared for and now she feared she was stuck – open, vulnerable.

'I know we agreed to keep things casual between us and I'll never blame you if you *can* separate the two. It's my fault for not realising I wasn't keeping my side of the bargain, but you meant something to me from the moment you turned off the fridge, despite every-thing you thought of me at the time.'

The words were coming more easily now, visible in the way his shoulders rose and fell. The hand that wasn't holding hers came up to gesture for emphasis and here was onstage Mattia, pouring out his emotions.

'Those few days together completely changed my perspective, made me realise how much I'd been holding myself back. I was stuck with a single vision of myself. Then you were there, throwing the truth in my face, but making it all okay. No matter what prob-lems I fixated on, you pushed me to manage them. You believed I could.'

'Of course you can,' Kira said fiercely, tears threat-ening in earnest now.

He smiled then. Raising his spare hand to her face, he splayed his fingers over her cheek and into her hair with more of that magic. 'You have no idea how beau-tiful you are when you growl like that.'

'I'm not *beautiful*,' she contradicted automatically. 'And I'm not growling.' There was less conviction in her voice for the second sentence.

'I felt some amazing things in Austria – all of them while I was looking at your face.'

'You don't have to say I'm beautiful just because we had great sex,' she muttered.

He straightened. 'You're only supposed to say "okay" and "no", remember? I'm not finished yet.'

'I can't imagine how much more you'd have to—'

'You're beautiful because I know you, Kira. It hasn't been a long time, but I know you better than almost anyone else does.'

It was a presumptive statement, but she couldn't contradict him. She wanted him to know her. Maybe he was afraid of fire and fridges, had never seen snow before this year and lost his shit in a gondola, but she couldn't doubt what he was saying right now when the truth was evident in his whole body.

'I don't want to lose what we had. It's too important to me. I want to build on it. If you mean this much to me after a single week, I can't wait to find out how I will feel about you in a year. It wasn't a casual fling – it was a miracle. At least that's what it was to me.'

A tear tumbled down her cheek. She was used to hoarding doubts, protecting herself with scepticism and shunning hope. But Mattia was standing in front of her, a mirror of her own feelings, and she couldn't doubt any more.

This was something, between them. This might be

it. She should have been horrified at the thought, but she wasn't.

Her feelings weren't a mistake – they were exactly *right*.

She couldn't imagine feeling more for him than she did then, but his words curled around her heart, making her want it too: being together. One day, she'd tell him she loved him. The conviction shook her.

'There's one more thing,' he said. 'I'm moving to London.'

Her jaw dropped. 'Okaaaaay.'

'I haven't quite got a job yet, but I've had good feedback from two of the auditions – the third one was a fire from the depths of the inferno, so please remember it's a miracle that I'm here and still halfway hoping you'll want to see me.'

'Okay,' she responded with a faint smile.

'My manager thinks London is a good base for building my career.' He paused and she gave him an encouraging nod. London was several hours away, but it was so much closer than if they were several countries apart and she'd take it. 'That's not really the thing that appeals to me about London. I thought, if I were there, I could come and see you?'

'Okay,' she said with an easy nod.

A smile twitched on his lips. 'Would you... I'd like to go out for dinner – with you.'

'Okay.'

'Lots of times.'

'Can I say something other than "okay" now?'

'Only if it's "yes, please".'

She was the one to come closer this time. 'Yes, please,' she said softly.

He slipped his other hand into hers and tangled their fingers. 'Maybe we could keep doing the...'

'Yes, please,' Kira said with a grin.

'Can I call you my girlfriend?' The eager spark in his eyes made her laugh.

'Okay,' she agreed. 'Only if I can call you my opera boy.'

'You do anyway,' he said with a doubtful look. 'But I like the sound of *your* opera boy.'

She sneaked her arms around his waist and held on, enjoying the moment his hand ventured into her hair.

'This is not how I pictured it,' he said absently.

'It's not?'

'Honestly, I thought you'd be harder to convince, that I'd have to be your friend for a few years before you'd see how good we are together.'

'With benefits, I assume.'

'Allora, I did hope.' His sheepish shrug made her smile and press a kiss to the middle of his chest. 'But I would have stayed without. I might have been a little miserable, but... I've never felt this way about someone before.'

'Me neither,' she mumbled into his shirt.

He stilled, as though the truth of returned feelings was just as astounding to him as it had been to her, and Kira realised it was her turn to say the difficult stuff.

'I don't think it was ever casual for me either, Mattia,' she admitted.

He drew back to study her. 'But you said—'

'So did you,' she reminded him, 'to Alessandra, the day before the wedding, and it bugged me so much.'

'Ahi, no! I was lying shamelessly. I knew I was lying too. I didn't think I *could* lie, but... I'd promised you.'

'You hadn't promised,' she assured him. 'It was my fault for resisting what my heart was trying to tell me. I missed you, these past weeks. It was terrible.' She pressed her cheek to his chest.

'I'm so sorry,' he said into her hair, wrapping his arms more tightly around her. 'I'm sorry it took me so long to be brave.'

'You're here now, even though I did everything I

could to push you away. You're stronger than you think.' She gave him a shove for emphasis.

He just nodded in reply. 'When you say it, I believe it. I want to be strong with you.'

Winding her arms around his neck, she peered up at him. 'Just don't lose your wonderful ability to feel things deeply. You changed my perspective too. You made me realise I can acknowledge my emotions and survive it,' she admitted with a wry smile.

'I am very glad we can both survive deep feelings,' he said solemnly. 'And declarations of them. How about I protect you from your deep, scary feelings and you can protect me from all the fires and fridges and ticking clocks we encounter?'

'It's a deal.'

'God, the rest of us almost didn't survive!'

Kira wrenched her head up at the sound of Reshma's voice. She was tapping her foot by Toni's desk, a hand on her hip. Toni sat watching them with a grin, miming popcorn.

'Usually you just say, "Do you want to go out with me," and the other one says, "Yes!"' Reshma continued. 'You two are hopeless.'

'Is that what you said to Willard?' Kira shot back, making Reshma colour. 'I didn't think so,' she mumbled. 'You might want to close your innocent eyes. I'm about to kiss him.'

'Put the poor boy out of his misery!' Toni called out cheerfully.

Mattia grinned down at her, clutching her tightly around the waist. 'Yes, put the poor boy out of his misery. I've waited five weeks for this.'

Lifting her chin, she went up on her toes until her lips were a breath from his. 'I think I've been waiting my whole life.'

EPILOGUE

The guides at Great Heart were dropping like flies. In another life, Toni might have called it the happiest time. But, like everything else in this life – her life – it was bittersweet to watch her friends find committed relationships and take their first steps as a couple. It was busy too.

Toni had to tear herself away from her scheduling challenges on the computer. It was a Monday evening, her day to close up the gym, as it shut early. Although the big hall felt strange when it was completely empty, she enjoyed the quiet rhythm of the work and the fact that she had the flexibility to do it, now her parents were happy to help out with childcare.

Although the merger between Great Heart and I Do had begun as a worrying development that threatened her job, she now found she had more work than she could easily complete and was earning more from the extra hours as well.

The adventure tour business had picked up a little as the merger had led to more general marketing and Toni found herself a jack-of-all-trades, a job she enjoyed, but there were days when she wished she didn't have so many balls in the air.

'Bye, Toni! See you on Wednesday!' Kira called as she burst out of the changing rooms, her hair still damp. She was doubtless rushing off to Woking, where Mattia had found an apartment, although he seemed to be in Weymouth just as often. Reshma had even nabbed him to sing at a handful of upcoming weddings. For a pair who should have been an odd couple, they had one of the most harmonious relationships Toni had ever seen. Sophie and Andreas enjoyed their bickering, but Kira and Mattia were soulmates.

While Toni was still widowed, the object of pity. She wouldn't change anything, because she had Cillian, just turned nine years old, but sometimes, it chafed.

She was still reeling from everything she hadn't

understood about Kira's past, but at least Kira's future now appeared bright. Toni had never had the luxury of keeping secrets. She would always be the one who had lost her husband in tragic circumstances while she was pregnant with their child.

After disinfecting the rental shoes and tidying the ropes, she went to shut down her computer as the last glow of daylight faded from the sky outside. But she paused when she noticed that a message from Gabri had dropped in. If her old friends were starting out on a new journey and leaving her behind, at least this wedding merger had brought her one good thing: her online friendship with Gabri, the florist I Do regularly used for weddings on the Italian island of Elba.

Toni had never even spoken to Gabri on the phone, let alone met her in real life, but they'd started exchanging messages last summer, when Toni had ordered the flowers for an I Do wedding. Gabri was chatty and friendly and Toni had enjoyed the fact that this new online acquaintance didn't know her tragic history.

Another Elba wedding was coming up in three months and Toni had been more than happy to work with Gabri again and take some of the pressure off Sophie, the lucky one who would actually go to the wedding on the sun-drenched island in August.

She sat down to read the message:

Ciao Toni

Sophie was in touch with me today, but she sent three emails that all contradicted each other and she even got the date of the August wedding wrong. I asked if she was okay and of course she said yes, but it was strange.

Anyway, can you make sure for me that everything is okay with her? She said maybe she will hire me to help with some tours as well.

Oh, and there was something funny I thought you'd like: I took a group on a foraging tour today and there was a plant I didn't know the name of in English. We say 'lassana' in Italian. When I got back, I looked it up and it sounds horrible! NIPPLEWORT.

Baci e abbracci

Gabri x

Toni pulled her chair out to reply straight away. Gabri always had something interesting to say about the plants on Elba or the flowers she was working with.

Ciao Gabri

That's kind of you to be concerned about Sophie. I'll check on her. She's probably just busy. She should be planning her own wedding, you know. She's sickeningly in love with my friend Andreas.

Nipplewort sounds like a disease! Maybe it's lucky you didn't know the name in English. But a foraging tour sounds fun. Is that another one of your many offerings for tourists? How do I book on??

Toni x

She clicked 'send', ruefully imagining if she truly did book herself a holiday and turn up on Gabri's doorstep. A week on an island with a girlfriend drinking wine and going on walks sounded too good to be true. She hadn't even mentioned Cillian to Gabri, although that omission was beginning to feel less natural as they exchanged messages more often. But these jokes and the glimpse into Gabri's life on the island were one of the few things she had for herself.

An answer popped up almost immediately:

No need to book. If you ever make it here, you'll have a personal tour guide and a free room, if you don't mind a rustic place full of orchids and snorkelling equipment.

God, it sounded like a dream.

The door to the meeting-room behind her banged open and she stood to hide the computer screen, as though someone might catch her daydreaming about a holiday. She turned to find a bleary-eyed Sophie emerging, and a prickle of worry crept over her skin.

'Sophie! What's up? Why are you still here?'

She rubbed a hand over her eyes. 'I just got so incredibly tired after my last meeting. I thought I'd better just close my eyes for a few minutes before I drive back, but it was more like an hour. Sorry I scared you.'

Suspicion rose in Toni's mind. 'Sophie, are you...?'

Sophie locked her gaze on Toni's, her expression tight and wary, and that was enough of an answer for the moment. Toni nodded, reaching a hand out to squeeze Sophie's, saying nothing even as the enormity of what might be happening settled in her stomach.

Andreas... Oh dear. The situation would be complicated.

Sophie's gaze fell absently on the computer screen. 'Oh, you're messaging Gabri Orzati. He's so sweet,' she mumbled. 'Anyway, I should get on the road.' She managed a smile at Toni. 'Tomorrow's another day – another wedding to plan.'

* * *

MORE FROM LEONIE MACK

The next book from Leonie Mack is available to order now here:

https://mybook.to/AdventureWeddings3

ACKNOWLEDGEMENTS

Every book is a team effort and this one was no different. I'm grateful for the early feedback from Eden Campbell and the tireless cheering from Tatiana that always keeps me going.

I'm also so grateful for the feedback and encouragement of my agent Saskia who really 'gets' what I'm trying to do with my writing – I value this so much. My editor Megan stepped in, doing a great job to help me whip this into shape and keep the focus of the story. Also, the copyeditor and proofreader as always performed their essential tasks with an eagle eye – thank you.

Special thanks as usual to my community of writers who offer me perspective, encouragement and a listening ear. For this book, I'm also thankful for the strong women in my life who inspired me to be brave and write a strong, complex woman who doesn't apologise for being who she is.

ABOUT THE AUTHOR

Leonie Mack is a bestselling romantic novelist. Having lived in London for many years her home is now in Germany with her husband and three children. Leonie loves train travel, medieval towns, hiking and happy endings!

Download your exclusive bonus content from Leonie Mack here:

Visit Leonie's website: www.leoniemack.com

Follow Leonie on social media:

ALSO BY LEONIE MACK

ALSO BY LEONIE MACK

My Christmas Number One

Italy Ever After

A Match Made in Venice

We'll Always Have Vegas

Twenty-One Nights in Paris

A Taste of Italian Sunshine

Sunny Days With You

A Wedding in the Sun

In Italy for Love

Falling for the Italian Dream

Snowed in at the Wedding Chalet

An Italian Island Love Story

Boldwood
EVER AFTER
x♡x♡

JOIN BOLDWOOD'S
**ROMANCE
COMMUNITY**
FOR SWEET AND
SPICY BOOK RECS
WITH ALL YOUR
FAVOURITE
TROPES!

SIGN UP TO OUR
NEWSLETTER

HTTPS://BIT.LY/BOLDWOODEVERAFTER

Boldwood

Boldwood Books is an award-winning fiction publishing company seeking out the best stories from around the world.

Find out more at
www.boldwoodbooks.com

Follow us on social media for brilliant books, competitions and offers!
@BoldwoodBooks

Sign up to our Boldwood newsletter here:

https://bit.ly/BoldwoodBNewsletter